To So Few

In the Beginning

To So Few
In the Beginning

by

Cap Parlier

SAINT GAUDENS PRESS
Wichita, Kansas & Santa Barbara, California

Saint Gaudens Press
Post Office Box 405
Solvang, CA 93464-0405

Saint Gaudens, Saint Gaudens Press
and the Winged Liberty colophon
are trademarks of Saint Gaudens Press

Print edition ISBN: 978-0-943039-35-0

Library of Congress Catalog Number - 2014914385

Printed in the United States of America

Dedication

—

To all those who have gone before us, and given their last full measure of devotion to the cause of freedom and the defense of those freedoms.

See other great books available from Saint Gaudens Press
http://www.SaintGaudensPress.com

Visit Cap Parlier's Web Site at http://www.Parlier.com

Acknowledgments

—

To John Richard and Roger Benefiel for research assistance.

To the late Colonel Bob Clapp, USMC, for his patient tutelage on the finer points of aerial combat when Cap was a young aviator.

To my wife, spouse, partner, sponsor and cheerleader, Jeanne, who tolerated the hours, days, weeks, months and years of research, writing and discussion. She has and continues to tolerate my love of flight and the need to tell a story about the greatest event in human flight.

To my reviewers: my wife, Jeanne; John Richard; and Leta Buresh, for their patience, reflection, opinions and suggestions. I believe they made it a stronger story.

Chapter 1

The dream, alone, is of interest.
What is life, without a dream?
--Edmond Rostand

Saturday, 10.September.1938
Wichita, Kansas, USA

The earth below had no relief – no depth – although the features were clearly discernible, like the green of the trees, the golden color of the ripening wheat and the glint from the sun reflecting off the occasional stream or pond. Buildings and roads marked the existence of man despite the two-dimensional character they possessed from an altitude of 8,000 feet. The infrequent motion of an automobile or horse drawn wagon offered some signs of habitation. Somehow the little realities of life seemed so insignificant, and yet the beauty and wonderment of the scene always brought Brian Arthur Drummond an exhilarating, overwhelming and rewarding sense of greatness.

"Watch what y're doin' there, Brian," shouted the old man, Malcolm Bainbridge, over the grunting of the engine and the whistling of the air.

They called him the 'old man' because he was the oldest pilot any of them had ever known. Malcolm Bainbridge was a man of moderate height and build who had survived not quite a half century of tumultuous events in life and history. His salt and pepper, unkempt hair along with his scarred, often stubbled, craggy face contributed to the folklore surrounding him. Malcolm had been, or so he told them, the oldest pilot in a pursuit airplane squadron in the Royal Flying Corps during the War to End All Wars – the Great War. He had been shot down twice, parachuting from his burning plane on one occasion and walking away from a rather nasty impact with a group of trees on the other. To his credit, eight German fighter planes and two observation balloons were eliminated by the synchronized, through-the-propeller, twin machine guns of his Sopwith 1½ Strutter, followed by his favorite Sopwith F.1 Camel fighter. Malcolm Bainbridge was an ace, an accomplished fighter pilot, and God only knows for what reason, a patient and persistent instructor of the fine art of flight.

"Watch yur airspeed," barked Malcolm from his position behind Brian in his attempt to bring his young pilot back to the task at hand.

A quick look into the cockpit at the few instruments populating the small panel in front of Brian yielded the cause of Malcolm's concern. The thin white needle was bouncing frantically in the vicinity of 50 miles per hour, not much above the stall speed of the Stearman C-3R Speedster. Brian gently pushed the stick forward, watched the nose of the airplane slowly point below the distant horizon and checked to see the airspeed climbing above 80 miles per hour, looking for 100. The rush of the air tugged at the skin of Brian's distinctively chiseled, unblemished face and his wavy, light brown hair. If it was not for the tattered pair of motorcycle rider's goggles, his renowned grayish-blue eyes would be watering, blurring his keen vision.

Brian Drummond had been an aviation enthusiast for as much as he could remember of his seventeen, plus a little, years. His first flight with a barnstorming, rather careless pilot by the name of Harry Johnson, occurred when he was nine, and most notably, without his parent's knowledge, or consent. Brian worked at the various airfields scattered around East Wichita every spare moment after school and on the weekends. The boy's commitment had convinced Malcolm Bainbridge to give in to his request for flight instruction nearly five years ago. Brian looked older than he was and although Malcolm never really challenged him on his age, his skills spoke for his ability and maturity. The young man continued to demonstrate an uncanny aptitude for the mechanics of an airplane, and he possessed an instinctive ability to control the aircraft in flight.

"Why are ya so distracted?" yelled Malcolm over the rush of the wind and the dull roar of the engine. Losing track of his airspeed was unusual for the young pilot. Such a slip was contrary to the native instincts Brian usually displayed in the cockpit.

Brian could only shrug his shoulders, not really wanting to acknowledge his complacency. The distraction on this day came in the form of his girlfriend. The thoughts of her crept into his consciousness through the uneventfulness of this particular flight.

It was probably his three hundredth flight, plus or minus a few. The first vestiges of the realization of his destiny occurred, to his recollection, somewhere after his tenth flight. He knew he belonged in the wicker seat with the thick leather belt across his lap soaring above the ground making the machine do as he commanded. The simple straight stick between his legs along with the two bars, the pilots called pegs, for his feet enabled the young aviator to perform smooth, aerobatic maneuvers like a graceful bird born to rejoice in the freedom of flight. The little lever he held with his left hand controlled the sound, the vibration, the power of the 120 horsepower, reciprocating engine mounted just in front of him. It was an awe inspiring sensation for the young man not yet out of high school even after the 525 flight hours he had accumulated.

"Brian, look down behind the left wing," Malcolm shouted. "D'ya see 'im?"

Brian searched the ground. A few buildings, orthogonal roads delineating large, mile square fields and lines of trees were all he could see. Then, something moved from behind a small, puffy cloud. His eyes were instinctively drawn to the point. There it was – another airplane climbing in the opposite direction. Turning his head further to the left looking into his instructor's face, Brian answered, "I've got him."

"They're comin' up ta get us."

"What do we do?"

The old man knew exactly what to do. He also instinctively knew it was time to take young Brian to the next level in his aviation education.

"Watch," Malcolm said with authority. "I'll take her. Follow me on the controls. Feel what I do."

Brian released the pressure on the stick and rudder pegs to feel the controls move under his hand. The aircraft's left wing dipped slightly as Malcolm adjusted their heading toward the edge of a billowing, cumulus cloud. Brian continued to watch the other airplane rise toward them and wondered why Malcolm was not turning to face their pretend adversary. Malcolm increased power to the engine, building speed. The cloud was growing in size although the other airplane did not appear to be getting any closer as it continued to climb.

"Why don't we turn to face him?" Brian asked eventually when his curiosity could no longer be contained.

"In huntin' terms, we're settin' the bait," came the response.

Now, Brian knew instantly what was going to happening. As an accomplished hunter himself, Brian quickly began to assimilate the events in the context of the hunt. A large grin grew across the young man's face.

"We know he's there," Malcolm continued. "He doesn't know we know. We have the advantage in terms of knowledge, altitude and speed," he paused for another quick assessment and flight path adjustment. "All ta the good," he added almost imperceptibly.

The additional explanation was not necessary as Brian continued to marvel at the fine points of this pending engagement. The picture in his head began to come into clear focus. They would act as if they were simply cruising along, then when the cloud obscured their adversary's line of sight, Malcolm would position the airplane for maximum advantage.

The cloud passed between the two airplanes. Malcolm turned to skirt the edge of the cloud, dropped the nose to gain speed, then pulled the stick straight back. The propeller noise changed as the machine groaned under the acceleration, several times the force of gravity the pilots called g's, of the vertical maneuver. Brian felt his whole body become very heavy as the nose continued to move through the vertical . . . straight up. Why is he doing a loop right now, Brian asked himself trying to understand what the old man was doing?

As they reached the apex of the loop, Brian strained to look up above the wing. He saw the browns and greens of the earth below come into view among the openings in the clouds. Airspeed fell precariously as the engine and propeller labored to maintain as much speed as possible. With the nose of the airplane approaching the horizon inverted, Malcolm abruptly rolled the aircraft to the upright position.

"Wow!" exclaimed Brian. "What was that?"

There was no answer from the rear cockpit, and Brian knew enough not to repeat the question with the old man concentrating on the engagement before him. Malcolm quickly turned into a tight circle staying close to the cloud. Brian watched Malcolm scanning the visible area below them yielding nothing. They continued to wait.

The bulging, boiling, white, fluffy protuberances of the cloud beside them attracted Brian's eye. While they had flown near clouds many times before, this was the closest he had ever been. As Malcolm continued to hold his tight turn, the visible boundary of the cloud seemed so close Brian could reach out and touch it, or step off the wing and stand on the bumps.

"There he is," Malcolm shouted as he adjusted the plane's path to move in the opposite direction to their adversary. "Check the sun." It was high above the cloud on their right side. Brian knew what Malcolm was looking for. Their target was now passing behind the left wing. "Let's go get 'im," he said as the aircraft rolled once again to the inverted position followed quickly by the nose dropping toward the ground below. The Stearman picked up airspeed rapidly as they dove toward the unsuspecting aircraft below them with the sun at their back.

The other biplane grew in size as the distance between them decreased rapidly. Their target, a venerable, but slower Curtiss JN-4H Jenny, was clearly visible directly in front of them through the propeller disk. The closure rate was still high although their flight path was not quite horizontal again, and they continued to descend upon their target.

Just as Malcolm began to make a machine gun sound yelling – tat-tat-tat-tat – over the volume of noise around them, first one and then the other pilot turned to see them. Brian shouted, "Yahoo," as they passed across the tail from left to right. He could see every detail of the airplane and the two pilots.

Malcolm pulled back on the stick in a maneuver like a loop except skewed over on its side. Again, the added weight on their bodies from the acceleration of the maneuver provided positive reinforcement of the ensuing engagement. When Brian could look back over his shoulder and see the ground below, the other aircraft was not detectable. Malcolm kept the nose of the laboring biplane coming around, until he saw their target.

The other guys were turning and climbing to follow Malcolm through the turn in an attempt to gain an advantage position. Their nose was still well behind the Stearman.

"Mistake!" Malcolm exclaimed.

"Why?"

Malcolm broke off the vertical maneuver holding the airplane at their higher altitude and continued the turn. "We have the advantage and as long as he follows me, he'll never get the advantage."

Brian absorbed the sequence of events and correlated the movement of the aircraft and Malcolm's control inputs with the aerial dance the two airplanes were now entwined. The two machines rolled and twisted in the sky, then in a wild maneuver combination, their adversary appeared directly in front of them, not fifty feet away.

"We've got 'im now," Malcolm shouted followed quickly by the distinctive sound effects of make-believe machine guns.

The other aircraft twisted and turned, climbed and dove, to no avail. Malcolm seemed to have a death grip on their prey. No matter what action was taken, Malcolm now kept his Stearman just behind his adversary, on their tail, at roughly the same distance.

The surrender did not take long. The wings of the other aircraft steadied up straight and level, and two sets of hands could be seen beside their heads. Malcolm maneuvered the aircraft alongside their now docile adversary. Everyone smiled and their opponents saluted Malcolm as recognition of his superior maneuvering. The old man had won yet another mock battle in the sky.

Malcolm returned the salute, and then rolled away from the other aircraft. "Take us home, my boy," he said.

Brian took the controls, descended below the base of the clouds, took several minutes to orient himself on their location and turned the aircraft to head for their home airfield. The flight back was uneventful and quiet including the approach and landing in the narrow, grass field they sometimes referred to as homeplate. Brian taxied the airplane across the field stopping in front of the large barn that served as a hangar for three aircraft.

With the engine stopped, Brian unstrapped and jumped out of the cockpit. A new animation possessed him as he stood on the wing facing the rear cockpit and Malcolm Bainbridge.

"That was the most fantastic ride I've ever done," Brian spoke rapidly. "How did you do that? Is that what air combat is really like? When can we...."

Malcolm raised his hand to stop the verbal onslaught of his pupil's enthusiasm. Slowly, Malcolm extricated himself from the small hole in the top of the fuselage without looking at Brian. The silence continued as the old man led the way to the ground. A long stretch of his body made the scene take on a bizarre change as if Malcolm had just completed a barroom brawl and was trying to see how many bruises he had acquired. Brian stood beside him, nearly half a foot taller, with a broad, anticipatory smile across his face.

"Let me get somethin' ta drink first, then I'll answer yur questions," Malcolm said without waiting for an acknowledgment or consent. His wife, Gertrude, always had a small tub of water with chunks of block ice chilling numerous bottles of Coca-Cola during the hot summer months of the Great Plains. Malcolm popped the tops off two bottles, handing one to Brian. After a few long draws on the elixir and a resounding belch, which was also part of the ritual, Malcolm sat in a large, rocking chair motioning for Brian to sit on the stool across from him. "OK, now, that was a minor taste a aerial combat," he began.

The conversation between the two pilots bounced back and forth with young Brian driving the direction and tempo. Malcolm, who was not a particularly talkative person, generally chose to let his actions do his talking. However, as a teacher, he had to talk. Malcolm carefully recreated the event.

The subtleties of every aspect of the recent mock aerial battle were regurgitated and digested in intimate detail. What had Malcolm been looking for? What was he trying to do with each maneuver? More important to Brian, although neither man knew or could have known, was the apprentice discussion of the principles of aerial combat.

Phrases like: 'the best defense is a good offense,' 'keep the sun at your back,' 'never underestimate your adversary,' 'always check your tail,' were presented and analyzed at Brian's insistence. There was a vein of pride in Malcolm's voice as he continued to bait young Brian and revel in the lad's enthusiasm for the intricacy of flight's greatest challenge – flying against the unpredictability of another human, or even worse, a group of adversaries who meant to do you harm.

Short snippets of Malcolm's experience flying against the Germans in France two decades earlier reluctantly intermingled among the lessons of flight. Brian was enthralled. Although the ravages of war were in the receding past, Malcolm also felt the responsibility to bring the human cost of conflict into graphic resolution for his young pupil. Injury, maiming and death were the macabre colors of the picture presented among the glory of flight.

"Malcolm," shouted Gertrude Bainbridge, the wife and earthbound caretaker of the aging aviator, "Brian's mother just called. She wants him home."

Brian hesitantly looked past Malcolm's wave of annoyance to the source of the words that would terminate their session for this day. The shapely figure of Missus Bainbridge, ten years younger than her husband, retreated into the small clapboard house among the trees beyond the backside of what Malcolm called his hangar. It was a certain indicator she considered the task accomplished. At that moment, Brian's awareness of the colors of dusk brought confirmation of the passing time. The two pilots had been absorbed in the collection of review, lessons and remembrance for nearly four hours without a concern for time.

The interest and enthusiasm Brian demonstrated helped Malcolm consider the next step for his young protégé. There were several attributes of a natural fighter pilot. Flight aptitude was certainly one, and Brian possessed all the skills needed. Another characteristic, and maybe even more important, was an instinctive hunting ability. Of course, expert marksmanship never hurt.

"What do ya think about a little huntin' next Saturday?"

"Great."

"We'll need an early start, say three o'clock in the mornin'."

Without the slightest hesitation, Brian responded. "No problem. I'll be ready."

"Don't ya need ta ask yur parents?"

"I will, but they have never objected in the past. There won't be a problem."

There was no need to ask him about a shotgun since most households on the plains had hunting weapons, rifles or shotguns. In fact, Brian had his own shotgun, a gift from his grandfather.

With copious appreciation to Malcolm for his time, patience and acceptance, Brian began the 75 minute bicycle journey home. Dreams of the next adventure roamed among his mental review of the day's lessons. The events of this late summer day were the concrete, irrevocable validation of what he wanted to do with his life. Brian instinctively knew he was born to fly. He felt it. He tasted it. He knew it.

The ride home seemed shorter than all the previous occasions. Brian's thoughts that afternoon became the thriving seeds of his dream, his vision, and his focus. Aviation had become nearly his sole objective – an obsession. Not the slightest doubt clouded his view. He decided to be better than all the others – the best pilot in the world. He wanted to be everything Malcolm Bainbridge was and more. The thrill, the challenge, of aerial combat on this summer afternoon gave him a taste of a powerful opiate, and he relished the intoxication. Without realization, Brian Drummond was addicted. His path was set. Then, the image of Rebecca Seward came to him as she had during the slow segment of the day's flight. Becky might be an obstacle. No, he told himself, he could not let that happen. He simply had to avoid the conflict.

Other than the illuminating bare bulb over the front porch, the broad swath of light emanating from the back of the house provided the only clue to where his parents were waiting. After leaning his bike against the side of the house by the back door, Brian entered the large, country kitchen with the seductive aromas of his Mother's cooking. He was the only person smiling among the three people sitting around the kitchen table. The slap of contravention brought his excitement, enthusiasm and dreams crashing back to earth as he stood behind his vacant chair.

His mother was the first speak. "Brian, you've got to stop wasting your time with Mister Bainbridge. You've got chores here and school work you must do, if you are going to succeed in this world."

His father was quick to add, "We've tried to allow you room to grow, but you are growing in a direction which cannot be successful."

"Plus, Brian, you are our only child. We want you to be safe and able to have your own family. There is no future around those flying machines," came the impassioned statement he had heard many times before from the woman who had given him life, "and, they are dangerous."

Brian stood stone still choosing to listen without reacting to the accusations. There was no way he could begin to convey to them the source of his smile. His parents thought he was doing odd jobs, and hanging around the airplanes and the old man that flew them. Brian was convinced, if they knew he had been flying, the words he was hearing would be more focused and harsh. His heart stopped when Rebecca Seward, his beautiful, brown haired, full bloomed girlfriend of not quite a year, began to say something and stopped.

"You've got to stay away from that place," his mother said with some emphasis and conviction.

Neutrality was the position Brian needed Becky to maintain in this discussion. She was the only one among his three antagonists who knew the truth about his experience as a pilot. The frown on her face and the concern in her gentle brown eyes along with the several attempts to interject her own feelings confirmed Becky's agreement with his parent's concerns.

"Are you going to answer your mother?" demanded George Drummond.

Brian did not want to say anything, but knew he had to respond quickly, or the tone of his father's words would soon change drastically. "What can I say?"

"You can say you're not going to waste your time at old Bainbridge's."

"I like it there. I'm getting my homework and my chores done."

The retort surprisingly stopped his parents. All three of his inquisitors sat looking at him as he served himself some fried chicken, green beans and mashed potatoes. Becky and his parents had already eaten. The sporadic conversation as Brian ate his supper revolved around other activities that might attract Brian's attention and keep him away from the airfield. Brian tried to walk the thin line between acquiescence and reluctant consideration.

Fortunately for the young man, his parents were reasonably predictable. With the expression of their concern and the evening meal complete, they both moved to the living room leaving their son to clean the dishes and utensils.

"I'd better go home," Becky finally said.

"It is getting late," came the rather feeble response. "I'll walk you home."

The short walk to the house four driveways down the street was at first performed without words. The two teenagers held hands as they walked slowly down the dark and empty street. The sky was clear and the stars lit up the heavens above the trees. The moon was not in sight, yet.

"Brian," said Becky hesitating for her boyfriend's acknowledgment. The only change was a shift of focus from the stars to her eyes. "Your parents are right. You've got to stop flying. If they ever find out you've been flying with Mister Bainbridge, they will be furious."

"You know I can't."

"They're going to find out what you are doing, sooner or later."

"Probably."

She was not getting the reaction she wanted from him. "It's dangerous, Brian. Something's going to happen to you."

"Might."

"Please, Brian, I don't want anything to hurt you."

"Nothing's going to happen. Mister Bainbridge," Brian always used the proper address for his instructor except to Malcolm in deference to his elder's wishes, "is the best there is. He's teaching me really well."

"That may be, but it is still dangerous."

The remainder of the walk to Becky's home was completed the way it had begun, cool and quiet. Brian wondered what was going to happen between them. At first, Becky had thought his flying was exciting and romantic in a strange sort of way, but several well-publicized aviation accidents elsewhere in the country over the last year brought a price to the excitement.

The front porch light at Becky's house was fortunately not lit. Brian looked forward to a good night kiss. Maybe that would help calm the troubled waters between them. Somehow, he had to make her understand how important flying had become to him. The three steps to the porch were shots of adrenaline as Brian anticipated what was to come.

Becky swiftly removed her hand from Brian's and reached for the door handle and thumb tab that would open her front door. Without looking at him, she said, "Good night, Brian. I'll see you tomorrow."

The implicit slap stopped him dead in his tracks. His mouth opened, but not even a breath came out. Becky was through the door and closing it behind her before Brian could muster up a response. "Becky," he said with the bleating of a lost lamb.

"No, Brian, a kiss isn't going to make it all better."

"Wait, Becky. Can't we talk?"

"We can talk tomorrow," she said with fire in her eyes. "I don't want to talk tonight."

"You don't understand," said Brian as he continued his pleading.

"Yes, I do." The fire was burning his consciousness. The pain was perceptibly real. "You love flying more than you love me. You want those airplanes more than you want me."

"That's not true, Becky. It's different." His strength was returning although the open door and the threshold separating them made a demonstrative defense inadvisable. "We've had so much together," Brian whispered, not wanting her parents to hear.

"Becky," came the voice of her father, "is everything OK?"

"Yes, Daddy," she responded. "Brian and I are just talking." She stepped out onto the porch closing the door behind her. Her eyes expressed her thoughts, so what are you going to do now. The arms crossed under her chest conveyed the determination and defiance Becky projected.

"What do you want me to do?"

The fire in her eyes remained as she stared at her boyfriend. The pause seemed like an eternity for Brian. "Do something besides flying."

"Like what?"

"Maybe baseball. Why don't you play basketball or baseball? You are very good at it."

The short, nervous chuckle was a sign of his frustration. "They're not the same thing. Why are you so against flying?"

"It's dangerous," Becky barked, stomping her right foot and shaking two fists beside her hips. "It's dangerous and you could get hurt."

"Can we sit down and talk about this?"

"It's getting late, Brian."

"Please."

Becky took Brian's hand moving toward the long, wooden, bench chair on the porch. The words were from Brian's heart as he tried to convey the feelings, the excitement and the rewards of flight. Becky recognized the importance of flying to her boyfriend. The struggle with good and bad, safe and risky, was within Becky as she had said many times. For Brian, there was no struggle other than with Becky, his parents and the other doubters.

The growing frown conveyed the frustration. "I've got to go in. It's late," she finally brought their talk to an end with a kiss on his cheek and a shade of defeat in her voice.

"Why don't you come out to the airfield and watch me fly? Maybe Mister Bainbridge will let you fly with me."

"Maybe I will, Brian, but I'm not going flying with you."

"Great!" came Brian's excited acknowledgment.

"Great?" Becky responded sarcastically.

"We . . . we . . . ," Brian stammered with recognition of his *faux pas*. "Well, not great you won't fly with me, but great at least you will come see me fly again."

Becky smiled as the two young people stood facing each other holding hands. The petite, porcelain features of her face illuminated Brian as he felt his body flush with warmth and feeling. Smiles from their lips to the locked brightness in their eyes confirmed the mutual feelings they shared.

Their lips touched in a soft, gentle kiss. Several slow repeats followed leading to the parting of their lips as their kisses became more intimate. A mutual giving passed between them with the growing passion. Becky lifted Brian's right hand placing it on the firm mound of her left breast. The feel, the touch of her, melted him as surely as a flame melts butter.

The arousal of nature's sustenance was equally as positive as the power of her touch. The change did not escape Becky's awareness as she reached for him to not only confirm, but to communicate her awareness to Brian.

"Doesn't that feel good?"

"Oh, Becky," he moaned softly as the hormones of perpetuation raced like lightning bolts through Brian's veins.

Her body stopped its motion as she backed away from him ever so

"It has all the makings, Mister Bainbridge."

A strange combination of grimace and sneer was clearly discernible even in the early morning light. "Why the formality all of a sudden?"

"It's an honor to be here with you."

"Well, we can dispense with that crap right now."

Both men laughed, enjoying the kinship events like these usually brought with them. There was something magical about the hunt, something neither man had invented, something that had been known for generations, centuries, if not millennia, across continents since humans began to hunt for food.

The shotguns were checked and ready. Jackets, game bags, canteens, all the accouterments of the hunt were ready without further words. With the preparations completed, Malcolm stood up stretching his shoulders back, cradled his shotgun in his left elbow and looked Brian straight in the eye.

"Which way?"

Brian did not recognize the beginning of probably his most important test. The boy's enthusiasm for aerial combat was the gateway of an inevitable path. Malcolm needed to know Brian's foundation, his basis, the core of his character.

After a quick final scan of the area he had already searched, a deep breath absorbing the smells of the wild country and most importantly, determining the wind direction, Brian responded. "I'd say we should work our way off in that direction." Brian nodded and pointed toward a wide, gentle draw branching off the main stream bed.

A smile silently acknowledged Brian's passing the first test. A perfect choice. Wind, vegetation, terrain, likely shelter for pheasants, all were just as he would have picked them, the best probability for success.

"Good choice, son."

Brian did not react to Malcolm's first reference to a paternal relationship, however figurative it might be. He liked it. Similar feelings drifted through his thoughts on occasion over the last year or so. Yes, indeed, he liked it.

They moved carefully upwind watching their steps. Malcolm noted with pleasure the way Brian moved, like a cat, with precision, skill and fluidity, always staying in the proper position. The distance between them left enough room for either man to keep a clear firing arc with the possible bird sites.

As good hunters, they were prepared. Two colorful males flew out of the small group of bushes. Initially, the birds flew toward them, then instantly banked away. Both men raised their guns at the same moment.

Malcolm fired first intentionally low on the birds. Brian fired a hair's breadth later. As fate would have it, the birds were in the wrong place at the right time. The shot pattern from Brian's A.H. Fox, Model XE, 20-gauge, side-by-side shotgun covered both birds that fell like rocks to the ground.

"I'll be damned," exclaimed Malcolm. "It's not often ya get ta see a shot like that."

"Thanks."

"Well, I must say, that didn't take long. Y're a hellava shot, Brian."

"Thanks, again."

"Let's pick up yur birds." As they walked to the fallen prey, Malcolm began the essential conversation. "Brian," he hesitated as if considering his words, "so ya liked the mock combat we flew last weekend?"

"I sure did."

"Aerial combat is very much like the hunt. Same techniques, same skills, same instincts. Y've gotta respond ta the situation, feel the shot, and definitely not think about it. The speeds of modern fighters are three or four times what we flew in France. The speeds will require quicker reflexes and a sharper eye, but it'll still come down ta the skills of the hunt. A fighter pilot must be a good pilot, not necessarily a great pilot. He must be aggressive, instinctive, ruthless and a great marksman."

"I can do that. I have those traits."

"Yes, ya do, Brian. But, war's killin'. Ya've gotta think of yur adversary as no different from those birds ya just killed. The sole difference is the birds ya'll face in the air shoot back. They're tryin' to kill ya. Y've gotta be cold, focused and single-minded. Y've gotta kill or be killed."

Brian absorbed the words as he retrieved the two pheasants, but had another question in mind. "Do you really think there's going to be another war in Europe?"

It was not the question Malcolm expected, but appropriate nonetheless. "At the rate things're goin', yes, I do."

"Why?"

"A very good frienda mine is a relative of Winston Churchill. Do you know the name?"

"Yes. My history teacher says he's single handedly trying to start the war."

A chuckle accompanied the response. "Well, then, I suppose we know the politics a yur teacher, however misinformed she might be."

"She's a he."

"Then, that explains it."

"What do you mean?"

"Never mind." They walked more casually for the moment with no bird havens nearby. Neither man could find the words they wanted. Silence with the soft rustle of the prairie grass marked their contentment with the status quo. Brian struggled with understanding what was said. He decided to try again.

"Do you think Churchill is a warmonger as some people say?"

"I'm afraid I don't. Sad ta say, I think he's a prophet."

"Really?"

"Since 1932, he's been consistent with his message, and he's been right on every occasion. Hitler has visions of a grand Teutonic state of Europe. He calls it the Third Reich, the empire that will last a thousand years, so he says. He's also lathered up the German people with talka retribution for the burdens of the Versailles Treaty."

"How do you know all this?"

"I have friends too, Brian. I've seen war in all it's ugliness. I've feelings. I sense what is happenin' and I know Churchill is right."

"Are we going to have another world war?"

"I believe so."

"With the Japanese included?"

"Donchya remember our discussion last spring about the rape of Nanking? In the matter of a couple of weeks, the Japanese slaughtered innocent civilians by the thousands. Yes, I think there is going to be a war – a big war – much bigger than the last one. And, from what John Spencer tells me, the Germans aren't much better than the Japs."

"It will be a heckava war, then."

"I'm 'fraid so."

"You don't think Hitler will stop as Prime Minister Chamberlain says?"

"No."

"Then, what," Brian's sentence was cut off by a small female pheasant taking flight. Both men aimed, but did not shoot allowing the bird to live for future generations. Almost in unison, both men took a deep breath to relax the effects of the spurt of adrenaline. The guns returned to the cradle of their left arms and the walk continued.

"Where were we? Oh, yeah, y're goin' ta ask somethin'?"

Brian thought for a moment, but could not make the connection. "I can't remember."

"Well, then, let me ask, with everything I've said, ya still think ya want ta be a fighter pilot?"

"Even more."

"I hope y're not lookin' at this as some sorta adventure. Combat is nasty business, no matter how ya cut it."

Brian Drummond thought about whether he should tell Malcolm about his real feelings, his thoughts, his dream. Greatness, and more specifically greatness in aviation, was what he sought. Brian wanted to be recognized, as Malcolm was recognized by pilots everywhere, as an aviator of accomplishment; of tested, demonstrated performance. "Flying is what I want to do. Hunting is what I'm good at. It seems to be a match."

"Maybe so," Malcolm left the response choosing to consider the words, and what they would mean in the probably not too distant future.

The casual walk through the sparsely vegetated Flint Hills continued until mid-afternoon although they both knew game encounters were less likely. The words passing between them formed the foundation of a new region of growth in the maturation of a new generation, fighter pilot.

———

Chapter 2

We have to distrust each other.
It's our only defense against betrayal.
--Tennessee Williams

Thursday, 29.September.1938
Heston Aerodrome
Heston, London, England

The drone of the British Airways, twin engine, Lockheed L-14 Super Electra announced the approach of the aircraft transporting Prime Minister Arthur Neville Chamberlain, MP. The tensions everyone felt about the impending war kept the conversation of the waiting dignitaries to a minimum. The journalists among the crowd did not share the same solemnity. The meeting with *Reichkanzler* Adolf Hitler had been up and down for the last few days, and weeks for that matter. The cable indicating Chamberlain's return to Great Britain had been simple enough.

The thoughts of many Britons focused on the Prime Minister's journey to the Continent. The newspapers and the BBC filled their minds with the closeness of a war, maybe even the war. The urgency surrounding the PM's mission was unmistakable. Hopes for peace were strong.

Group Captain John Henry Randolph Spencer, DFC, Staff Secretary to Fighter Command, Royal Air Force, happened, not coincidentally, to be at Heston Aerodrome for the Prime Minister's return. Other dignitaries were also present including Ambassador Jan Masaryk of Czechoslovakian to the United Kingdom, standing two shoulders from Spencer. Without question, journalists armed with their notepads and cameras made up the majority of the waiting group. The mixture of expressions and animation in the assemblage presented a graphic contrast to Spencer. The effervescent, almost jubilant, excitement of some of the reporters brought out the white against the black of the Czech minister's stone cold stare and rigid posture.

The robustness of the engines died quickly as the aircraft stopped in front of the group. The door soon opened allowing the gaunt, tired-looking Prime Minister to exit acknowledging the applause with several waves of his hand. The distinctive flashes of light from the cameras recorded virtually every movement. Lord Halifax, the Foreign Minister, the next man to emerge from the airplane, took his position behind his leader.

The Prime Minister of the Great Britain stood before the assemblage more like a mechanical device with an artificial smile, almost painted on, waving to no one in particular. The applause, given for an as yet unknown reason, seemed to provide a modicum of strength to the career politician and leader of His Majesty's Government.

Then, as if he had extracted as much energy as possible from the recognition, Chamberlain raised a piece of paper in his right hand. He waited for the bustle of the crowd to die. "I have here a signed agreement with *Herr* Hitler which shall preserve peace in Europe." The Prime Minister's words were interrupted by more applause. Words of support, hope and guarded optimism mingled with the clapping of hands. "This is a truly historic occasion." More applause.

This time, Group Captain Spencer standing among other military officers overheard an admiral, whom he did not recognize, ask the naval captain next to him if he could see anything on the paper the PM was holding. John Spencer, as well as several others, looked intently. True enough, the paper actually appeared to be several blank sheets. No words were discernible on them.

"My good friends, this is the second time in our history that there has come back from Germany to Great Britain peace with honor. I believe it is peace in our time."

The applause and cheers from many in the crowd did not drown out the less inquisitive and now offended comment from the admiral. "My God, man. Now, he's quoting Benjamin Disraeli. I've heard enough," he concluded with disgust as he turned to walk away. The captain followed a few steps behind the admiral giving one last glance over his shoulder at the assemblage. John Spencer's curiosity remained strong enough to keep him in place.

As the journalistic questions continued for Chamberlain, Masaryk leaned over to say to Lord Halifax, "If you have sacrificed my nation to preserve the peace of the world, I will be the first to applaud you. But if not, sir, God help your mortal souls!"

Spencer looked quickly from the relatively short ambassador to the tall, lanky, foreign minister. In that instant, John Spencer knew precisely that the ambassador's admonition provided the defining description of what Chamberlain presented to the world.

Foreign Minister Lord Halifax stood stunned for a brief moment. "I hope and pray time shall prove us right."

Masaryk chose not to respond. He too, as the admiral and several other listeners chose to simply leave and return to their waiting automobiles.

The feelings John came to recognize were those of false hope and expectations, and disappointment. He knew all too well, from listening to his uncle, what the Prime Minister's words meant to Great Britain, to Europe and probably to the World.

Chamberlain undoubtedly felt the mood change as well. "Thank you, ladies and gentlemen." With one last wave, the Prime Minister disappeared into the waiting limousines with his entourage for the return to Whitehall and Downing Street. John waited for a good portion of the crowd to disperse. The journalists, without stimulation to support their frenzy, lost interest as they cogitated over their latest news story. Most seemed to like what they heard. It was the professional military men who grumbled and complained about the Munich Accord.

Friday, 30.September.1938
Wichita, Kansas, USA

The several weeks of distant history passed with Brian Drummond stretching the limits of his parent's constraints to continue his clandestine flying with Malcolm Bainbridge on some of his contract flying assignments. Malcolm flew for fun and did not need the money, but still felt the pretense of making a living with his machines of the air should be maintained. The relationship between tutor and student flourished with Malcolm deriving the enjoyment of passing his knowledge to an exceptional pupil while he received the young man's labor to maintain his aircraft. The understanding that cemented their relationship was based upon mutual respect from entirely different perspectives. Brian viewed the older man as the venerable keeper of the faith willing to pass his plethora of knowledge to his blessed brain, while the image from the other direction was that of a potentially flawless gemstone with the first few facets chipped off.

Malcolm, despite his avocation in a fledgling time, was a realist who recognized the need to extend, to pass, to hand down his passion to the next generation. Brian was, virtually without exception, one of the most instinctively skilled pilots he had ever flown with. The boy combined the hunting skills learned with his father and uncles throughout his youth with the manipulative prowess and air sense of a veteran pilot. The boy was simply great.

The routine mail, small freight and aerial photography flights were on occasion flown by Brian, with mail, packages or a photographer in the front cockpit. The training flights also continued expanding the lad's experience in numerous areas, precision aerobatics and low level maneuvering, mock aerial combat against multiple adversaries, and most notably, dead reckoning navigation over flat, near featureless terrain.

Part of Brian's aviation education relied on Malcolm's fame with the pioneers who began their companies around Wichita – Walter Beech, Clyde

Cessna and Lloyd Stearman. Visits to the plants where some of the aircraft of their time were conceived, designed, built and flown helped Brian understand aviation. The infant companies offered a unique facet to the illustrious history of Wichita, the Midwestern cattle town with a legacy nearly a century old. With Malcolm's guidance and the generosity of his friends, Brian was exposed to some of the finer aspects of aircraft including propulsion, aerodynamics and control. The more Brian was exposed to, the more voracious his appetite became for information and knowledge.

This particular Friday, the principal at his high school gave the students a day off, an extended weekend. The reason provided referred to some requirement for the teachers to meet with several state officials. None of the pupils actually cared why they were given a day off from school, they simply accepted it with every intent to enjoy it. Brian took full advantage of the extra time to pursue the passion in his life with Malcolm Bainbridge's assistance.

To that end, the old and the new, Malcolm and Brian, were returning from a flight delivering a package to Fort Worth. Brian was in the front cockpit piloting the aircraft.

"Remember what I told you about crosswinds," the old man offered to his rapidly maturing young pilot.

Many thoughts flashed from his tutor's catalytic reminder. Hold the crab angle until near touchdown, then push on the top, or opposite, rudder pedal to align the nose with the landing area, and lower the opposite wing into the wind to compensate and maintain the attitude. He had practiced the technique many times, and performed it well. As they approached Malcolm's little airfield, the wind looked stronger than expected, and it was unusually almost perpendicular to the length of his relatively narrow, grass, landing strip. The waves of the strong wind rippled through the grove of elm trees on either side of the strip.

The landing conditions did not look acceptable – too many things changing too rapidly. Wisely, as he had been taught, Brian pushed the throttle lever forward. The engine groaned in response, but did not fail to increase RPM with the propeller biting into the air.

As they passed down the strip, buffeted by the roiling wind, Brian looked off his left wing to see the bright yellow blouse under the worn blue overalls along with Becky's waving hand. Instinctively, Brian returned the wave although he quickly realized she was probably responding to the rocking movement of the aircraft's wings as he worked to keep the machine level.

The circuit to return for landing was tight, uniform and well corrected for the crosswind. The approach was normal. As he passed over the last line of trees, Brian applied right rudder to keep the nose of the aircraft pointed straight down the landing strip and lowered the left wing into the wind. With the wheels a few feet above the grass, a flash of brown and black darted out of the treeline to the left. A big dog chased a zigzagging rabbit directly in front of the aircraft. Brian jammed the throttle forward to miss the oblivious animals to no avail.

The left main wheel struck the dog's right shoulder causing the left wing to dip even more, contacting the ground. The aircraft cartwheeled creating a swirl of dirt, grass and fragments of the wings as the aircraft broke apart. The aircraft fuselage, or more appropriately, the cockpit containing the two men, tumbled three times jostling the occupants violently against the sides. The remains of the Stearman finally came to rest in a tangle of wires, broken wood and rags of semi-rigid, doped fabric shrouded in a ball of dust. The two men were suspended upside down hanging in their harnesses.

"Quickly, lad, unbuckle and get out," came the familiar authoritative voice of Malcolm Bainbridge.

As Brian released the buckle allowing himself to fall to the ground, a strong hand grabbed the back of his jacket. Malcolm dragged him away from the broken machine as he struggled to stand.

Events were still happening very fast. Brian became aware of the screams of a woman at about the same moment he felt the heat from the flames now consuming the broken aircraft they had just departed.

"Oh, my God," Becky screamed as she ran toward them. "Brian, are you all right? Oh, my God." Becky stopped about ten feet in front of the two men, hunched over as if it was she that was in mortal pain and placed both hands over her mouth and nose so only her eyes were visible. "Are you all right?" came the muffled question once more.

Brian tried to quell his shaking body to regain control. "I don't know," was the feeble, disturbed response that ushered forth.

Her arms enveloped him as she pressed her face into his chest with tears streaming down her cheeks. Becky was now shaking as much as Brian was. "We've got to get you to the hospital."

All Brian could do was look down at her. He did not know what he should or should not do.

"No need," came the commanding voice beside them. "He's not hurt."

By now, Gertrude Bainbridge was at the scene to investigate the consequences of the burning pile. "Are you OK, Malcolm?"

"Yea, Gerty. We're OK. The boy just had a pass with bad luck. Hit the Seaver's dog on landing."

"Are you going to take him back up?"

"I've gotta."

"What?" Becky screamed at Mister Bainbridge with an uncharacteristic vehemence. "You're not going to kill him!"

"No, I'm not Miss Seward, but he's gotta go up, or he may not fly again."

"No!" she continued to scream. "You can't do that! You're not going to kill him. He's not going to fly anymore."

It was at that moment Brian began to show some signs of recovery. He looked first at Becky still scowling at Malcolm, then he looked into the determined eyes of his instructor, and finally at Missus Bainbridge who simply smiled and nodded her head. There was considerable hesitation in his still shaking body and growing apprehension in his consciousness.

Malcolm saw the mechanism of self-doubt beginning to turn within his young protégé. If they waited much longer, Brian might not ever have the same edge and fine touch he had just demonstrated a few minutes earlier. "Come on, Brian, y've gotta get back on the horse."

"No, no, no," Becky shouted with her own determination as she pulled on his right arm in an attempt to extricate her boyfriend from the clutches of the devil, as far as she was concerned.

Gertrude Bainbridge stepped in to hold Becky saying the reassuring words that began to soothe the hysterical girl as Malcolm wrapped his strong arm around Brian and led him off toward another aircraft. Brian knew what Malcolm was trying to do having been literally tossed off a horse a few times before, so he submitted to Malcolm's directions.

To Brian's staggered surprise, Malcolm stopped short of the second Stearman C-3R and began opening the barn doors to his pride and joy, a compact, distinctive shaped, Sopwith F.1 Camel, painted in the markings of his old Royal Flying Corps unit, No.43 'Fighting Cocks' Squadron. The skull & crossbones on the black wheel covers distinguished the otherwise camouflaged aircraft. "No, Malcolm. I can't. I can't do it. I'll crash the best aircraft you've got." The words did not deter Bainbridge from continuing his preparations as if he were totally oblivious to Brian's protestations. "There's only one cockpit," Brian said feebly as if Malcolm did not know the configuration of the venerable fighter.

With Brian wheeling the propeller, the engine of the renowned, Great War fighter started with ease. Malcolm taxied the aircraft out of the barn beside the other Stearman. Brian placed the triangular-shaped, wooden blocks in front of both wheels, chocking them in case the aircraft decided to move. Malcolm got out of the cockpit leaving the engine still running at idle. The old man walked toward Brian who was now shuffling backward away from his approaching benefactor.

"No, Mister Bainbridge," Brian said resorting to the formal now. "I can't do it."

With the fighter's 150-horsepower, Bentley BR.1, rotary engine still chugging in the background, Malcolm reached for both of Brian's shoulders and said with some force verging on anger, "Y're one a the best, most gifted pilots I've ever flown with. Ya can fly the piss outta this machine. Y're goin' ta do it, and do it as well as y've done everything else." The older man hesitated for a moment as he studied the reaction of his words. Malcolm Bainbridge stood as straight as he could, pulling his shoulder back to force his chest out. "This is yur destiny. Yur born for this." He released Brian's left shoulder, swung slightly away and pointed directly at the idling fighter. "There is yur destiny," he added with a firm, ardent voice of conviction and an arm pointing over Brian's shoulder toward the Camel.

A strong hand began to push him toward the fighter, and then fell away. A strange mixture of fear, elation, apprehension, doubt and eager anticipation filled the young man's head. A bizarre concoction of the wavering mind made him hesitate a few moments every few yards, and yet compelled him to continue. As he passed behind the tail of the aircraft and felt the propwash mixed with partially burnt gasoline, the magnetism of the beckoning cockpit began to take control of his mind. The reality of his first flight in one of the most famous fighters in the world took control of his reservations. The fulfillment of a dream was now what occupied his thoughts.

The descent into the tight confines of the cockpit felt like a glove compared to the relative spaciousness of the Stearman's cockpit. As he strapped himself to the seat, Brian scanned the cockpit instruments and controls as he had done in the hangar many times before. There was a familiar-ness to this place almost like a distant, inaudible voice telling him he was home.

Another reality shot bolts of electricity through his brain. "Oh God. I can't," he said to himself as his mind began to consider the consequences of another mistake. "I can't!" His chin fell to his chest and his eyes went blank as self-doubt began to work its venomous way into his concentration.

From the corner of his right eye, something moved. Instinctively, he looked up and toward the motion. Malcolm was standing beside him two wing lengths away. About 100 yards beyond him stood Missus Bainbridge with her arm around Becky who was back to covering her face with both hands. Beyond them were the still smoldering remains of the aircraft they had just left.

What attracted the most attention, however, was the broadest grin he had ever seen plastered across the weathered face of Malcolm Bainbridge. There was energy in his eyes, the energy of confidence that passed between them like an unseen force of nature.

Once Malcolm knew he had Brian's attention, he raised his right hand to full height above him with his fingers spread wide apart, then clenched a fist, held it for a few seconds and pumped the large balled fist several times signaling Brian to launch.

Brian signaled for Malcolm to remove the blocks in front of the wheels. Without looking into the cockpit, Brian's left hand reached for the throttle lever pushing it slightly forward. The engine turned over a little faster and the wind currents around him became stronger. The aircraft moved forward.

Turning the aircraft to point down the remaining grass strip that was still long enough, Brian checked the wind. Doubts filled his head, again. Was the crash his fault because he miscalculated the winds? Had he made a simple, but terrible mistake?

Again, the motion, this time from his left. There was Malcolm Bainbridge still grinning and pumping his fist.

Brian lowered his head and said aloud, "Please God, don't let me make any mistakes." With that short aviator's prayer, the throttle moved forward. The nimble Camel swiftly built up speed to Brian's pleasant surprise. The tail skid rose off the grass followed shortly by the distinctive bounce of the wheels as the fighter leapt into the air. Brian quickly corrected for the crosswind and checked his instruments. Everything was normal.

As the ground fell away from him, so fell all his doubts. The thrill of flight in the historic airplane took command of his mind and body. Numerous control inputs helped him gain the feel for the agile fighter. This was a lot more machine than he had ever flown, and it was all his for the moment. The roar of the engine had an invigorating and yet calming effect on the young pilot.

Finding the airfield was a simple task with the streamer of smoke from the remains of the Stearman blown over by the wind pointing directly to his intended landing spot. Brian made a full throttle, low pass down the strip. Only Malcolm could be seen waving as he passed. To convey the triumph over his fears, Brian pulled the nose up to about 30 degrees, pushed forward slightly as he had been taught and rolled the aircraft completely over one and a half times. With a short hesitation in the inverted position, he pulled the nose down toward the horizon and rolled some more to lose some of his altitude to enter the downwind portion of the landing circuit.

There was plenty of room to land, and the smoke from the Stearman was blowing away from the landing area. With regained confidence, Brian executed a near perfect, crosswind landing. He taxied back to the barn, turned and stopped the Camel beside the remaining Stearman. The reluctance to shutdown was overcome by the approaching presence of Malcolm.

"Magnetos off," Brian said aloud to himself. Quiet returned except for the whisper of the wind.

Malcolm pulled himself up on the wing to face his young pupil. Offering his hand in congratulations, he confirmed the impression, "Ya did good, lad. I hope ya feel better now."

"Yes, I do, Malcolm. Flying this," patting the side of the fighter, "was the greatest." The smiles and brilliant eyes of both men communicated more than their words. Brian knew this had been a momentous occasion no matter how you cut it. "Thank you for trusting me."

The older man leaned over and swatted Brian's head. "Oh, the hell ya say. This has nothin' ta do with trust. This is belief. Like I told ya, boy, this is yur destiny."

"Well, thanks anyway."

"Y're welcome. Now, get the hell outta that machine. The ladies are waitin' for us at the house."

A sense of loss passed through his consciousness as he extricated himself from the cockpit. After a few admiring strokes, the two men pushed the classic airplane back into the barn and shut the doors.

The walk to the house was filled with the talk of flight and reinforcement of the lessons learned this day. Brian was dumbfounded by Malcolm's almost nonchalance toward the accident and the loss of one of his aircraft. Malcolm Bainbridge made the younger man feel as if he had been lucky to have crashed. It was a strange, but curiously attractive feeling.

Their arrival was greeted with a hug and a kiss from each of the women accompanied by the appropriate appreciation. The change in Becky was in stark contrast to the earlier emotions conveyed after the crash. Although she seemed to be happier and more relaxed than when he took off, Becky still had a distant troubled glaze to her expression that began to erode any remaining brightness. Brian could not help wondering what had caused the change and in so short of a time. A cold Coca-Cola provided a refreshing punctuation to an eventful day.

Brian recounted the tales of the day in glorious detail as the four of them sat in the living room nearly oblivious to the quiet, stern and inward expression on Becky's face. Although Brian overcame the doubts of an accident, Becky was not so quick to let go of the potential consequences of the dramatic afternoon.

After several questions of affirmation directed toward his girlfriend without a flicker of a response, Brian could not avoid her mood. "What's wrong, Becky?" Brian asked as if he did not know.

"You know perfectly well what's wrong," she answered with some fire in her voice.

Brian could not find the words as he looked from Becky's angry eyes to Gertrude and Malcolm Bainbridge with an expression asking for help.

Missus Bainbridge made the first move. "Becky, you've got to understand flying."

Like gravy taken too far in the thickening process, Becky crossed the cliff's edge. "No I don't," she spat back as she rose quickly to leave. "Thank you for the soda," she added without looking back.

The screen door slammed shut as Brian stood. Dumbstruck by the eruption, Brian looked from one set of bewildered eyes to another. "I'd better go with her."

"Sure, Brian. We'll see ya tomorrow." Malcolm waited for a nod from his young pilot. "Give her some time. She'll come around."

Brian was not so sure, but he knew he had to follow the advice and hope for the best. "Thanks for everything today. Flying the Camel was great." No reference was made to the accident although it was in Brian's thoughts as he left the house.

Rebecca Seward's headstart required some extra effort and a few minutes to eliminate. She pedaled her bicycle with vigor and purpose. The thought of trying to talk to her passed quickly.

The ride home in the late afternoon was equally distant as Brian thought about the words of Malcolm Bainbridge, and what they meant to the future while Becky undoubtedly considered ways she might be able to get Brian to stop flying. She wanted him safe without alienating him forever.

They split in town with only a quick kiss between them.

———

Friday, 30.September.1938
Headquarters, Fighter Command
Bentley Priory
Stanmore, Middlesex, England

The dark wood paneling and high ceiling spaciousness of the Commander's conference room reflected the bright burst of remaining sunlight streaming through the enormous French doors. John Spencer joined several of the senior staff already assembled. This was the latest of the daily gatherings that had grown from the weekly war meetings called by their leader, Air Chief Marshal Sir Hugh Caswall Tremenheere Dowding, GCVO, KCB, CMG, Air Officer Commanding-in-Chief, Fighter Command. The precipitously mounting tensions of the late summer and early fall of 1938 brought the entire British armed forces to full war alert. Taut nerves and senses represented the anticipation, expectation and resentment.

"Good afternoon, John," came the first greeting from Air Vice-Marshal Keith Rodney Park, MC, DFC, the New Zealander transplant and Air Officer Commanding-in-Chief, No.11 Group. Park's area of responsibility included the Southeast approaches to London, the most likely direction of attack, if the Germans invaded the Low Countries and the primary Channel crossing lanes.

"Good afternoon, sir."

"What does the Chief have for us today?"

"More of the same, I'm afraid."

"Now, now, John," said Air Vice-Marshal Trafford Leigh-Mallory, CB, DSO, of No.12 Group, the central segment of the Air Defense system of Great Britain – the ADGB. "After yesterday's triumphant return of the PM, it simply cannot be more of the same. After all, he has saved the world from the brink."

John did not miss the sarcastic tone. "That may be, sir, but I'm afraid it is still more of the same, nonetheless."

Other members of the staff completed the group as they waited for their leader. Tea was served as they stood about the room. The conversation remained at a social level. Spencer always noted and was always impressed by the calm and ease of these men who were on the verge of leading the still maturing air force in the impending and inevitable war. Without the uniforms, these men could be mistaken for any educated, active group in business, government or the charities for that matter. Most of these men were accomplished pilots, three were aces in the Great War and each of them were career military professionals. They also spanned the full range of military disciplines, operations, logistics, intelligence, administration and support, and yet their conversation included the changing weather, the fall colors, the latest antics of their dogs and other topics not related to their profession. The characteristic, John rationalized, probably stemmed from the pressures upon these pilots – these leaders – these men of destiny.

The side door joining the conference room with Dowding's office opened. The tall, thin stoic figure of Air Chief Marshal Dowding entered the room. The man they called 'Stuffy' in recognition of his quiet, somber, often interpreted as aloof, demeanor commanded respect within the circles of the Royal Air Force. Many professionals considered him the messiah also in recognition of the visionary religious fervor and commitment he consistently, methodically and persistently applied to the strengthening of Fighter Command during the bleak and blind years of appeasement. Many considered him to be the single greatest force behind the maturation of Radio Direction Finding, the command and control system and the modern, mono-plane, fighter aircraft. If they were successful in defending Great Britain, they would have Dowding to thank.

"Good afternoon, gentlemen."

"Good afternoon, sir," came the chorus of responses.

"Apologies for my tardiness. I thought it best to receive the latest from the PM's responses at question time in Commons. Please be seated."

The staff took their usual seats with Dowding at the head of the long conference table with his back to the glass doors.

"Shall we begin, then? Mister Leonard."

"Sir, all units remain at full alert. No unusual activity in the past few days. We remain at a level of 60% of prescribed full strength although aircraft deliveries are showing some signs of improvement."

"Everyone agreed?"

Nods around the room confirmed the assessment Air Marshal Geoffrey Leonard, DFC, Chief of Operations.

"Very well, then." Dowding looked to his Chief of Air Intelligence, Air Commodore James Hogan, DSO. "Anything new with our friends?" he asked with a sarcastic reference to the implications in some segments of the press regarding relations between Britain and Germany.

"No sir. Production remains quite high. Operations remain normal for the Germans." Normal flight operations for the *Luftwaffe* meant sustaining the highest level of routine and simulated combat activities of any country in Europe, if not the world.

"Good. Well then, until the dust begins to settle, we shall stay at full alert. Let us remain on our toes and ever vigilant. Our chum, Adolf, has certainly demonstrated a propensity to take unannounced and precipitous action." He paused to verify the agreement of the staff. "Any other old business?"

No responses came from the group.

"Very good. Then, I suppose we should move to the current events. Group Captain Spencer attended the Prime Minister's return and has reviewed the agreement between His Majesty's Government and the Third Reich. Your assessment, Mister Spencer."

"The press reports seem to be fairly accurate with respect to the mood at Heston Aerodrome. The overwhelming impression reflected relief, enthusiasm and support. There were also a few quiet dissenters, principally officers, although I did hear a rather stern admonishment by the Czech ambassador to Lord Halifax."

"Quite right, John. Vice Admiral Foley called me last night," interjected Air Vice-Marshal Park.

John Spencer immediately attached the name to the face he saw in the crowd at Heston. The disgusted admiral was none other than Vice Admiral Sir James A.J.X. Foley, KBE, DSO, the rather well-known and highly regarded destroyer commander and submarine hunter. John felt an inner embarrassment for his inability to recognize the famous admiral at the time. After all, Admiral Foley gained his reputation in the Great War as the most successful destroyer commander in any Navy. He was soon to be the commander of Naval Forces, Southern Approaches, which included the entire length of the English Channel and the Thames Estuary. In essence, Admiral Foley would command the seas of the most likely invasion route given another global war.

"What did Sir James have to say?" asked Dowding.

"He was a bit disgusted, actually," Keith Park responded.

Several mumbled words of agreement came from other members of the staff.

"I believe he reflects the same sentiments as the rest of us," Dowding added. "Has everyone had the opportunity to read the text of the agreement?" Several members of the staff had not read the document, yet. "I made sure we received an official copy of the text from the Air Ministry. John, if you will please pass our copy around for those who may wish to read the famous words."

Group Captain Spencer retrieved the copy from his file folder, passing it first to Air Vice-Marshal Park on his right.

AGREEMENT

Germany, the United Kingdom, France, and Italy, taking into consideration the agreement, which has been already reached in principle for the cession to Germany of the Sudeten German territory, have agreed on the following terms and conditions governing the said cession and the measures consequent thereon, and by this agreement they each hold themselves

responsible for the steps necessary to secure
its fulfillment:

1.   The evacuation will begin on the 1st
October.

2.   The United Kingdom, France, and Italy
agree that the evacuation of the territory
shall be completed by the 10th October,
without any existing installations having been
destroyed and that the Czechoslovak Government
will be held responsible for carrying out
the evacuation without damage to the said
installations.

3.   The conditions governing the
evacuation will be laid down in detail by
an international commission composed of
representatives of Germany, the United Kingdom,
France, Italy, and Czechoslovakia.

4.   The occupation by stages of the
predominantly German territory by German troops
will begin on the 1st October. The four
territories marked on the attached map will
be occupied by German troops in the following
order: the territory marked No. I on the 1st
and 2nd of October, the territory marked No. II
on the 2nd and 3rd of October, the territory
marked No. III on the 3rd, 4th, and 5th of
October, the territory marked No. IV on the 6th
and 7th of October. The remaining territory
of preponderantly German character will be
ascertained by the aforesaid international
commission forthwith and be occupied by German
troops by the 10th of October.

5.   The international commission
referred to in paragraph 3 will determine the
territories in which a plebiscite is to be
held. These territories will be occupied by
international bodies until the plebiscite has
been completed. The same commission will fix
the conditions in which the plebiscite is to be

held, taking as a basis the conditions of the
Saar plebiscite. The commission will also fix
a date, not later than the end of November, on
which the plebiscite will be held.

6. The final determination of the
frontiers will be carried out by the
international commission. This commission
will also be entitled to recommend to the four
Powers, Germany, the United Kingdom, France
and Italy, in certain exceptional cases minor
modifications in the strictly ethnographical
determination of the zones which are to be
transferred without plebiscite.

7. There will be a right of option
into and out of the transferred territories,
the option to be exercised within six months
from the date of this agreement. A German-
Czechoslovak commission shall determine the
details of the option, consider ways of
facilitating the transfer of population and
settle questions of principle arising out of
the said transfer.

8. The Czechoslovak Government will
within a period of four weeks from the date of
this agreement release from their military and
police forces any Sudeten Germans who may wish
to be released, and the Czechoslovak Government
will within the same period release Sudeten
German prisoners who are serving terms of
imprisonment for political offences.

Adolf Hitler
Neville Chamberlain
Edouard Daladier
Benito Mussolini

Munich,
September 29, 1938

Dowding waited patiently and quietly until each of his officers read the Munich Agreement between the Four Powers. He resumed, "In my humble opinion, for what it is worth, the Munich Accord has virtually assured that we shall have war. The words upon that piece of paper leave me cold. However, within every dark cloud, there is a silver lining, if you choose to see it."

Although there was no one in the room who disagreed, silence provided the accent to the reality they all felt.

"Since we seem to share the same assessment, you might be interested to hear what Mister Churchill had to say in Commons this afternoon." Referring to a small piece of note paper, Dowding continued, "The Prime Minister's question time was delayed a day. Commons appeared to be in a particularly raucous mood. Mister Churchill's questions to the PM conveyed his skepticism and dismay with the Accord. He is apparently holding to his position that we are on the path toward general warfare on the Continent, if not the whole of Europe or the world, for that matter."

"Quite," was the only verbal agreement from Park. The others added their agreement with head nods. Park looked to John Spencer. "I do believe your uncle has hit the nail squarely on the head, once more, John."

Group Captain Spencer acknowledged Marshal Park's comment without a smile. Being correct did not make anyone feel good about the specter of war so near, John Spencer's uncle included.

"I might add my own comments to Mister Churchill's."

A knock on the large, oak, conference room door halted the discussion. A WAAF corporal from the subterranean communications room entered the room smartly and professionally handing a single piece of paper to Dowding. He read it, nodded his head in acknowledgment to the corporal and allowed her to depart. Dowding reread the message.

"The Air Ministry was informed by the Foreign Office not quite an hour ago that the Polish government has issued a 24-hour ultimatum to the Czech government demanding the immediate return of the Teschen District."

"Damn Poles are going to get this row started, if they are not careful," commented Air Marshal Leonard.

"Dare say," added Hogan.

Dowding remained pensive and withdrawn as the discussion continued. John Spencer focused on his boss and could only wonder what thoughts had to be coursing through his mind. The pressures on him had to be enormous although the stoic leader of Fighter Command generally did not share his innermost feelings, thoughts and concerns.

"Has His Majesty's Government taken any action?" asked Leonard.

Dowding looked up, but did not respond for several seconds. "It does not appear so."

"I'll be damned," added Leonard.

"Yes, well, as I was saying, I would like to add my comments to Mister Churchill's." Dowding paused, scanned the room to ensure he had everyone's attention, and then he continued. "It is my considered opinion we owe a good measure of thanks to the Prime Minister."

"Excuse me, sir," came the words of incredulity from Air Vice-Marshal Charles Rantford, Chief of Logistics. Everyone's eyes were riveted on Dowding in an effort to read his direction although, as usual, no one could.

"I believe this agreement has brought us back from the brink of war, if only temporarily," Dowding said with a heavy, remorseful voice as if the words turned his stomach, but needed to be said nonetheless. "I might add, as each of you I am sure recognizes, if this country went to war today, Fighter Command, indeed the Royal Air Force, if not the entire armed forces, would be ill prepared, inadequately equipped and would most likely be quickly overwhelmed by the Nazi war machine." Not one disagreement surfaced, nor were there any disagreements held within. "The Prime Minister has brought us, inadvertently I suspect, the most valuable commodity we need, we seek, indeed, we must have . . . time. Time to continue to build our meager force. Time to prepare our pilots, our controllers, our fitters, our RDF operators, for the onslaught which is soon to be upon us." Dowding paused to let the message sink in. "Each of you recognizes the reality we face. We must make every effort humanly possible to take full advantage of the time, however short it may be. We have no alternative but to make our utmost efforts to be prepared for this inevitable conflict. I suspect Hitler will not attempt general warfare until weather improves in the spring."

The remainder of the afternoon and early evening of this particular Friday were spent discussing the preparations each of the major staff members had ongoing. Pilot training, intelligence collection, aircraft production, squadron status and deployment were all discussed and agreed upon. Periodic exercises of various magnitudes were planned to operate elements as well as the entire system under simulated combat conditions. They all knew the inescapable was nearly upon them. There was precious little time remaining.

Saturday, 1.October.1938
Wichita, Kansas, USA

The cool caress of the early fall air brought a welcome relief from the long summer heat and winds. The eternal rhythm of the planet began the next phase yielding the vibrant colors along the periphery of the newly harvested fields. The Great Plains, America's breadbasket, were finally showing signs of recovery from the nearly fatal droughts and dust storms of just a few years earlier.

The changes, although not of a direct impact on the day-to-day life of Malcolm Bainbridge, were nearly transparent to the youthful enthusiasm of young Brian Drummond. It was a great Saturday morning with crystal clear, blue sky above Brian's head as he completed the bicycle journey from town to Bainbridge Airfield, as the other aviators called it. This would be a payback day for Brian where he compensated Malcolm for his generosity and tutelage. Maintenance and repair on the two remaining aircraft under Malcolm's ownership, completion of the clean-up of the skeletal remains of the crashed Stearman, and other various minor chores around his home and airfield.

Although he would rather be flying the machines, the next best thing for Brian was working on them or around them. Often times, just the sight of one of the majestic airplanes brought a smile to his face and a warm sensation to his heart. Brian's labor on the ground was the price he was willing to pay for the pleasure of flight. Brian used the servicing time to touch and stroke the airplanes. He also used the time to evolve, develop and extend his dream. The process gained strength as his experience grew and his exposure bloomed. The more he learned, the more he wanted to know. The more he experienced, the more experience he desired, needed and demanded.

There was no motion or other indication of activity around the Bainbridge house, the large barn plus add-ons that served as a makeshift hangar or other miscellaneous buildings. The assignment for the day was essentially the same as it was every Saturday. Each aircraft had to be carefully checked for holes or tears in the doped fabric – the skin of each aircraft. Minor, usually cosmetic, damage was always present from a rock thrown up by a wheel, from an occasional bird strike, or for one reason or another. Brian varnished the patches to cover the damaged areas.

The inspections of the two aircraft indicated an unusually low amount of injury to the airplanes. The completed patches would take several hours to dry sufficiently for them to be painted. Malcolm liked his aircraft well maintained and looking good, and Brian tried to meet the old man's expectations. All the other equipment, engines, propellers, control cables and instruments, were checked to complete the physical inspection and repair.

The last task on the aircraft involved driving the small field tractor with the fuel and oil tanker wagon, the pilots called a bowser, to each machine and filling them with gasoline and oil, if required. The smell of the gasoline brought feelings of power, not influence, but horsepower, speed and energy. There was just something about the distinct odor that made Brian feel good.

After servicing the airplanes, Brian exchanged the bowser for a mower deck that had to be hitched to the rear fittings and connected to the drive pad on the back of the rear axle. The tractor with the mower attachment made quick work of the large grass area around the hangar and the Bainbridge house. The big parts were finished in less than thirty minutes. The hard part remained, pushing the hand mower around all the trees and trimming the edges of the lawn as defined by Malcolm.

Nearing the end of the mowing task, Malcolm Bainbridge finally emerged from the house. He waited on the porch sitting in the large wooden rocking chair that was implicitly his without a name on it. Beside him, Brian could see a hefty pitcher of iced lemonade undoubtedly freshly made by Gertrude Bainbridge. Although the temperature was inconsistent with the attractiveness of the cold lemonade, Brian was ready for the refreshment to offset the accumulation of sweat he had built up despite the chilly temperatures.

With the last of the trimming accomplished and the hand mower properly returned to the work shed, Brian joined Malcolm on the porch.

"Good mornin', m'boy," came the greeting from Malcolm along with a large glass of cold lemonade.

"Good morning," Brian answered taking the glass. "I hope I didn't wake you by doing my chores."

"Not really."

The two men sat looking out from the porch through the quivering shadows of the trees, each content with their own thoughts. Brian was experiencing an emotional salivation with thoughts of flight while the older man was covered by a more somber mood brought on by events across the Atlantic.

An awareness of the peculiar mood did not dawn until Missus Bainbridge opened the screen door to say, "It's comin' on again, Malcolm."

With a nod of his head, the old man turned to his pupil. "Ya need to hear this, Brian. Y'll bear witness ta great events which are beginning ta happen."

Somewhat confused, Brian followed Malcolm into the house. The old man stood over the large, brown, wooden box containing the radio as if he was waiting for some creature to spring out. He motioned for Brian to sit.

The young man chose a wooden chair on the periphery of the room since he was still a bit sweaty.

After a few commercial announcements for the largest feed store and an automobile dealership in Wichita, the man on the radio began, "Now, for the ten o'clock morning news from CBS Radio.

"Our sole story this morning involves historic events in Europe.

"British Prime Minister Neville Chamberlain returned from Munich yesterday to cheering crowds in London. Holding a paper he said was an agreement with the German leader, he told the crowd, 'I believe it is peace in our time.'

"Reaction in Europe has been generally thankful. The drumbeat toward war has been silenced. A celebratory atmosphere accentuated the sense of relief, although Winston Churchill, virtually the lone dissenter in British politics, remains consistent in his condemnation of the Munich Accord.

"Further, we have a statement by CBS Radio correspondent, William L. Shirer, in Berlin, with another view of this historic agreement."

A different male voice, more scratchy than the announcer, presumably Mister Shirer, spoke, "It took the Big Four just five hours and 25 minutes here at Munich to dispel the clouds of war and come to an agreement on the partition of Czechoslovakia. There is to be no European war after all."

Brian Drummond looked toward Malcolm Bainbridge who continued to stare at the radio as the announcer provided a description of the geography of Southeastern Germany and Czechoslovakia, and more specifically the subject Sudetenland region. Brian, as an observer to the living room scene, needed little knowledge of topics to understand their significance. The stern, focused, almost angry expression on Malcolm's face and in his eyes added the most dramatic punctuation to the broadcast news story.

"A diplomatic source," the radio announcer continued, "indicates the agreement ceded to Germany, as their final territorial demand, part of Czechoslovakia, Chancellor Hitler has in the past contended was historically and ethnically German. There was no comment from either Chancellor Hitler or President Roosevelt regarding the belief that this truly was the final demand and that war in Europe has been averted by the historic agreement between Prime Minister Chamberlain, Chancellor Hitler, Premier Daladier and President Mussolini.

"We will bring you more news regarding events in Europe as they come in. We return you to the regular program." The broadcast ended and the music returned.

Malcolm moved slowly to a large chair opposite the radio. His shoulders drooped and his head hung low. He almost fell into the chair like a pile of mush plopping into a bowl. Further gravity was added when he buried his face in both hands with his elbows on his knees.

A young man's curiosity broke the silence between them. "Are the Big Four, Britain, France, Germany and Italy?" Brian asked knowing the answer, but not knowing what else to say.

No sign of response from Malcolm brought Gertrude Bainbridge into the conversation. "You are correct, Brian."

"Then, how can they decide to divide up another country like that?"

Missus Bainbridge looked to Malcolm for the answer, but none appeared to be forthcoming. "I don't know. It does seem strange, but maybe the Czechs agreed to it also."

Without further prodding, Malcolm raised his head. "We're goin' ta war, again," he said with a heavy voice and no eye contact.

"What?" was the simultaneous response from Gertrude and Brian.

"We're goin' ta war, I tell ya," he answered with more force to his words this time. "Chamberlain sold out ta Hitler. The bastard won't stop now."

"Malcolm, that's not what the announcer said," Gertrude protested as if he had not heard the words correctly.

"I know what he said, Gerty," Malcolm reacted with a growing fire in his eyes. "Ya remember the letters I've been gettin' from John Spencer, the British pilot I flew with in the Great War?" Malcolm waited for the affirmative nod from his wife. "In his last letter, he said this might happen. I share his opinion of Hitler."

"What do you mean?" Gertrude Bainbridge asked.

"John has been keepin' me posted on events in Europe. The British and French have been carvin' up Europe to feed Hitler's appetite for land. The more they feed him, the more he wants. Now, it's part of Czechoslovakia. Next, it will be the rest of Czechoslovakia, or maybe Denmark, or even France for that matter."

Brian was a distant witness to this curious conversation being conducted in a small house in the middle of the United States of America. He did not feel the need to involve himself in the conversation, choosing instead to listen and learn as much as he could. Malcolm Bainbridge was quite certainly convinced great things, bad things from his mood and tone, were about to happen.

"How can that possibly affect us?"

"Ya may mark my words, Gerty, there'll be war within the year is my guess."

"No, Malcolm, you can't possibly mean that."

"Go ahead, mark the calendar. Go ahead. We're goin' ta war," the older man said as he rose and quickly walked out of the house.

Gertrude Bainbridge and Brian Drummond watched out the living room window as Malcolm disappeared into the shadows of the woods surrounding their house. Neither of them moved nor spoke for what seemed like a long time as their thoughts reviewed the words just spoken and the implications of those words.

"I'd better finish my chores."

"No need, Brian."

"I'd rather finish if you don't mind, Missus Bainbridge."

"Suit yourself," she said as she sat down in one of the overstuffed chairs raising her apron to her mouth as if she needed to wipe something away.

Leaving the house and returning to the airplanes changed the focus of Brian's thoughts. He remembered the events in the air of a few weeks back, the stories, however brief, Malcolm told him about flying in the Great War, and about Malcolm's forecast of impending war. The mechanics of his remaining agreed-to chores came automatically as Brian considered other possibilities.

With the inevitable conclusion to his voluntary Saturday morning task, Brian accepted another ice-cold glass of lemonade.

"Would you like some lunch, Brian?"

"No, thank you, ma'am. I really should be going, I guess."

"I'll tell Malcolm you finished and went home."

"Thank you," responded Brian as Missus Bainbridge entered the house.

Although there were no guarantees or even agreements for any flights this day, Brian, as he usually did, had hoped for a flight. Anytime he was near airplanes he wanted to fly. He finished his lemonade and rose to leave as he saw Malcolm returning.

"I finished my chores."

"Good. Thank ya, Brian. Sit for a moment, I'd like ta talk about what's happenin'."

Brian did as he was requested. Malcolm poured two more lemonades from the pitcher on the small table.

"Ya need ta understand these events, Brian." The young man waited patiently for his tutor to continue. "They're playin' right into the hands of that crazy man, Hitler. They're givin' him just what he wants, hopin' he won't take any more, but they're wrong."

Somewhat confused by the announcement and Malcolm's words, Brian could not quite see the connection. Deduction told him Malcolm knew more than what had been stated on the radio. "I don't understand."

"Ya ever watched a pack of wild dogs in a feedin' frenzy over a pig's carcass?"

"Something like that."

"Well, that's what this Mister Chamberlain has done. He's a thrown a carcass in amongst the pack of jackals, and we will see the feedin' frenzy."

Missus Bainbridge must have been listening as the screen door opened and she, once again, joined the conversation. "Oh Malcolm, you're just bein' dramatic."

"Maybe so," he responded without looking at her. His eyes appeared to be focused on his boots as if the words he wanted to say were written across the toes. "I happen to believe what John Spencer and his uncle, Mr. Churchill, are sayin.' Appeasement will not stop the mad man."

Brian's mind was now rolling through a world of thoughts from the geography of Europe, he had learned in school, to the history of the Great War, and the experience of a not-so-young pilot fighting in that war. The possibilities, the consequences, the glory of what might happen in those places of school books and an old man's stories were as powerful as any narcotic on the unsuspecting and inexperienced mind of innocent youth. "War?" was the only word softly spoken with an inquisitive tone from the depths of his considerations.

Both of the Bainbridges looked at Brian, into his eyes, in an effort to see what he was seeing. The way the word sounded did not have the same meaning to each of the Bainbridge couple. Malcolm heard curiosity and wonderment while he could see in Gertrude's eyes the vision of this young man going off to the wastage of his youth and life.

Gertrude turned to her husband and spoke with fire and sparks in her voice. "Malcolm Bainbridge, you stop this foolish talk right this moment. I want to hear no more of this."

"Now honey. let's not overreact here."

"Overreact, my foot," she continued with the same emotion. "I watched you go off to Europe, fightin' their war. I worried myself nearly to death while you were gone. I almost died each time I received a letter or a notice, thinking you had been wounded or shot down. So, you don't tell me not to overreact. There can be no such thing as overreacting to talk of war."

Only the soft notes of a Glen Miller tune could be heard in the Bainbridge living room. Gertrude stood over Malcolm without motion for what seemed to Brian an eternity before she decided to withdraw to the kitchen. Malcolm returned his stare to the toes of his boots, his thoughts off somewhere else.

"I'd better go now," said Brian wanting to extricate himself from the uncomfortable situation and feeling the scene from yesterday was being repeated.

The spell over Malcolm broke when he looked to his young protégé. "Nonsense. There's no need ta go." A slight smile washed across his face. "Gertrude's just real sensitive 'bout the war even though she knows I won't be goin'."

"Then, why would she care?"

"She feels for ya and the other young men who'll have ta fight this one."

Malcolm could see the possibilities flash into Brian's head as he tried to relate the stories from the Great War to what might happen in Europe now, if war was to come. The discussions about the changes in aviation encompassed many things including the successes of General Billy Mitchell, the speeds of modern aircraft, and the use of aviation. Brian heard him say many times the next war would be fought in the air. Mixed with these thoughts of world events and technological progress were Malcolm's comments about destiny. Malcolm knew Brian understood what he was saying.

"When?" was all Brian could ask.

Malcolm knew the subject of the young man's question without asking. "Less than a year, I'd say."

"Will it be big?"

"It'll be bigger than the last one, I'm afraid." Only the music from the radio filled the space between their thoughts. Malcolm wanted to say more. "My friend, John Spencer, is a group captain, the equivalent of a colonel, in the RAF. He says the Brits have been preparin' for war since a few years back when this mad man, Hitler, started his saber rattlin'."

"How have they been preparing?"

"They're buildin' those new monoplane fighters I've been tellin' ya 'bout. Real fast, from what I hear. And, they've been trainin' pilots ta fly the new machines."

Considering for a moment what he was about to say, Brian said, "Malcolm, I want to be a part of this."

The short laugh was more to relieve the tension building within the old man rather than a humorous response. He knew exactly what was racing through Brian's mind. He also knew there was no sense resisting the force of nature so recognizable in the young man. Nonetheless, Malcolm thought he would make an attempt to distract Brian.

"We're not goin' ta be in this one, Brian. The mood in the country is ta stay outta any fight over there."

"I know," answered Brian. The sigh of relief from Malcolm was premature. "I want to join the RAF."

The thunderbolt hit as anticipated, but in an unexpected spot. Malcolm twitched and fidgeted as he struggled for the words he might use to dissuade Brian, but in his heart, he knew what the lad was thinking and feeling, and he also knew there was not much hope in changing his mind.

Fresh air was the elixir needed for the pressure of the moment and topic. Leading Brian on a walk into the afternoon of mixed shadows of the trees with leaves just now beginning to turn their annual colors and the spotty puffs of clouds above them, Malcolm began what was to be a long discussion with Brian. This conversation was more from a father to the son he never had rather than tutor to pupil.

All the things a father would say to his son in situations like these were said. The frustration of war. Their fight, not ours. Why risk your life for a cause that is not ours? Many of the words spoken by Malcolm were not entirely believed in his own mind, but they were words that had to be said to an impressionable young man who possessed visions of glory and patriotism in the face of what was portrayed as a universal evil. Malcolm even tried to convey the horrors of war, the mutilation, the loss – the loss of life, the loss of friends, and the loss of innocent people you love.

Consideration was the best word to apply to Brian's deliberations over Malcolm's descriptions and dissertation. The young man was pensive and inquisitive beyond his years. It was Brian's response to the topics that swayed Malcolm the most. During those steps and among the words exchanged by the two aviators, Malcolm knew he had no choice but to help Brian in his personal quest. He recognized the mind set of his pupil. He knew with the approach of war and Brian's attitude the young man's departure across the Atlantic was only a matter of time. He also knew Brian's best chance for survival was fighting on his terms rather than by the dictate of the government.

As the questions and answers continued on that long afternoon walk, Malcolm determined his process for dealing with Brian's sense of adventure and perceived duty. He would not make the task easy. Solicitation of support was the first of numerous obstacles Brian would have to overcome to fulfill his stated objective. Group Captain Spencer would receive a letter requesting his surreptitious evaluation of Brian's flying skills under pressure. If John considered him worthy, the gates of entry into the RAF would have to be met. Malcolm knew the requirements were different than they had been twenty plus years earlier, but he did not know how difficult they might be especially without a declared war. The last set of obstacles would be making his way to England for his training and initiation, if it ever got that far. He knew he had to make it difficult to find out, to prove Brian's commitment and be able to face Brian's parents and girlfriend when the wrath descended upon him for his assistance.

"OK, Brian, I'll help ya. Y're goin'a hav'ta prove yurself."

The obvious excitement in his bodily gyrations and the tremor of his voice told the story. "Oh God, that's great, Malcolm. Thanks. Thank you so much. I won't let you down."

"Brian, don't thank me. This is not a game I'm sendin' ya into."

"Oh, I know."

"Maybe ya do," Malcolm continued with a subdued tone. "Have ya thought about what y'll tell yur parents and Becky?"

The young man's hesitation offered a complete answer. "No." The realization of what was ahead was the first actual dampening of Brian's enthusiasm and excitement. "They'll just have to accept it."

"That may be, young man, but ya'd better prepare yurself because it won't be easy."

Despite the obstacles presented by Malcolm, Brian knew what he wanted to do, knew what he had to do, and was glad he was going to get some help.

Chapter 3

Unto the man of yearning thought
and aspiration, to do nought
is in itself almost an act.
-- Dante Gabriel Rossetti

Wednesday, 5.October.1938
House of Commons
Westminster, London, England

The Right Honorable Winston Leonard Spencer Churchill, Member of Parliament for Epping, moved slowly through the aisles of the chamber not really acknowledging comments, both for and against him. The comments spread across the spectrum although most balanced toward ridicule.

The green benches of the lower chamber, the House of Commons, began to fill. Nearly full attendance was expected to hear the Prime Minister's report upon returning from Munich. With the hall nearly full, the Prime Minister entered to take his position on the seat before the majority leader's rostrum.

The Speaker called the House to order. The normal amenities and procedures were followed with the usual precision, respect and tradition. The floor was turned over to the Prime Minister of Great Britain, the leader of the Conservative Party, the Right Honorable Neville Chamberlain. The years and rigors of high office showed on his entire person and demeanor.

"Honorable members," he began. The words came through with some difficulty initially. The beginning of his speech recalled the significant events that led to Munich and more specifically, the Munich Accord.

Churchill's thoughts were more focused. For more than eight years, he had been banished to the back benches of the ruling party's side of the House. Virtually the lone voice for strength and firmness regarding any activities directly or indirectly related to the German regime of Adolf Hitler, he chose the horrendously burdensome role as conscience, voice and rapier for the minuscule minority of members, and citizens for that matter, calling for caution and preparedness.

On this particular day, Winston concentrated on the words of the speech he would deliver in response to the Prime Minister's presentation. He felt no satisfaction, no joy, no enthusiasm for what he had to say, but the message had to be strong medicine for a governing body leading the nation into war – a war that would be devastating to all who participated or touched by its evil flame.

Chamberlain droned on about the virtues of the agreement he had forged with Hitler. The expected cheers, grunts and other words of encouragement normal to Commons punctuated his speech. The excitement among members was inescapable which brought an inner depression to Churchill. He remained convinced of what was about to happen. The disappointment over the blindness of those in power, or near power, made the depression more pronounced, but also provided a growing strength to present the contrast – the reality – the truth. Occasionally, Winston returned with purpose to the press reports of the Prime Minister's return to England yesterday.

Without question, the country wanted peace. So much so, everyone seemed willing to accept anything that might preserve the peace even for a brief moment longer. The memories of the Great War and the pain, suffering and sacrifice within individuals, households, communities and the nation made the thoughts of anything other than peace almost unbearable. The remembrance of brothers, husbands, sons and fathers who lost their lives on the muddy, scarred and deadly Flanders fields twenty years earlier brought an enormous tolerance as well as the safety of blindness. There was an element of desperation to their collective desire for peace.

Those memories were not lost on Churchill, son of Lord Randolph Churchill, a distinguished member of an aristocratic family. Unfortunately, he knew too much and knew too well the mind of the German leader. The reports from Germany from various sources were too graphic, too blatant, too ominous to be ignored. He had committed himself to being the voice against the wind, but no one could say he was not a steadfast, consistent and determined voice.

As Winston listened to the distant words of his leader and rehearsed his own soon to be delivered speech, his thoughts occasionally and briefly recounted the press reports of Chamberlain's words at Heston. Shots of incredulity punctuated his recollection. Despite all his warnings in this very chamber, in the halls of Parliament and in the privacy of social gatherings, Chamberlain chose to ignore the cautionary guidance and calls for strength. There was little satisfaction in being correct since the result would be another incomprehensible slaughter of young life.

From his seat among the backbenchers, Churchill now listened more closely to the words. Even the opposition accepted the Prime Minister's explanation of the agreement and shared the PM's belief that Hitler was satisfied and finished with his acquisitions. As the congratulatory words continued, the twinges of depression began to gnaw at him, but he resisted, needing his concentration.

Then, with the proper timing as a member finished the delivery of his accolades to the Prime Minister, Winston stood. There was silence.

"The Chair recognizes the Honorable Member from Epping."

"Mister Speaker, it is with a buoyant heart I listen to the words of my colleagues." He paused letting his low, gravely, lisping, somber voice come forward in stark contrast to the words. The usual muffled comments from members were missing. This was not what they expected from the consummate oracle of dissent. "The Prime Minister has returned to this Chamber with an agreement from *Herr* Hitler which I am certain he believes has brought us back from the brink of another world war. Listening to the words of praise how could any intelligent man not be impressed, encouraged and just perhaps even ecstatic."

A few members adding their here-here's began to show signs of animation drawn out by Churchill's message of support, however false it might be. Winston lowered his head, as if disappointed by the response.

"All is over. Silent, mournful, abandoned, broken, Czechoslovakia recedes into darkness. I think you will find that in a period of time, which may be measured by years, but may be measured only by months, Czechoslovakia will be engulfed in the Nawzee regime.

"I do not begrudge our loyal, brave people who were ready to do their duty no matter what the cost, who never flinched under the strain of last week – I do not grudge them the natural, spontaneous outburst of joy and relief when they learned that the hard ordeal would no longer be required of them at the moment; but they should know the truth." The grumbling of the House punctuated his speech "They should know that there has been gross neglect and deficiency in our defenses; they should know that we have sustained a defeat without a war, the consequences of which will travel far with us along our road; they should know that we have passed an awful milestone in our history, when the whole equilibrium of Europe has been deranged, and that the terrible words have for the time being been pronounced against the Western democracies; 'Thou art weighed in the balance and found wanting.' And do not suppose this is the end."

The disagreement of many MP's reverberated through the Chamber. The expected challenge took full bloom. Clearly, despite the proximity of war these last few weeks, very few members recognized, or chose to recognize the true threat. Churchill knew he had to continue in his role as conscience for the government and the country.

"And do not," Churchill raised his voice slightly to regain control of the floor. He tried several times until reasonable quiet returned, and then he continued. "And do not suppose this is the end," he repeated. "This is only the beginning of the reckoning. This is only the first sip, the first foretaste of the bitter cup which will be proffered to us year by year, unless, by a supreme recovery of moral health and martial vigor, we rise again and take our stand for freedom as in the olden time." Winston paused again to let the raucous response die down. "You were given the choice between war and dishonor. You chose dishonor, and you will have war."

An uproarious objection filled the hall from both sides of the aisle before he could be seated. Nearly the entire house was on their feet for recognition. As was usually the case, Winston struck directly at the exposed nerve ends of all those so satisfied with Chamberlain's enormous efforts to find peace through appeasement and those few who sympathized with the German process of renewal. There was a certain sliver of enjoyment in touching those peculiar nerve ends although the message still brought sadness to his heart. He did not want to be correct, but he knew without question he was precisely on the mark.

Although the press provided descriptive, general details regarding his solitude, Churchill was not alone. There were Members of Parliament whom shared Winston's beliefs and convictions regarding the threat to peace. Although not truly alone, Churchill served as virtually the sole voice of dissent and remained very much the lonely bulwark against the prevailing current. He was comfortable with the mantle he had carried so many times in his political career.

The Speaker of the House struggled to regain order through the pandemonium. As he sat among his colleagues who stood shouting their protests and waiting for recognition, Winston knew he had struck resonance within the House of Commons. The growing numbers of converts, disciples and believers buttressed him against the storm. He thought the Speaker was about to lose his voice when he finally threatened expulsion. As the protest began to subside somewhat, the Speaker looked to the Leader of the Opposition, who chose not to speak, and then recognized the Right Honorable Alfred Duff Cooper, MP.

The First Lord of the Admiralty stood at the far end of the Government bench. "The Prime Minister has confidence in the goodwill and in the word of *Herr* Hitler, although when *Herr* Hitler broke the Treaty of Versailles, he undertook to keep the Treat of Locarno, and when he broke the Treaty of Locarno he undertook not to interfere further, or to have further territorial claims in Europe. When he entered Austria by force he authorized his henchmen to give an authoritative assurance that he would not interfere with Czechoslovakia. That was less than six months ago. Still, the Prime Minister believes that he can rely upon the good faith of Hitler."

The House roared once again although without the fervor that greeted Winston's words. The Members sensed, as some already knew, they were not the usual words of protest especially when they were delivered by an important government minister.

"Honorable friends, I do not share the Prime Minister's faith in this evil man." Again, the protests.

This time a backbencher shouted, "What do you want, war?"

"No," Cooper shouted back. "I want peace, not war. But, it should be painfully clear the policy of appeasement has not brought us peace, only closer to the singeing heat of the fire. As my Honorable Friend from Epping has said, '. . . we have sustained a total and unmitigated defeat.' And," he shouted against the protests, "and, I cannot with a clear conscience serve in a government that continues to cling to a sinking ship. We have reached the time for strength – resolute, defiant strength. As such, I humbly and regrettably tender the resignation of my post as First Lord," he concluded and sat down.

The debate continued for another hour before the call of a vote was made. As members filed out of the Chamber and into the respective lounge signifying their vote, forty members of the Conservative Party lead by Winston Churchill remained in their seats choosing to neither support the government's policy of continued appeasement, nor vote against their party. In less than 20 minutes, the House refilled and the vote was read. "The ayes, three six six. The nays, one four four. Abstentions, four oh. The vote to accept the Munich Accord passes."

———

Saturday, 8.October.1938
Wichita, Kansas, USA

The unusually early, unexpected blast of Arctic cold across the Great Plains shaved off some of Brian Drummond's enthusiasm. It took away most of Malcolm's desire for a tutorial or recreational flight. Although offered another sortie with Malcolm's beloved Sopwith F.1 Camel, Brian sensed his mentor's equally unusual desire to talk. Instinctively, he knew the topic of concern had to be important. He likewise had several questions he wanted to discuss. The warmth of the modest Bainbridge living room bathed in the golden glow of the hardwood fire made the surrender to talk, in deference to flight, much easier to justify and accept.

The seductive and catchy rhythms of Artie Shaw and His Orchestra playing 'What Is This Thing Called Love?' bolstered Brian's patience. He simply knew Malcolm wanted to talk and yet the words just did not come. The tapping of his foot to the beat of the music probably helped his mentor pass whatever obstacle he had faced.

"Brian, I'm not quite sure how ta approach this delicately. The only way I know is ta jump straight at it." The younger man nodded. "I know here recently y've been listenin' ta me and my ramblin' 'bout the war'n'all." Brian lost his eyes as Malcolm contemplated his next words. "Ya may think it's glorious adventure to fly in combat, ta test yur skills in an ultimate stakes contest, but it just ain't that way, m'boy."

The pause most probably indicated a solicitation of response. Brian could not think of exactly what Malcolm was getting at, nor how he might answer if he did understand. He suspected this was about to become an argument to abandon his dream. Brian hoped that was not the case. He needed Malcolm's assistance and guidance. Without it, he knew there would be no way for him to make contact with the RAF, or figure out how to get across the Atlantic Ocean.

"War's ugly business like I've told ya many times before. It's nasty, brutal, bloody and tragic. I was foolish when I volunteered for the Royal Flying Corps. I was stupid and ignorant ta let my love of flyin' affect my judgment like that. I don't want the same thing ta happen ta ya. Gertrude and I are both concerned. I know yur parents would probably be angrier than a riled up hornet's nest if they knew what y're thinkin' a doin'.""

His heart rate jumped up several notches. Oh God, please do not tell my parents, Malcolm, he told himself trying not to show his worry. Brian's brain raced through possible counter-arguments to keep Malcolm on his side.

"Don't worry, I'm not goin'ta tell yur parents . . . at least, not yet. But, I do want ya ta think real hard before ya do anythin' foolish like I did twenty-three years ago. I'm not goin'ta lie ta ya. Part a flyin' in France was great fun, but it was still ugly. Watchin' yur buddies auger in, seein' guys blown apart or burned near ta death all mount up on ya. Ya must think 'bout the enormous downside in this dream a yurs."

"You've told me many times, Malcolm. While I haven't experienced the ugliness as you say, I've listened carefully to your words and your warnings."

"Why, Brian? Why do ya want ta do this?"

"I want to be the best pilot in the world."

"Y're goin'ta be, trust me. I've never seen such a natural pilot as you. Y've got the touch and y're a quick learner. Ya don't need ta go ta war ta prove yurself, m'boy."

Brian sensed the undercurrent. "Would you have done it?"

"That's not a fair question."

"Sure it is. Tell me honestly . . . . Would you have done it over again?"

Malcolm hesitated, undoubtedly considering whether or how to answer. "Yes."

"Why?" Brian went on the offensive.

"Ya really want this, doncha?"

"Yes, I do."

Malcolm thought some more. "It's some a the grandest flyin' y'll ever do. The friendships y'll develop will be as strong, if not stronger than family, but it is still ugly business. It is deadly serious work."

"I think I understand that."

"Maybe ya do, Brian. Maybe ya do."

"I need your help, Malcolm. I want to join the RAF. I want to be in this fight. I want to be the best there is, and I want your help to get there."

"Y're goin' ta be the death a me, boy."

"I hope not, but will you help me?"

Malcolm looked out the window. The wind continued to strip the trees of their multi-colored, dead leaves. "Sure, I will. Ya know I will."

"Thanks, Malcolm."

"Y're not goin' ta thank me when y're in the middle a this thing."

"So, when can I go?"

"Whoa, now. Y're way ahead a yurself. First, ya must promise me y'll finish y're schoolin' before y'll get any help from me. Second, I think ya should get yur parents' consent ta this idea a yurs. Third, ya need ta figure out how or what y're goin' ta tell Becky."

Brian felt the warmth of reward. He needed Malcolm's support and anticipated there might be conditions. "Will the war wait for me to finish school?"

"I don't know, but it's not negotiable."

"I'll be eighteen in April."

"Stop! I know what y're thinkin'. If yur parents don't agree ta this, they'll be after me for sure even if y're of age . . . more so if y're not, and the law will be behind 'em."

"But, they're never going to agree. Hell, they won't even give me permission to fly."

Malcolm Bainbridge stood, moving to the window. Turning sharply, he said, "Foul language is not acceptable, first."

"I'm sorry."

"Second, y've put me in a very uncomfortable position, Brian. We've been flyin' for better than five years and y're just now tellin' me yur parents not only haven't given their permission, but don't know 'bout yur flyin'. Is that about it?"

"Yes, sir, but they will never agree, and flying is the only thing I've ever wanted to do since as long as I can remember. They just don't understand."

"Have ya given 'em a chance?"

"I tried several times."

Malcolm stared out the window for many minutes as if answers to big questions might float by on the chilly wind. Brian tried to anticipate what Malcolm might or might not do given the current situation and his dream. He also considered what other options he might have if Malcolm rejected his request for assistance. No achievable or acceptable options came to him.

Without turning away from the window, Malcolm reopened the discussion. "I've stood in yur shoes, more or less, many years ago. My parents thought I was insane for wanting ta throw my life away, risking life and limb with those new-fangled flying machines." He paused for another long time. Brian wondered what could trouble his mentor so much. Surely, he was not the first young man to contemplate such a move. "While I was away in France earning my spurs, as it were, both my parents passed on. No one told me until I returned to the States after the war. I've never forgiven myself for not squarin' things with 'em." Another pause and Brian wanted to jump in to say, his parents were young, healthy and safe, but he could not. "I don't want ya ta carry the same burden." He turned to look directly into Brian's eyes. "Ya need ta figure outta way ta help yur parents and Becky understand yur dreams. Ya need ta give 'em a chance."

"I can't, Malcolm. I know how they will react. They will stop me from everything, including flying with you. I can't. I just can't give that up."

"Brian."

"No, Malcolm. It won't work. I'll wait until I graduate in the spring, and then I want to go as soon as possible after that. Once I'm over there, I'll be eighteen and legally on my own. I'll write to them to help them understand what I must do."

Malcolm Bainbridge searched Brian's eyes looking deep into his soul testing for himself the veracity of Brian's words. "All right. I'll help ya."

"Yahoo."

"Wait. Just because ya want it, doesn't mean the RAF is goin' ta take ya. First steps first."

"I'll make it. I'll do whatever they need me to do."

"That's the right attitude, but y've got one other problem – Becky. She knows quite well y're flyin' and she doesn't like it. Does she know ya want ta join the RAF?"

"No, and I think if she did, she'd spill the beans to my parents just to keep me here."

"She's a strong-willed young woman, Brian. One lesson ya should never forget is, never underestimate a determined woman. They've their ways a gettin' ta a man when they want ta. While she's young and probably not in full realization a her powers, she's demonstrated how strong she can be. I think she truly loves ya, Brian, so be careful with yur heart and hers."

"I will."

Malcolm laughed more deeply than Brian had heard in a long time. "I'm sure ya will, m'boy." The smile disappeared. "Just remember this, y're at a crossroads in yur life. If ya go through with this, y'll never be the same again. There'll be a war in Europe, if not the whole world this time, and if y're in it, it'll change ya forever and those around ya. So, y're really sure this is what ya want ta do?"

"I'm as sure as the Sun."

"Then, so be it. We'll get crackin' on things."

———

Saturday, 29.October.1938
Wichita, Kansas, USA

The telegram response Malcolm sought from his friend and squadron mate from the Great War – the War To End All Wars – took just over three weeks to arrive. The time was longer than usual which was probably indicative of the pressure on John Spencer.

As Malcolm suspected, his English brethren thought Chamberlain's capitulation to Hitler at Munich was a travesty of justice and the inexorable prelude to war. It was noteworthy his reference to his Uncle Winnie's public pronouncements to the same effect although the British government held virtually the opposite position. Much to his surprise, however, John indicated the RAF was keenly interested in highly skilled pilots from almost any source to fill the cockpits of Fighter Command. This fact, probably more than any other, was the true indicator, at least the Royal Air Force's assessment, of the likelihood of war. He agreed to take a look at young Brian during his next visit to the United States that was an official tour of United States Army Air Corps facilities and aviation companies in the spring. The plan was begun.

This Saturday, well into the fall season, was essentially the same as previous weekends. Brian Drummond was outside doing his obligatory tasks early. The need to cut the grass was disappearing as the colder and colder air was sending most of the vegetation into its seasonal hibernation. The airplanes, however, needed their routine upkeep regardless of the time of year.

"Well, Brian," began Malcolm's disclosure to his pupil, "y'll have yur chance ta show yur stuff early next spring."

The excitement over the news was readily apparent. "Great. Fantastic. When do . . . ? What do I . . . ? How do . . . ?" The incomplete sentences were the best he could muster up at the moment.

The deep, loud laugh from the older pilot provided the recognition of the humor in young Brian's response. "Hey, settle down. It won't be tomorrow, and y've gotta lot a preparation ta do, if ya truly intend ta go through with this."

Several deep breaths provided sufficient calming to his excitement. "OK. OK. What do I have to do?"

"Some a the details still need ta be worked out, but there are a series a air meets in the spring and summer. I'm sure y're familiar with these air meets." A nod of Brian's head confirmed the assessment. "It was one a Billy Mitchell's ideas that caught on."

"Oh my gosh, I can't believe it," said Brian as he continued his weekly repayment for Malcolm's instruction.

On this particular day, Malcolm decided to assist Brian in the completion of his chores as they talked about the sequence of events. Weather and Malcolm's spotty winter business permitting, a refinement of Brian's specific skills would be carried out during the cold months before spring. The plan as Malcolm laid it out involved attending at least three air meets. At one or more of those meets, Brian would be observed by a representative of the RAF although he did not know it would be Malcolm's friend who would do the evaluating. An independent determination, without Brian's knowledge, would be made whether any further contact or effort would be undertaken. If the decision was to proceed, a clear set of requirements would be presented which would enable Brian to voluntarily initiate joining the Royal Air Force.

After a short flight for Malcolm to demonstrate some of the skills Brian would need to perfect, the young man thanked his benefactor profusely and departed for town with the same enthusiasm and excitement that exploded earlier. The next step he took would come closest to derailing his progression to fulfilling his dream.

The clouds had thickened during the afternoon although there were no immediate indications of rain or snow when Brian pedaled his bicycle up to Becky's house. She could tell her boyfriend was excited about something and wanted to tell her. The decision to go down to the drug store for a soda was an easy one.

The counter at the soda fountain of Reardon's Hardware and Drug Store was almost empty. One older couple sat at the far end as Becky and Brian ordered their usual Saturday afternoon drinks, a strawberry soda for Becky and a Coca-Cola for Brian.

"OK," Becky began, "what are you so excited about?"

"Well," he began, then stopped to take a long drink of his Coke. His chest heaved from the contained belch resulting from the carbonation. "You've got to promise me you won't tell anyone."

"Why? What is it?"

"You've got to promise."

"All right, I promise," she answered with some annoyance and little commitment.

"Well, I'm going to fly in some air meets," Brian said with a proud, confident voice. He did not want to tell her the rest of the story for obvious reasons. He knew she would probably go crazy, if she learned he was planning to fly for the RAF.

"What are those?"

"They are like contests where pilots fly through special maneuvers to show their skills."

"What for?"

"Like I said, to show my skills."

"To whom?"

"What do you mean?" asked Brian.

"Who are you trying to show your skills to?"

Brian stopped to think. He should have anticipated the question. The complete answer would not make her very happy. What could he say to get past this question? His hesitation brought out a more pointed question.

"What are you hiding, Brian?" she probed.

"I'm not hiding anything," he responded entering a lie he knew he had to pull off. Why did I ever start this, he asked himself? "They're just contests to show your skills to other pilots, that's all."

"You do that all the time right now," she said challenging his response and waiting for a more forthright answer. Becky looked directly into his eyes trying to see the tell-tale flickers of deceit.

"It's just a contest, Becky, nothing more," he said looking down at his drink.

Becky knew at that moment there was a lot more to this story, and she also knew she would not get the rest of the story by challenging him. A more subtle incisive approach would be needed, and she knew what she had to do. "OK. It's just a contest." His excitement and hesitation probably meant something really big, something he knew would upset her and his parents. She had to know what this was all about. It would take more than just talk, she told herself, as she leaned over and kissed Brian on the cheek. The gesture of affection brought a smile to his face and a new brightness to his eyes. "Let's go out to our place," she said finally referring to the old barn belonging to the family of a friend from school where they found the privacy they needed.

The bicycle ride was easy enough as they moved down the streets past the edge of town and into the empty fields. The road surfaces changed from the smoothness of the concrete pads joined by strips of tar to the hard packed dirt and gravel characteristic of country roads.

The waning afternoon sky was completely overcast now although the clouds were not particularly dark. The temperature of the air was still rather moderate, but Brian knew it would probably change by tomorrow. The wind was light at the moment although it was probably going to change as well.

Other than a few waves to friends on their journey accompanied by some pearls of gossip as they rode, there was no conversation as each was occupied with their own thoughts. Brian's mind wandered from recognition that Becky was not satisfied with his announcement, to where they were going and what they were probably going to do, to the challenge and excitement of the air meets and what they might bring. He was definitely not as focused as Becky. Her thoughts were of Brian and the unexplainable sensation she felt which was telling her she was about to lose Brian. Lose him to what she did not know, but the feeling was strong and she did not like it.

A quick check of the area confirmed their isolation prior to opening one of the large doors. Inside they leaned their bikes against one of the posts supporting the hay loft. All the livestock stalls were empty with a couple occupied with field implements. A rather new Ford tractor was parked in the open area off to one side. The overcast sky made the interior rather dark, but all the features were still clearly discernible.

Satisfied the interior was also devoid of unwanted human companions, Brian began to climb the straight ladder to the loft. He knew that was where they were headed without any prompting from Becky, and he also knew he had to go first, against his training, because Becky did not want him looking up her skirt if she had gone first.

Brian opened the loft door and pulled a bale of hay closer to the opening so they could look out across the fields and down the road toward town. He waited by the makeshift bench until Becky completed her climb. Looking at her never failed to make his heart race a little and today was no exception.

Her rich brown hair was pulled back tight against her head and gathered in a ponytail at the back. Her light blue and white checkered dress buttoned down the front and accentuated her chest while the full skirt hid the exquisite shape of her long legs. The white socks and brown and white saddle shoes practically covered the remainder of her legs below her skirt.

"Oh, Becky, you are so beautiful," he said with clear appreciation in his voice.

"You always say that when you don't want to talk," she answered implicitly indicating her desire to the contrary.

"No, I mean it."

"Thanks, Brian," she acknowledged not wanting to ignore his compliment entirely. Becky smoothed her skirt against her backside as she sat down on the left side of the bail looking out the opening. She arranged her skirt to make sure there was a clear space for Brian.

Brian took the hint and sat down beside her taking her right hand between his and looking at the side of her soft, smooth face. Waiting for her to speak seemed like an eternity. Just about the moment he started to speak, she began.

Without looking at him, Becky said, "Brian, I'm so afraid I'm going to lose you."

"Oh, Becky. You're not going to lose me. Nothing's going to happen," he answered with conviction.

"Maybe," she hesitated, "but it's still the feeling I have."

Brian was not sure what to say, or whether he should even respond. Her concern was unmistakable and in many ways he felt sorry for her. The pleasure that flight brought to him seemed to only cause her pain and anguish. According to Malcolm, the dilemma was virtually universal and was simply a struggle they would have to work through. He did not know how to make her appreciate the enjoyment flying gave him. "I don't know what to tell you."

The thought of raising the subject discussed at the soda fountain came to her, clearly, but her instincts told her to wait. "Just tell me you love me."

"Jesus, Becky," he said squeezing her hand and turning toward her. "I do love you." Brian took a few moments to gather his thoughts since Becky was in no hurry to speak. "I have loved you since we first got together." Their first date, more or less, occurred just over two years ago, right after school started, and they found an attraction sitting next to each other in most of their classes. "I even liked you when the guys were teasing me about you."

The thought of the changes in them and their friends over the last two years made her smile and laugh a little. They were old enough now where it was the right thing for boys and girls to be together. Just a few years earlier, they were thought to be crazy, if they were interested in the opposite gender. Their relationship had grown from attraction, to love and continued growing in intimacy. The progression seemed natural and irresistible. They knew some of the kids had gone all the way even against the teachings of the church. The forces were too strong.

Becky leaned toward Brian and kissed his lips. After a moment of minute separation and sparks between their eyes, Brian returned the kiss with more feeling only to be greeted by Becky's arms wrapping around him as she pushed him back into the loose hay behind the makeshift bench.

"Oh Brian," moaned Becky with her soft, seductive voice.

The kisses became deeper, more involved as their hands began the inevitable search for the soft round spots that were so attractive to their gender. Becky's voice, her movements and the attraction of her body were more than Brian could resist.

He managed to gush her name between kisses as their hands feverishly began to disengage the buttons of his shirt and her dress. Fragmented words of passion and endearment passed between them, which seemed to only fuel the raging fire within their young bodies.

Then, as more and more of their flesh was exposed to the cool air, his hands began to move up the ever so soft skin of her inner thighs. Becky began to cry quietly at first. The tears seemed to slow her motion and quiet the fire within her. The change was unavoidable for Brian.

"What's wrong?" was all he could ask. The tears and heaving of her chest added to his confusion. "I'm sorry, if I did something wrong," he said as he considered the rapidity of his action, or going too far. There was no answer, but her crying was not what he expected with the blazing heat inside him. Brian moved away from her raising his torso on his left elbow as he looked into the welling tears of her soft, brown eyes. "Becky, what's wrong?"

"Oh, Brian, I don't know," she finally answered as her breathing continued to be choppy. "I guess it's just that I like the feelings we have between us and yet I know I'm going to lose you."

"Nothing's going to happen."

"You keep telling me that, but something inside me says you're not telling me the whole truth."

"Why do you do this?"

Becky looked into his eyes and captured them as firmly as any clamp. "I don't want to lose what we have. I want us to be together forever."

He wanted the same thing, but he also wanted something else. Should he tell her what he was planning? Should he trust her with the secret of what Malcolm Bainbridge was helping him to do? Brian wanted both. He wanted to be with Becky. He loved Becky, but he also wanted to fly in the greatest event that would probably happen in his lifetime. Brian saw no conflict between the two desires, the two wants. Reality told him Becky did not share his views of flight and would probably not react well to the idea of him going to England to fly for the RAF against the Germans. Somehow he needed to reassure his girlfriend.

"Nothing's going to happen to me." Brian's word did not have the desired effect. "Malcolm says I'm the best instinctive pilot he has ever known." His words still did not have the desired effect. "What do you want me to say, Becky?"

"I just," she said among her sobbing, "I just feel I'm," more sobs, "I'm going to lose you."

Her crying was like a hot acid quickly eroding the strongest metal. The feelings Becky referred to were uncanny. How could she possibly know what he had been talking to Malcolm about? Was it his continued interest in flying? Was it something else? Becky's emotional pain was hard for him to resist. Brian wanted to make her feel better, but telling her he was planning to join the RAF and fly in the combat of the inevitable war would not make her feel better.

A different approach came to him. "Even if we're not physically together, Becky, we'll always have each other."

The crying became harder. "That's not what I'm talking about," she cried.

That did not work, he told himself. "Then, what are you talking about?"

"I'm talking about," came the words in jerks and spurts, "really losing you." Becky tried to gain control to no avail. "Not just being separated." Her hands joined his in wiping away her tears. "Something," her words still coming in jerks, "tells me I'm really going to lose you."

Now, Brian knew he could not tell Becky his plan. He wanted to share his excitement, but that was a distant emotion at the moment. He wanted to tell her about the choices, about the opportunity, and about the duty to defend freedom wherever it was in danger at the hand of tyranny.

"No matter what happens, Becky, I'll always be with you."

"So, something is going to happen," she whined, her convulsions increasing.

"Becky, nothing is going to happen," Brian said almost harshly as his patience wore thin.

"I want you to be with me. I want you to be a part of me."

"I am."

"No, Brian," she began gaining control of her pain. Her eyes took on a more probing and communicative sparkle. "I want more."

"What do you mean?"

Becky placed her left hand behind his head and pulled his lips to hers. They kissed softly at first, but they moved quickly to dancing their tongues among the warm, moist interiors of their mouths. The weight of his chest on her felt so good, reassuring in some small way. Becky moved her knees ever so slightly to convey her desire. This was the time. Brian's heart began pounding within his chest. It was time for them to become one. She wanted to have all of him, and the waiting was over.

"Oh Becky! Are you sure?"

Her eyes conveyed the clear message. "Yes, Brian. I want us to do this, to be joined. Now is the time. I want this as much as you do."

There was a sense of purpose consuming his girlfriend. Becky stood using her hands to make Brian stand as well. The questions on his face and in his eyes confirmed the signs she was now in control. Brian wanted this to be their special moment, and he wanted nothing to come between them.

Reaching for the buttons of his clothing, she undressed him completely. He stood in front of her completely naked without the slightest motion or sense of embarrassment. Brian knew what he wanted to do, but he was frozen as solid as a block of ice although his state of excitement was unavoidable.

Devoid of any hesitation, Becky completed the task for herself, but did not wait in front of Brian's searching eyes. She moved quickly to him. Their embrace was for the first time without any interference. The simple touch of their skin heightened both their heart rates and their desire.

Their eyes met. The message spoken was deep and dramatic to both the young lovers.

"Are you sure?" Brian asked again in the face of the fire he saw within Becky.

The answer came in her actions with a smile on her face and without another word passing between them. Becky slowly lay upon her dress pulling him down to her. The union they sought was finally achieved in the fire and passion of the moment. The slight pain of initiation quickly washed away in the flood of warm, gushing sensations and love Becky felt for the man whom she allowed to be closer to her soul than any person in her young life. The motions, the touches, the kisses came as naturally as breathing. The conclusion burst passed them, a reflection of their immature first steps toward pleasure.

The two young lovers lay upon the straw bed in the loft with the darkening sky before them still joined as the carnal heat subsided within him. Becky moved her hips as if she wanted more. She did not seem to be finished. The flash of the minute sun in the barn on this particular afternoon was more than Brian had ever imagined it might be while it was not quite what Becky wanted it to be. Physically, there was something missing for her, and yet emotionally she felt closer to Brian than ever before. The question she asked him several times was, did he feel closer to her? Was the bond now unbreakable? Could she extract from him the rest of the story?

The combination of thoughts brought tears back to her eyes, tears of joy mixed with confusion and concern. Brian's recognition of her changing emotional state took a few minutes.

"Why are you crying, now?" he asked as soon as he saw her tears.

Becky looked deeply into Brian's eyes with his face just above hers. "I want to know if you are leaving me?" with a soft sob to her words

The possibility of confiding in her the plan formulated by Malcolm crossed his mind and held him in limbo for a few moments. He wanted to tell her, to share his excitement and the sense of adventure before him, but his perception of reality stymied the idea. Brian instinctively knew what would happen. Becky simply did not and maybe could not see what he saw.

"No, Becky. I'm not leaving you," he lied. It was not a big lie to him. In fact, he rationalized, it was not yet a lie because he had not been accepted in the RAF. In his heart, though, he knew they would take him. "I'm only going to fly in a few contests."

"Sure, Brian," she answered with just a touch of sarcasm in her voice. At that instant, she felt an overwhelming urge, part shame for her nakedness and loss of virginity, and part need for the security of her home. Becky gently pushed Brian off her and quickly got dressed. Despite Brian's attempts to talk, trying a number of subjects, he was not able to get her to talk.

Becky was down the ladder and on her bike almost before Brian finished getting dressed. It took him nearly a quarter of a mile to catch her. She was pedaling rather fast. After one brief attempt to determine what was bothering her, Brian wisely chose to let silence descend between them.

———

Sunday, 30.October.1938
Wichita, Kansas, USA

"**I**s Becky coming to dinner?" asked Susan Drummond of her only son.
"Yes, Mom."

"Good, I can use a little help here."

"I'll help, Mom."

Missus Susan Drummond stopped peeling the potatoes looking to her son with amazement in her eyes. "All right, what is it you want?"

"Nothing, Mom, I just thought I'd help."

"OK, then, what have you done wrong?"

The laugh punctuated an underlying nervousness. "Nothing!" he responded with emphasis.

"Now I'm really getting suspicious."

"Well, this is a great way to start Sunday dinner. I think I'll just leave."

"Oh, Brian, don't be so sensitive."

"Hello," came Becky's voice as the knock preceded the opening of the kitchen door.

Susan Drummond looked at her son. "Saved by the bell. Hi, Becky. You're just in time to save Brian from the inquisition and to help me."

"What trouble is Brian in now?" asked Rebecca Seward before giving her boyfriend a kiss on the cheek.

"That's it. I'm leaving."

The two women ridiculed Brian in a friendly, spirited way as he left the room. With some frustration, Brian sat down in the living room across from his father. Even the Sunday Wichita Eagle newspaper spread to full span could not hide his son's presence. "Having a little trouble with the ladies?"

"Not you too."

The pleasant, smooth tones of the Artie Shaw Band evened the rough edges as George Drummond let the exchange die. Brian's thoughts wandered to more germane subjects. He looked at the clock on the mantle. A few minutes until the news came on insured his silence.

Maybe more news from Europe would enable him to ask his father about the unraveling events. He reviewed the opinions and views Malcolm provided, and thought his father would probably not share the same views.

His assessment gained validation after a short discussion with the opening of a brief reference to the continuing speculation of the press. Most of the news on this mid-afternoon broadcast covered predominately local and state items that only recently became of little concern for Brian. George Drummond could easily be counted in the majority since he saw little connection with events in Europe. Brian wanted to share his thoughts and desires about what lay ahead, but knew there was no choice. He had to keep the possibilities to himself.

The late afternoon Sunday meal enabled the concerns of another continent to remain in the distance. The usual fare of fried chicken, mashed potatoes and green beans gave them all the room they needed to talk about other things like the weather, school, business and just plain gossip. Wichita certainly gave the community plenty of gossip being a small city straddling the Arkansas River fairly well centered on the Great Plains.

Appropriate compliments brought the quite common, humble acknowledgment from Susan Drummond. She also made sure Rebecca received her appreciation for the assistance. All four contributed to clearing the table, washing, drying and putting away the dinner dishes.

The four retired to the living room with George Drummond turning on the radio for some background music. Another quick glance at the mantle clock revealed slightly less than ten minutes to the hourly news and another opportunity for Brian to sample the waters.

The conversation remained light and airy. Then, almost instinctively, all four of them listened to a rather strange announcement as the news was supposed to begin.

"For the next hour, CBS Radio will broadcast a special performance by Mister Orson Welles and the Mercury Theater Players. This is a theatrical presentation and does not represent real events."

"That's a strange announcement," observed George.

They all listened as the apparently normal hourly news program began. After several normal news items about Congress and State Department activities related to events in Europe, the announcer referred to astronomical observations of explosions of an unknown origin on Mars.

Each of them checked the others, looking for some expression of affirmation. Did they really hear what they thought they heard? None of them spoke choosing to let the announcement pass as unimportant. The news portion of the program gave way to the invigorating rhythms of swing music. The rhythms eventually brought them, or at least the Drummond's, to the usual gossip topics regarding the latest events in the neighborhood.

It did not take long for Brian to acknowledge Becky's continuing quiet and pensive mood. He let it pass with only a few winks that received a frown and averted eyes. Brian could tell his girl had something important on her mind, and he felt quite certain he knew the issue.

An authoritative voice on the radio began, "We interrupt our normal program for a news flash. Objects of an unknown origin have been reported landing in New Jersey. Sources at the scene tell us of numerous objects having very strange shapes landed from the sky. We will try to keep you posted as information develops." The music returned as though nothing happened.

Again, they all looked at each other. "Do you think that's really happening?" asked Susan Drummond.

"Didn't they say it was not real at the beginning?" responded Brian.

"Yeah, but was that statement real, or are these announcements real?"

"We interrupt again," came the same voice with much more urgency. "Creatures have been spotted coming from the spacecraft. We believe they are Martians fleeing from their planet."

The announcer went on to interview several eyewitnesses. Then, screams could be heard in the background, and they started shouting about death rays coming from these Cyclops like creatures with long spindly necks. People were dying. The National Guard and then the Army were called up to fight against the attacking Martians.

"It can't be real," observed George Drummond.

"It sure sounds real."

"I wonder if anyone will believe it?" asked Becky.

About that moment another announcement was made about this hour being a theatrical presentation.

"Sure. That must be it. It's just a story like Fibber Magee and Molly."

They all continued to listen intently as the story evolved into cataclysmic events several of the radio people began to call, the War of the Worlds. Their attention remained riveted to the radio as they listened with growing enthusiasm and interest. The sound effects, the excitement and panic, the story seemed so real like the Martians were truly attacking the earth. People had fear in their voices. Everything sounded so believable and yet out of this world. Only the several disclaimers kept them away from reaction.

Toward the end of the hour, the Martians began to weaken like they were becoming sick. Some of the characters began to speculate the Martians could not cope with human diseases. They eventually all died. At the end of the program, they repeated the statement about the presentation not being real.

Shortly after the conclusion of the story and the recognition of the Mercury Theater Players who performed the various characters, Mister Orson Welles told all the listeners there was no reality to the story. Actual reports, or maybe they were part of the story, said panic-stricken citizens in New Jersey and New York had fallen victim to the realism portrayed in the story. Several more requests for calm were made in an attempt to stop mass evacuations.

Finally, the assembled group in the Drummond house returned to their own reality.

"That was really something," said Brian.

Comments from his parents conveyed their agreement while Becky remained distant.

Brian saw a safe opening to test the waters. "What if it had been real?" he asked his father. "Would you have gone to fight the Martians?"

He received a hearty laugh. "First, that's what we have the Army for. Second, what would any of us be able to do against a death ray?"

"We'd have to do something."

"Like what?"

"I don't know, but I'd go fight them."

"No, you wouldn't!" exclaimed Susan. "You're just a boy, Brian."

The young man resented the maternal reference, but wisely chose not to respond. All three stared at him as if the answers to all their questions were written on his face. The passions within him bolstered the strength of his character. There was no question that what he was planning to do was right. Recognition that his contemplated action would be a serious disappointment to his parents and Becky softened the passion, but could not quench the fire within him.

"Somebody has to fight the wars," Brian blurted out without thinking.

The reaction was predictable. All three sprang upon him.

"So, that's what this is all about," Susan said quite strongly. "You think you want to be a soldier and fight in this so-called European war. Well, there's not going to be any war, and even if there was, you are not going to be a part of it."

Becky glared at him, but thankfully for Brian she chose not to speak.

"You're mother's right. It's ridiculous for you to even think such things," his father added.

A desperate inner voice wanted to shout about honor, responsibility, commitment to a cause that was right, all the things he had seen in Malcolm. The urge to speak grew quickly, but wisdom won out over passion as Brian left the group for the sanctuary of his bedroom.

Brian cursed himself for bringing the subject up. He had come so close to exposing the sprouting plan to realize his destiny. His future lay in the air. He felt it. He knew it. Why couldn't anyone else see it?

His head was buried in his hands at the desk when his mother entered the room.

"Brian, Becky has gone home," she began. "I don't think she was very happy. She seemed quite troubled by something."

There was no movement or response from her son.

"Do you have something to tell me?"

"No, Mom."

"Brian, listen to me," she continued with her soft, soothing voice. "If you are thinking about joining the Army after you graduate, you've got to get those thoughts out of your head. You are the first in both families to go to college. You've got such a bright future. You simply can't waste your life fighting someone else's fight." She stopped, waiting for a response.

He wanted to tell her she did not understand. She had no way to understand what was going on within him. Despite all the urges to confide in his mother, to seek her advice and counsel, he knew any discussion would end his prospects. Susan Drummond was kind and gentle, but also persistent and ruthless when she needed to be.

"Sure, Mom," he said with as much of a smile and brightness on his face he could muster up. The next step for her would be to extract a promise, a commitment from him. His brain raced through the possible responses he could think of.

"OK, then," she said with a pause. "Maybe you should go talk to Becky."

Brian breathed an enormous sigh of relief. "Sure, Mom."

———

Thursday, 17.November.1938
Westminster Palace
Westminster, London, England

Churchill seemed to chew on his unlit, Havana *Imperial* cigar as he listened to the fractious discussion around him. The Member's Lounge was nearly full as they awaited the call into session for the Prime Minister's Question Time. Everyone knew there would likely be only one central topic this particular evening – the most recent events in Germany.

Seated near him and engaged in the conversation were many of his longtime friends and supporters; Duff Cooper, the recently resigned former First Lord of the Admiralty; Robert Anthony Eden, the highly regarded, youthful, intellectual touchstone of the Conservative Party; Lord Beaverbrook, the successful newspaper publisher who was originally known as William Maxwell "Max" Aitken; and Maurice Harold Macmillan, the young rising star in the Tory ranks.

"It is absolutely amazing what excuses the Germans will use to further their aims," observed Lord Beaverbrook.

"Wasn't it a Jewish refugee they claim started this ugly affair?" asked Macmillan.

"According to our sources at the Daily Telegraph, a 17-year-old boy who happens to be a Jewish refugee assassinated the Third Secretary at the German Embassy in Paris apparently in protest to the repressive conditions in Germany."

"Sure, Max, that is what the press provides," challenged Eden, "but, how could that possibly justify this rampage?"

"They are calling it *Krystallnacht* – Night of Broken Glass."

"How apropos," said Eden.

"What were the damage reports?"

"According to the report to the Foreign Office, 7,500 Jewish shops were smashed and looted, and an untold number of assaults, murders and rapes," said Macmillan.

"All from that foul, little man Goebbels. It took them barely more than a day to incite this riot, this outrage, this atrocity," Eden said sadly.

Winston listened distantly, but intently to the discussion. He shared their sense of revulsion. He also knew more than he could let on even in the protected domain of the Member's Lounge. For a week, he received detailed reports from the intelligence community as well as his own friends inside Germany. All the indications that could be seen or heard told them the damage, injury and fatalities were far worse than anyone was reporting. Virtually the entire country erupted against the Jewish community remaining in Germany. Winston recalled a conversation of slightly more than a year ago with his friend, the renowned physicist, Doctor Albert Einstein. The pre-eminent scientist predicted almost precisely what would eventually happen. His prediction or premonition had come true.

"It had to be more than Goebbels," suggested Eden.

"This has Heydrich's fingerprints all over it," interjected Winston, catching himself before he said more.

"I suppose it does."

"Why do you say that?" asked Duff Cooper.

"Who is he?" asked Macmillan.

Winston thanked the young Macmillan silently. Maybe Duff Cooper's probing question would pass. He did not want to get into a discussion about sources.

"*SS-Obergruppenführer* Heydrich, chief of the *Sicherheitsdienst*, the principal department of Himmler's SS," answered Eden. "Winston is probably correct. Heydrich appears to have been the mastermind behind these so called excuses."

"The House will now convene," announced the caller.

The members of the House of Commons from the various parties moved into the chamber and respective seats. The conversations continued until the House was called to order. The Prime Minister gave a short report of events on the Continent. The indignation of the House punctuated each statistic, each fact, each observation. Winston knew with a heavy heart that this latest monstrous act was simply another mile marker on the inevitable journey begun half a decade earlier.

Churchill listened to the questions and answers with interest as he waited for the correct moment to seek recognition. As he stood, the House fell strangely silent. He looked around for some other cause and found none. He turned his eyes down and left toward the Government Bench and the back of the Prime Minister's head.

"Is not this the moment when all should hear the deep repeated strokes of the alarm bell, and when all should resolve that it shall be a call to action, and not the knell of our race and fame?" Winston challenged, and then sat down.

The House erupted with many Conservative MP's shouting defensive phrases on behalf of their beleaguered leader as well as others on both sides of the aisle cheering for the challenge. Winston absorbed the pandemonium around him as he considered his next question.

The Prime Minister stood at the podium and without looking at his antagonist he responded. "As my gallant and honorable friend has been so eloquent in the past, the goal of His Majesty's Government is peace, simply peace. While the events in Germany are without question deplorable, we believe they are the regrettable act of hooligans caught up in the frenzy of nationalistic fervor. We must not let the senseless actions of a few derail the noble intentions of the many."

Winston stood again. "At the Lord Mayor's banquet, this month, at the Guildhall, he told us that Europe was settling down to a more peaceful state. The words were hardly out of his mouth before the Nazi atrocities on the Jewish populations resounded throughout the civilized world." The House erupted again. The Tory backbenchers turned more hostile toward their elder member. Winston waited for quiet so he could ask the requisite question. The Speaker demanded order numerous times before the cacophony died down. Winston waited for several moments longer for the last protests to drift into silence. "What does His Majesty's Government intend to do about this outrage?"

The House was surprisingly quiet. Winston could only surmise many Members shared his concern. The Prime Minister stood once again without recognizing Churchill. He waited for a long minute before he spoke. "The Foreign Secretary has transmitted our official concern. The German Government has repeatedly stated their position that this was an unfortunate, random act of criminals, not an orchestrated attack. We have no choice, but to continue watching activity within Germany."

Further objections, this time for the Prime Minister's meager reply, came from both sides of the aisle. The Leader of the Opposition and the Labor Party, the Right Honorable Clement Richard Attlee, MP, stood to take his turn. Winston Churchill watched the Labor Leader look across the hall at him and nod. "I yield my question time to the Honorable Member from Epping." Some members objected, but parliamentary procedure had been served.

Winston stood once again. "The Prime Minister is persuaded that *Herr* Hitler seeks no further territorial expansion upon the Continent of Europe; that the mastering and absorption of the Republic of Czechoslovakia has satiated the appetite of the German Nawzee régime," he said purposely slurring the label of the National Socialist Party. "By this time next year we shall know whether the Prime Minister's view of *Herr* Hitler and the German Nawzee Party is right or wrong. By this time next year, we shall know whether the policy of appeasement has appeased, or whether it has only stimulated a more ferocious appetite. What evidence does His Majesty's Government possess which might shed some precious light upon this rather dark place?"

Chamberlain stood quickly and turned with rare fire in his eyes to face his principal antagonist. He stared for several long moments before turning back around to grasp the podium. "Perhaps my gallant and honorable friend should concentrate his renowned powers upon the situation on the Continent rather than his dogged harassment of the honorable ministers of His Majesty's Government."

Churchill knew instantly the tide had turned. The government had to hold its collective face up to the challenge, but the weight of their arguments had disappeared. They no longer could defend the policy of appeasement. They knew it, but they could not admit it.

The venerable member from an aristocratic and political family stood for what would be the last time in this session. "What is the use of sending members to the House of Commons who say just the popular things of the moment and merely endeavor to give satisfaction to the government whips by cheering loudly every ministerial platitude, and by walking through the lobbies oblivious of the intrusions they hear? People talk about our parliamentary institutions and parliamentary democracy; but if these are to survive, it will not be because the constituents return tame, docile, subservient members and try to stamp out every form of independent judgment. The government should not expect support for a flawed, erroneous and injurious policy."

"What is the Member's question?" admonished the Speaker, which raised a flurry of here-here's.

Winston waited for the noise to dissipate. "When will His Majesty's Government see the light and take a more stern course with *Herr* Hitler?"

The House of Commons exploded with strong feelings from both extremes. The volleys of questions and retorts continued for another forty minutes without a respite. While the Prime Minister's Question Time was not the proper forum for debate, the message they all derived from the tone of this period was unmistakable. The support for the government policy of appeasement was eroding rapidly. More members saw the signs of impending war, and they were growing uneasy that Winston might have been correct all along. The Conservative Party Whips worked hard through the evening hours to retain control of the majority.

The emotions stirred up by the scandalous incitement of the less reserved segments of the German population were difficult to repress among the often-callused Members of Parliament. Many of Winston's colleagues saw the events surrounding the Night of Broken Glass as possibly a watershed moment in history. For him, *Krystallnacht* was just one more consistent indication of the true colors of Adolf Hitler and the Nazi Party he spawned. This was the remorseful confirmation of Hitler's intention to take Europe and maybe the world into another great war. The unfortunate reality, however, was the majority still believed Hitler's aspirations were legitimate, honorable and limited. The policy of appeasement would continue for the time being until the signs became absolute and irrefutable.

———

Chapter 4

Think where man's glory most begins and ends,
and say my glory was I had such friends
-- William Butler Yeats

Monday, 9.January.1939
Beech Aircraft Company
Wichita, Kansas, USA

The excitement of anticipation flowed like a torrent within Brian's body. The months of work with Malcolm brought dramatic progress in Brian's airmanship, and a clearer demonstration of his potential as an aviator. The young man's instructor and mentor suggested the extraordinary step of soliciting the assistance of Walter Beech, the successful local airplane builder. Brian knew this effort had to be extraordinary as indicated by Malcolm's obvious signs of discomfort being dressed in a suit and tie.

If Brian was going to have a chance in the airmeet competition, he needed a decent airplane. While Malcolm's stable of aircraft was certainly acceptable for his courier service and training school, they were not the best tools for competition. Likewise, although Malcolm Bainbridge's business was reasonably successful, it would not support the acquisition of the most recent competitive airplanes. Malcolm and especially Brian needed the assistance of someone who possessed considerably more ability with respect to competitive aircraft. Walter Beech met that requirement.

On this brisk, but sunny winter day, Malcolm Bainbridge and his young pupil, Brian Drummond had an appointment with their best hope, or at least that is what Malcolm had said. They had one hour of Mister Beech's time.

As they walked toward the main factory office doors of the Beech-craft plant on Central Avenue, Malcolm felt the need to say, "Let me do all the talking."

The strange thing was Brian had never considered saying anything in the presence of such famous men as Malcolm Bainbridge and Mister Beech. He responded by simply nodding his head.

The attractive, young receptionist at a desk just inside the doors smiled at them both. "May I help you?"

"We've an appointment ta see Mista Beech."

"May I have your names please."

"Malcolm Bainbridge and Brian Drummond."

The expression on the young woman's face told Brian she recognized the name of his instructor. She dialed a short number into the telephone.

"Mister Bainbridge to see Mister Beech." She paused presumably to listen to the response, or allow Mister Beech's secretary to check his appointment calendar. "Yes, certainly." She placed the handset in its cradle, smiled at Malcolm, and said, "Follow me, please, gentlemen."

The receptionist led them down an elegant wood paneled corridor to an equally elegant carpeted office area. Brian did have some difficulty absorbing his surroundings with his attention focused on the smooth contours of the young woman ahead of them. Despite the distraction, Brian did manage to make the short journey without running into anything. The distraction was broken by a subtle elbow from Malcolm.

Mister Beech's office was plainly marked by a small sign with his name and the title, President, below.

His secretary stood to greet them. "It is a pleasure to meet you, Mister Bainbridge," she said. "Mister and Missus Beech are waiting for you."

"Thank ya." Malcolm's discomfort seemed to grow even more with the middle aged woman's announcement.

"Mister Bainbridge to see you, sir."

Malcolm shook hands with both Walter and Olive Ann Beech, and then introduced Brian Drummond to the famous aviation couple. Missus Beech was an attractive woman with strong features and a distinctive air of confidence. Both had warm, firm hand shakes.

"It is a pleasure to see you again, Malcolm."

"And, it is an honor for me to finally meet you," added Missus Beech.

"The honor's mine, ma'am."

"Well, we won't quibble over platitudes, but it is not often we get to meet a famous war hero and fighter ace."

Malcolm's discomfort again became more pronounced. He was clearly not comfortable with the recognition.

"I know you're not here to be adored, Malcolm," Walter interjected. "What can we do for you?"

"I'm lookin' for a fast, easy handlin' airplane for young Brian here ta compete with in this comin' season's airmeets."

A short laugh from Walter punctuated the request. "We haven't designed a competition airplane since Clyde Cessna, Lloyd Stearman and I built the Mystery S ten years ago, and the Model 17 is hardly an airmeet machine."

"As a matter a fact, I was thinkin' of a Mystery S which is why I'm here."

The President of Beech Aircraft Company thought for a few moments. "Technically, the Curtiss-Wright Airplane Company owns the Travel Air drawings for the Mystery S. Have you discussed this with them?"

"Yes, sir," Malcolm answered promptly. "I talked ta Glen last Friday."

"And?"

"He said ya had a setta Mystery S drawin's, and he'd no problem with ya doin' the mods I'm thinkin' about."

Walter Beech continued to look deeply into Malcolm's eyes as he considered Malcolm's words. "There are only a few months until the first meet in Oklahoma City."

"I realize all that. I'm just askin' for some modification help."

"What kind?"

"I can get a good condition Mystery S. I need'a bigger engine and prop along with some drag clean-up and adjustments in the flyin' controls."

"Well, well. At least, you know what you want. What engine and propeller are you thinking of?"

Malcolm and Walter launched into a detailed discussion of the modifications requested. Brian had heard all the points several times while Malcolm was formulating his plan. What amazed Brian was the attention with which Missus Beech listened to the conversation. He had never met a woman who seemed so interested in the intricacies of aviation other than the occasional and rare female pilot like Jackie Cochran, 'Poncho' Barnes, or Louise Thaden whom he met in 1936 during one of their cross-country races. For a moment, his thoughts drifted to Becky. He wished she had the same interest, the same fire within her about aviation that Missus Beech seemed to have. It would certainly make life a lot easier for him, he knew. Olive Ann Beech was quite a bit younger than Walter, or so it appeared, and the stories of how they met were well known in Wichita even to those not interested in aviation. Brian could remember his parents talking about the secretary that married the boss. But, if she was after his money, she sure showed an undivided interest in this new proposition.

"Well, what do you think, Brian?" The question from Mister Beech brought him instantly back to the conversation.

"I think it's great, sir. And, I'll do well with the machine."

"I'm sure you will, son." Walter paused for a moment clearly not finished with his thought. "Do you think you can handle an airplane with that much power?"

"Yes, sir. Mister Bainbridge," using the formal reference to his elders, "taught me real well."

"You certainly had the benefit of one of the best fighter pilots in the world, so I should hope so."

"Yes, sir."

The President of Beech Aircraft Company turned to the fighter ace, now independent entrepreneur. "You have a deal, Malcolm. I'll get my chief engineer down here to introduce you, and then let you work with him on the details. Do you think you'll need any mechanic support?"

"No sir. I think we'll be able ta handle it, and yar modifications are most generous."

"Yes, well . . . I have only one requirement," he paused to look at Brian, "I want you to fly the hell out of the machine. This will probably be the last hurrah for the Mystery S."

"I can do that," Brian answered.

"Good." Walter Beech picked up the phone, asked his secretary to get Mister Marion down to his office. In short order, introductions were made, guidelines given, and gratitude and salutations passed. Charles Marion was, indeed, the Chief Engineer of Beech Aircraft. According to Beech, Charles Marion and Walter had been together professionally since the mid-20's.

The remainder of the afternoon was spent over a set of the Travel Air Mystery S drawings pulled from the archive. Without the distraction of an attractive woman, Brian threw himself into the technical details of the proposed modifications. Listening mostly, the young aviator absorbed the wealth of information passing between the two elder men as he considered what it was going to feel like with so much power and speed. There was an excitement about the details. The enthusiasm effervescing from Charles Marion and Malcolm Bainbridge spread like a virulent contagion. Beech employees began to gather as the word of the modifications floated through the drawing room. Speed was not a topic that had passed through the office in recent years, but aviation aficionados were quite aware of the speeds reached by Howard Hughes, and the monoplanes of Willie Messerschmitt at *Bayerische Flugzeugwerke* in Germany and Sir Reginald Mitchell at Supermarine in England. A modest return of a famous aircraft from ten years ago would have to suffice.

———

Tuesday, 17.January.1939
British Embassy
Berlin, Germany

Although sovereign territory of the Crown, the old German gothic mansion was typically heavy with dark woods and veined marble common of German architecture.

This day belonged to history despite the prerequisite for secrecy. Trevor Andersen knew the importance and why it belonged to history. British

Intelligence had waited patiently for this day since the revelations of *le Armée de Terre* intelligence Major Gustav Bertrand's agent, code named 'Ash,' several years earlier.

The operations manual for the Enigma coding machine was a God-send to the Allies. The small box was the brainchild and responsibility of *SS-Obergruppenführer* Reinhard Tristan Eugen Heydrich, chief of the SD – the *Sicherheitsdienst* – the principal enforcement arm of Himmler's *SchutzStaffeln*, the dreaded SS. Only eleven people knew the copy of the manual existed. The events surrounding the acquisition validated everyone's belief in divine providence. As Trevor knew misty details of the manual, 'Ash' was a disillusioned German military attaché in Paris. The man was simply trying to do his part for the preservation of peace. Many on the opposite side of the fence shared his concerns for the looming specter of war in Europe in barely twenty short years from the War To End All Wars. 'Diamond,' as Trevor Andersen was known within the dark world of the British Secret Intelligence Service, was the chosen operative. News of a possible exposure of a new Enigma machine had brought 'Diamond' to Berlin.

Trevor's hard leather shoes clicked loudly on the marble floor as he entered the small office of the Assistant Commercial Attaché. He always liked to accentuate his normalcy when in his public persona.

Recognition was instantaneous. "Good to see you again, Mister Johnston," came the greeting from Gordon Breather. "We've been anxiously awaiting your arrival."

"It is nice to be loved," responded Trevor Andersen, code name – 'Diamond,' alias Robert Henry Stone Johnston, alias several other assorted names depending upon circumstances.

"Yes, well, you shall be more loved if this endeavor is successful." A slight nod was the only response Gordon received. The young diplomat held a single finger to his lips as he unlocked a drawer and withdrew a small piece of paper. "We have the prospect of selling aviation grade hydraulic pumps to the Germans. I have several industry leads for your company to pursue."

The conversation continued along commercial lines as the young Mister Breather held up the paper for Trevor to read. The agent appreciated the extra caution against any eavesdropping, however remote the threat might be within Crown territory in the heart of Nazidom.

> EXPECT THE MACHINE TO MOVE FROM BERLIN
> TO DANZIG EARLY APRIL.   ANTICIPATE LOW
> PROFILE MOVEMENT WITH MINIMUM PROTECTION AND
> NIGHT TRANSIT.   FURTHER DETAILS MAY NOT BE
> AVAILABLE.

Their eyes met as the words of business prospects filled the room. Each man knew clearly what the message meant and what actions the simple note would produce. Both shared a common belief toward the evil that surrounded them although neither was aware of the other's feelings. Another slight nod acknowledged receipt of the message. With that, Gordon Breather struck a match, burned the paper and lit a pipe bowl full of fresh tobacco. The business conversation continued for the benefit of anyone, friend or foe, who might be listening, intentionally or inadvertently.

The breakthrough in access to the most sensitive piece of technology in the world brought a warm stimulation to the experienced intelligence agent. 'Diamond's mind had already begun the planning process, the approach he wanted to take. Possession of the relatively small wooden box that was the most sophisticated tactical coding device known to the world would give the Allies incalculable value when war came to Europe. 'Diamond' knew the importance, if for no other reason than the mission he was pulled off for this mission. A handful of people in the British and French governments knew that possession of an Enigma device along with the operations manual already in hand could, or more probably would, change the outcome, or at least the course, of any looming conflict with Nazi Germany.

"Thank you for your assistance, Mister Breather. We shall pursue this business opportunity with vigor," Trevor clearly stated.

"Brilliant. Then, your journey shall be worth the effort."

"Quite right, I do believe."

"Very good."

"With that, I bid you, adieu, Mister Breather, and thank you again."

"You are most welcome, and good luck," Breather said with a wink. "Good day to you." Trevor Andersen walked out the British Embassy to make other visits. He knew the importance of the little box and understood the significance the output of a real box in friendly hands would soon be.

Tuesday, 17.January.1939
Beech Aircraft Company
Wichita, Kansas, USA

As agreed just one week earlier, the Chief Engineer of Beech Aircraft, Charles Marion called Malcolm Bainbridge to present the modification plan. Brian could not miss another school day. The day away last week was a stretch for the school and Brian's parents, but the chance to shake hands with Walter Beech did not come around every day. This particular day would be solely devoted to the business at hand. Malcolm was grateful for Mister Beech's support.

The ten-year-old aircraft, a superior machine in its day, was just another vintage airplane. The changes that Malcolm asked for, and hopefully Beech would be able to make, should make the plane competitive in the hands of a capable, aggressive young pilot like Brian.

"Good afternoon, Mister Bainbridge," the receptionist said. "Mister Marion is waiting for you."

In a matter of minutes, the Chief Engineer appeared to gather up Malcolm. Words of energy filled the walk to the drawing office. There was certainly no doubt of Charles Marion's enthusiasm.

With the original drawings and numerous sketches, the changes began to take form. The calculations of improved performance added to the growing picture in Malcolm's brain.

"The engine will be no problem," Marion announced with pride. "The increased diameter will be accommodated by a series of slight bulges in the cowling and rerouting the ignition leads to save space. We've already begun fabricating new mounts to take the added torque. The control for the variable pitch prop is easy enough."

"That's great."

"Yes, but, the best news is we figured out a way to use a series of aluminum straps inside the wing skin along with some reinforcing to the wing joints so we can remove these external support wires."

"Ya're sure."

"Absolutely."

"Ya remember the bird'll have to take at least minus one, maybe up to minus two g's," Malcolm questioned, referring to the force of gravity or acceleration while in an inverted position.

"All the calculations say these straps will take it," he answered pointing to the specific points on the wing sketch.

"Then, ya're right, that's the best news."

"Our figures show nearly sixty mile-an-hour speed increase with all these changes."

"That should get us close."

"Do you know what you'll be competing against?"

"Not really, but I suspect Brian'll be up against some a Glen Curtis's latest work."

"The Gee Bee?"

"I don't think so. It's fast, but not good for maneuverin' and precision work."

"Out of curiosity, what types of airplanes has your young pilot flown?"

"Mostly, a Stearman C-3R Speedster, although he has flown a Sopwith F.1 Camel."

"This bird will have considerably more torque than any of those."

Malcolm knew precisely what Charles Marion's comment was directed at. Would the young and probably inexperienced pilot be able to handle an airplane with significantly more power? It was certainly a valid question, as Walter Beech had asked. He knew the answer to the question, but Marion as well as Beech Aircraft and its president needed some reassurance. "Good question, Mister Marion. The best I can say is, this kid is probably the best natural pilot I've ever flown with or know of. Ya can rest on this one." Malcolm said the words with confidence despite the perpetual question hinging on chance events like Brian's collision with the Reaver's dog.

The Chief Engineer of Beech Aircraft accepted the reassurance from the ace fighter pilot.

All the changes requested by Malcolm would be completed in just under two months. There would be just enough time for a couple of test flights by Malcolm to evaluate the handling and performance, and then a series of intense training flights for Brian to become comfortable with the machine. The early spring days would not leave much time after Brian's school time to practice, but there was no choice if he was to be adequately prepared for Oklahoma City, the first airmeet of the season.

"I'll get the airplane up here, the day after tomorrow."

"That should do fine. I've already got a few engineers working on the modification drawings, so we'll be ready to start the job. We've had to find the proper labor skills for this type of work, but I believe we've got 'em."

"Great. I'll fly directly inta Beech Field in a day or so."

"We'll be waitin' for ya, Mister Bainbridge."

———

Wednesday, 18.January.1939
The Admiralty
Westminster, London, England

Trevor Andersen sat in the dark wood paneled outer office of Vice Admiral Sir Geoffrey Ian 'Jumper' Pike, KCB, DSC, the elderly, but still strikingly vibrant Director of Intelligence Branch, Royal Navy. The journey through the hallowed halls of Admiralty House had been full of surprises. The field operative had not seen the transformation in activity and commitment that had taken place since the Munich Accord of last fall. The officers and civil servants scurrying about left him with the distinct impression the country was either at war or going to war, a sentiment he knew Admiral Pike shared with a few noteworthy individuals in His Majesty's Service.

Trevor possessed an inner calm that existed in stark contrast to the professional, but decidedly contained, excitement enveloping the news he carried from Berlin. Acceptance and activation of the capture plan waited for the proper approval.

"Sir Geoffrey will see you now, Mister Andersen," his elderly female secretary stated.

The woman opened the large door as Trevor approached and announced his entry to the admiral. The inner office was not spacious, but it was also not confining. Books lined the shelves while papers and maps cluttered the large conference table.

"Good to see you again so soon, young man."

"Good afternoon, Sir Geoffrey."

The venerable old man waited for the doors to close. "Enough of formalities. What of your news from across the channel?"

"I believe it is the best we had hoped for."

"Really."

"As you suspected, Admiral, the Nazi's appear to be preparing for Poland."

"Yes, yes, and . . . ," he said with impatience. Sir Geoffrey was one of the few that had predicted this particular event months ago.

"Apparently, our good friend, Heydrich, plans to move an Enigma machine from Berlin to Danzig sometime in the next few months to ensure his commando units in East Prussia and Poland have the latest machine before the first shot is fired."

"Are you saying, you believe that demented little corporal will attack Poland in the spring?"

"No sir, I suspect not, but I do believe your prediction of this summer is closer to correct."

"I see," Admiral Pike answered softly as he shifted to deep thought.

Trevor waited for his return. Sir Geoffrey was uniquely famous for the power of his intellect, rivaled by only a few. The pause did not last long.

"How did we come upon this little gem," he asked referring to the source of information.

"Ash," was the simple answer.

"Ah, yes, the conscientious Prussian in Paris."

"Yes, sir, but apparently he has been reposted to the Foreign Ministry in Berlin."

"Which I'm sure is where he found access to such an incredibly important bit of information."

"Yes, sir."

"Is it genuine?"

"I believe so."

"Well, then, let's hear of your plan."

"Do you have a current map of the Polish frontier?"

Sir Geoffrey rose from his chair, walked directly to the conference table and deftly extracted the appropriate map. Trevor needed only an instant to orient himself on the map.

"We don't know the route, but we do know the origin, destination and approximate time of travel. According to 'Ash,' the machine will be in a simple cargo shipment to the SS detachment in Danzig. Of all possible routes, I believe this is the most likely," Trevor said fingering the thin line leading from Berlin across Polish territory to Danzig.

"Can we cover all possible routes?" the admiral asked knowing the answer he would receive.

"No, sir. There are only a small number of 'Blocker's men we could trust with a mission of this importance."

'Blocker' was the code name for Colonel Stanislaus Pordonski, Polish Secret Police, a long time personal friend and colleague of Trevor Andersen. Although the details of 'Blocker's collaboration with the British were known only to a very few. Even more secret was the status and condition of the Polish Secret Police. There were only four men who could be trusted and each was known personally to 'Diamond.' They would gladly give their lives upon the appropriate command. Trevor knew this was the occasion for such a request.

"Then, we shall have only one pass at this thing."

"Yes, sir."

"Have you considered the site?"

"I have a complete plan."

"And?" the admiral said with inquisitive impatience.

"I propose to ambush the lorry at this point. A small stream along the carriageway within a moderate pine forest gives us the proper control. We'll use Brazilian blowguns and those particularly nasty Curare tipped darts." The Amazonian poison was quite fast acting and left virtually no trace especially in a burned body. "We'll retrieve the Enigma, replace it with a high quality copy since we know the basic structure from the ops manual, and then carefully create an accident and fire."

"Excellent."

"The Germans will surely investigate. We will leave no signs of our presence. The Gestapo will find the lorry, all its cargo and passengers in a slightly charred condition. With God's help, they'll believe the burnt remains of our forgery to be the genuine article."

"What then?"

"We'll move the box to our embassy in Warsaw as soon as possible."

"Then, we'll hold it there for a few months to see how the Nazis react."

"Yes, sir."

Admiral Pike returned to his pensive state. Trevor Andersen was fairly certain what the old man was thinking about. How would he sanction a covert operation within the sovereign territory of another nation? He knew they would not be able to address this issue with the Polish government. There were simply too many potential betrayers.

"This one is too big for me. Let's see if we can get Winston's help."

Trevor hesitated to ask the obvious question for fear of insulting Sir Geoffrey, but this time curiosity got the better of him. "Mister Churchill holds no position within the government. What can he do?"

"Well, young man, you shall come along to meet our future leader and most supportive Member of Parliament."

"I'd be honored."

"Yes, I'm sure you will," he said with a hint of sarcasm. "You shall meet one of the greatest men of our century, and then you shall know why we seek his counsel."

The words did not end Trevor's curiosity, but precisely ended his inquiry. The younger man felt a shiver of inadequacy. Admiral Pike turned away walking toward the window to view the dreary exterior.

"Have you met with Colonel Pordonski?"

"No."

"I should think we need to know, to make certain, of his support for our plan before we trouble Winston with this issue. So, if you will, make arrangements to visit the good colonel as soon as possible, then we'll take our plan to the former First Lord."

"As you wish, sir."

"Wait now, lad. This is not a command. It is quite inappropriate for me to involve myself with the details. Only you should decide if a contact is proper."

"It is, sir. 'Blocker' is a good chappie. He'll quite understand."

"Then, let it be so."

"Sir, if I may be so bold . . ." He received a nod from Sir Geoffrey. "Why are we running this as opposed to SIS?"

"First, you work for me. Second, it was your contacts that brought us the information. And third, 'C' and I have a gentleman's agreement to insure maximum likelihood of success. We'll use your relationship with 'Blocker' to get the device safely into Britain, and then SIS and the GCCS will take over for exploitation. I've kept 'C' informed of the situation."

"I see. That should work, I suppose."

"Quite, ol'bean.

"Thank you, sir. We'll get the bloody thing, if there is any way."

"I know you will, Trevor. I know you will."

———

Tuesday, 7.February.1939
Warsaw, Poland

The British Airways flight from London for Trevor Andersen set a new standard for cold, noisy and bumpy. He was not particularly partial to flying, but he found the airplane to be a substantial better tool for the intelligence business. People and things could move quickly from place to place. Not so surprising to Trevor, very revealing photographs could be taken of the ground beneath the airplane, an advantage the British and French were using as well as the Germans.

The quality of transportation added to the very early hour of his flight departure put the British agent in a coarse mood. His salvation was the importance of the meeting. With his feet firmly on the ground, 'Diamond' had two hours to make his way to the corner cafe agreed to with 'Blocker,' Colonel Stanislaus Pordonski, Polish Secret Police.

The taxi ride was uneventful. Check-in at the Bristol Hotel, the traditional hostelry for British travelers to Warsaw, was equally without concern. His assigned room was comfortable, clean and warm as usual. A quick wash brought welcome refreshment.

The three-block walk to the Tronka Cafe on Wadislav Street took the remaining warmth in his body. Fortunately, a pleasant fire inside cut the chill. The round face, dark features and slight smile of his friend and colleague made all the previous annoyance disappear. A quick scan of the patrons and proprietor allowed some relaxation although the usual anxiety about meetings of this nature kept Trevor on his toes.

Colonel Pordonski stood as his friend approached. "A true joy to see you again, Robert," he said in perfect English using Trevor's alias, Robert Henry Stone Johnston. Trevor spoke Polish as well as Pordonski spoke English although their common practice was to speak the guest's language, or switch languages every sentence when they were in other countries.

"Good to see you, Stan."

"If I didn't know better, I'd swear you have been avoiding me."

"Now, now, you certainly do know better."

"Yes, well, nonetheless, you have been away too long."

"I'll try to do better," Trevor responded in their personal code that told Pordonski there was an operation in the planning stages.

A broad smile washed across the rugged features of Colonel Pordonski's face. He knew without any further information the operation was against the Nazis and that simple little fact brought great pleasure to the veteran soldier. "The music shall begin soon." A simple nod was the only response. "Are you hungry, my friend? Can I interest you some good sausage and beer?"

"I'll take the sausage, but I'll pass on the beer. Some good Polish apple juice should be quite nice, actually."

Pordonski now knew an additional important detail. The mission they were soon to talk about must be extremely significant which made him even happier. The older man's growing enthusiasm was expertly contained. He motioned to the waitress. Colonel Pordonski reverted to his native Polish tongue as he ordered their meals from the moderate height, well shaped, but plain looking woman. She accepted his gentle pat of her buttocks with an expression of familiarity.

"A friend of yours?"

"You might say that although it has been some time now."

The discussion between the two before and through the light meal would be broadly called small talk. Stories of fishing, friends and family took up slightly more than half an hour. Both men enjoyed and discussed the subtlety of the high quality Polish sausage until the duet with an accordion and violin began to play and sing Polish folk songs.

With the soft native music and associated increase in voices of the other patrons, Trevor began the business of the meeting. With a casual last survey of the adjacent tables and their occupants, and in a hushed voice, 'Diamond' explained, "I don't want to offend you, my friend, but I simply must begin by saying this conversation is of ultimate secrecy and frankly did not occur."

Pordonski tried not to show his annoyance with the preface. He nodded his head in discrete acceptance.

"We have an opportunity to obtain one of Heydrich's magic machines."

"I truly hope you are not joking with me."

"I assure you, Stan, I am not."

"And then, the machine must be coming through Polish territory, I would guess, most probably bound for the Nazi enclave in Danzig."

"Yes."

"Is this the Enigma machine we first discussed nearly a year ago?"

"Yes."

"When?"

"We believe the transport will occur sometime in the next few months."

"Are you sure this is a real one and not bait for a trap?"

"As sure as we ever can be."

"What is your plan?"

Trevor scanned the room again. "We will need a small team of your most trusted men. We'll set up a 'slow down' on the road through the forest to the west of Pila. The key to the plan will be making the ambush a very convincing road accident."

"Guards?"

"We expect three SS stormtroopers from the Special Branch in addition to the driver. One will be in the cab, I'm sure, and the other two in the covered bed. They all will be dressed as teamsters, and as you would expect, armed with automatic weapons and handguns."

"I'm sure you have also thought about the method of dispatch."

"I think we talked about this some time back. We'll use the native Amazonian poison, Curare."

"And?"

"I propose we use blowguns with poison tipped darts."

Pordonski chuckled nervously with the thought of facing several *Erfurter Maschinenfabrik Werke*, 9 mm, MP-38 sub-machine guns with darts. "We'll slightly. Their eyes remained riveted to the other as they each searched for what they wanted to see.

"I'd better go in," she said.

"Becky," he protested, "you can't go in."

"I've got to." Several small steps separated them. "We'll finish this later." Becky gave Brian one last kiss on the lips.

The two young lovers relinquished their passion to memory as Brian watched Becky disappear into her parent's house.

The walk home was slow, distracted and contemplative. The images passing among his thoughts flashed from one love to another. The conflict between flying and the pleasures of his girlfriend's soft skin were like apple pie and peach cobbler. He wanted more of both.

———

Saturday, 17.September.1938
Flint Hills
Eastern Kansas, USA

Watching the pinks and oranges of the dawn mix with the grays of the scattered clouds made the drain of the very early morning departure worth the sacrifice. Both men from adjacent generations knew the best hunting came with the rising sun. This was the first hunting excursion without his father for Brian and also the first time he had gone to the field with Malcolm. The recent mock aerial combat experience brought new meaning to this particular outing although neither pilot mentioned the significance.

Malcolm's modest 1933 Ford Sedan stopped in a long draw, miles from the nearest man-made object. The only acknowledgment of any living creature was the cattle trail they were on. For the last several miles, the trail moved along a very small streambed that was dry most of the year. This day the trickle of fresh, clear water joined the melodies of the various prairie birds.

The pristine terrain, no matter how sparse the vegetation, always seemed to produce images of pioneers crossing the Plains for the first time, exploring the virgin land without maps, guides or clues.

The twinge of a morning chill added to the energy already fueling the excitement of the impending hunt. For Malcolm, this was a ritual performed for many decades with his own father, several uncles and numerous friends. This journey was different. For Brian, this was just another hunt although it was certainly special owing to the honor of accompanying Malcolm Bainbridge, a fighter ace in the Great War.

"What d'ya think, Brian? Will this mornin' do?"

have machine guns as well, right?"

"Yes, but we must make every attempt not to use them. Bullet holes in the lorry and the bodies of the guards will compromise the operation."

"I see," Pordonski responded with a pensive tone. "You are, of course, quite right."

The two men stopped their discussion with the approach of the waitress. After asking them if they needed a refill of their drinks, she received a soft 'no' and another pat on her posterior.

"We'll talk some more of the plan, but, right now, I would like to hear what you intend to do with the machine."

"The team should disperse immediately after the ambush. You and I will take the device in a Polish Air Force staff car to Warsaw. I propose you drop me and the device off at the British Embassy. We'll sit on it until we determine if the Germans accepted the ruse."

"Why shouldn't we keep it?" he asked knowing the answer.

"You know quite well, Stan. We can make arrangements for your crypto boys and ours to get a good look at the machine in a safe room buried in the embassy. Poland must be Hitler's next target, and if we are correct, this device could decide the outcome of the war."

"Having access to Nazi codes could do that."

Trevor simply nodded.

"Then, what if they attack?"

"We'll get the device out of Poland before the attack, and if England is attacked, it will go to America."

"I pray to God it does not come to all this."

"I as well, my friend."

"So, what do we do now?"

"Before we proceed to the next step, I must know if this operation is acceptable to you?"

"Yes."

"Can you form a small team, each of whom can be trusted with an operation of this importance?" Trevor asked even though the question was somewhat insulting to his friend.

"Yes, of course. You knew the answer before you asked the question."

Trevor offered the names of team members he would suggest from the ranks of 'Blocker's special units. Several of the men Trevor knew were not available. They discussed the strengths and weaknesses as well as specialties of the team, which they eventually agreed upon. He thought for a moment and decided he had to say, "If we fail in any way, this action could and most probably will provoke the Germans into attacking Poland. It would probably be the beginning of a second world war of this century."

"I am quite aware of that, Robert," he answered using Trevor's alias, again. "Let me ask you, do you think it is worth the risk?" Pordonski asked also knowing the answer to the query.

"Yes, I do, without question."

"Then, so it shall be."

"Good. Then, I would suggest we take a little drive tomorrow morning."

Colonel Stanislaus Pordonski knew precisely where his good friend, Trevor Andersen, wanted to go. The Pole paid the bill, winked at the waitress and said his good-byes. The two men shook hands and separated for a good night's sleep.

———

Wednesday, 8.February.1939
Pila, Poland

The 300 kilometers through the Polish countryside took slightly more than four hours at Pordonski's breakneck speeds. Trevor Andersen fully appreciated the thrills of fast cars on the narrow country roads of England, but Pordonski pushed insanity. The apprehension dampened any appreciation of rural Poland.

As the signposts indicated their approach to Pila, Stanislaus Pordonski, Colonel, Polish Secret Police, slowed the vehicle in a minor effort to avoid drawing attention to the two agents. Through the village streets and out the west side of town brought them to a small pine and spruce forest about 25 kilometers from the town center.

The cold winter day did not stop both men from lowering the windows of the staff car. The engine was practically at idle as they moved slowly through the forest. They listened and looked intently for any unusual signs they were being observed. Human voices, footprints in the snow, smoke, locals gathering fire wood, were all indicators they might be observed. Twice, they stopped, switched off the engine and listened intently to the winter silence. Neither of them found even the slightest evidence or reason to worry although Trevor knew their tradecraft demanded continuous suspicion and alertness.

"This is it," Trevor said.

"Yes."

"Let's drive to the other end. The western approach along this road is the expected route the lorry will travel."

"Right."

The forest occupied small rolling hills in the otherwise flat farmland of Northwest Poland. The Pila road from Trzcianka was the main route from Berlin to the port city of Danzig passing through this small forest. The road lay beside a small stream through most of the forest. Both men gauged the width of the road, about six meters, along with the drop off to the stream that varied from less than a meter to several meters.

After the second pass through the forest, each agent, independent of the other, focused on the optimum point of the ambush. Pordonski had the additional thought praising his friend for the selection of the area. There was a new level of appreciation for the skills of the English espionage agent. A map study alone enabled the Englishman to select the site. The ground reconnaissance confirmed and refined the selection.

"You've done well, my friend," Pordonski spoke first.

"Thank you."

"Let's clear this area before we draw attention to ourselves. We can drive into Pila and take an office in the police station to review our impression over a proper map."

"Very good. Quite right."

The local head of constabulary knew Colonel Pordonski on sight. The respect the Polish colonel commanded was impressive and indicative of the high regard to which he was held. Pordonski insisted upon the utmost secrecy and issued a demonstrable command not to be disturbed. The chief relinquished his office which possessed a detailed map of the streets of Pila and virtually every building, and a comprehensive terrain map of the surrounding area. The target site was detailed clearly toward the right edge of the chief's wall map.

"What do you think?" asked Colonel Stanislaus Pordonski.

As he stared at the map, Trevor answered, "I don't think we'll find a better location."

"I believe you are correct."

Trevor found a blank piece of paper on the chief's desk, made sure the desk top was hard enough so as not to leave an impression of any marks on the paper, and took several glances at the map before he started to draw. The road, the stream and a rendering of the small hills in the area provided the playing field. Trevor drew several X's and arrows on the sketch.

The two men thanked the chief for his hospitality and departed Pila, not wanting to take any chances of being overheard no matter how remote the possibility might be. Andersen asked Pordonski to pull off the road once they were well into the countryside east of Pila. Trevor extracted the sketch map from his coat pocket.

"I suggest we pull down a small tree. We should only block a portion of the road near this curve. The obstacle should be enough to slow the lorry down, not stop it. It must look natural. We'll need fresh snow on the fallen tree so it looks like it has been there a while and vehicle tracks around it." The pause for contemplation accentuated the consideration for the fine points of this event. "We'll need a man on each side to jump on the running boards, open the door and hit the driver and guard with darts. The other element of two men must hit the two guards in the back nearly simultaneously."

Without the slightest sign of emotion or response, Colonel Pordonski considered the suggestion. "The timing is too critical. I will have to rehearse the men, and we certainly will need to practice using your blowguns." A slight chuckle punctuated his words. "These weapons are not common to this part of the world."

"Quite."

"You and I should remain back until the guards are neutralized."

"Yes, yes," Trevor responded not entirely agreeing. The English agent enjoyed the action of a well-rehearsed operation, but he also knew the Polish colonel was right. If the Nazis even imagined a Polish colonel of the secret police along with a British espionage agent were involved, war would be an unquestioned certainty. Hitler did not need much of an excuse. "I'll carry the copy. You and I will search the cargo while your men stage the accident. We must make sure the cargo is in the exact same orientation when we are finished. German fastidiousness with detail must be served."

"How much time do we have?"

"A month, maybe a little more."

"Yes, well, not very much time to rehearse a tight sequence like this, but we shall be ready."

"I know your team will be properly prepared. You always have. But, while the strike timing is critical to immobilizing the lorry, we must quickly find the box among the other cargo and replace it with our copy. As we discussed earlier, the line between success and failure will be our ability to make it a convincing accident and cover every element of our presence. If we give the Nazi's even the slightest hint the Enigma has been compromised, we shall lose all our efforts and probably the single greatest tool with which to beat the Nazis on the battlefield."

"One of my men is an absolute genius at covering tracks in the snow."

"I hope so."

"You will be surprised."

"Maybe we'll be lucky to have the snow melt."

"No matter. This man can handle mud, gravel, snow, plowed fields, it doesn't matter. He is a genuine genius."

"Your expert could very well be the single man who will win the coming war."

"Then, he shall also save my country."

"Save us all, Stan."

"As you say."

Trevor looked back to the map. "We should make our way to this point, and then split. You and I will need to get to Warsaw as quickly as possible. The others should use different egress routes."

"Not a problem."

"Now that we have discussed this plan, Stan, what do you think?"

A broad smile grew across his rugged face. "I think we shall soon have Heydrich's magic machine and he shall be none the wiser."

"I hope so."

"God shall ensure our success."

"Then, can I return to England with your support."

"Absolutely."

The two intelligence operatives nodded their conclusion to the planning session and returned to the road. The drive back to Warsaw proceeded at a slower pace and was filled with refinement of the plan. Both men gained confidence as the details were redrawn with different perspectives, options, alternatives, outcomes and contingencies. They worked hard to cover every possibility from weather to mistakes.

The Polish capital rose before them in the early evening. A quick meal along with a last exchange relative to the method of communication prior to the operation provided a professional closure to the preparatory task. Trevor needed to gain final approval now that he had Pordonski's support. The Polish team would report the state of their readiness. They would know what they needed to know within a few weeks, if not days. History would be silently served.

———

Sunday, 12.March.1939
House of Commons
Westminster, London, England

The House was called to order for an unusual weekend session to hear a report of extraordinary, rapidly changing events. The newspapers buzzed with agitated excitement over the rapidly unraveling events in Central Europe. The Prime Minister recognized the importance of timing and did not want to wait until Monday for the report.

Winston tried to place himself in Chamberlain's position. The terrible, plummeting incidents that continued to draw all of them closer to war had an unavoidable debilitating effect on the progressively more wearied Prime Minister. Normally, the Foreign Minister would make an announcement of this sort, but Lord Halifax, as a peer in the House of Lords, was not permitted in the Commons chamber. Under less precipitous conditions, Lord Halifax's deputy would serve as his surrogate. Chamberlain obviously and quite appropriately felt this task could not fall to a non-Cabinet minister. Winston watched the tired man stand before the House.

The slumped figure of Prime Minister Chamberlain stood at the podium. "This morning our ambassador to Czechoslovakia reported that Dr. Hácha and the Czech Government capitulated to German demands." Muffled words behind members like the distant grumble of thunder punctuated the Prime Minister's announcement. "The effect of this declaration puts an end by internal disruption to the State whose frontiers we had proposed to guarantee, and His Majesty's Government cannot accordingly hold themselves bound by this obligation." Groans reverberated through the House. "The occupation of Bohemia by German military forces began at six o'clock this morning. The Czech people have been ordered by their Government not to offer resistance."

Winston Churchill slumped deeper into his seat as the weight of this protract, inexorable and grotesque descent into the abyss continued unabated. The territorial guarantees offered by the British and French Governments had meant nothing. Hitler achieved his aim in less than six months and His Majesty's Government chose to take the path of least resistance. They capitulated in their own manner in the face of growing strength of the now menacing Germany. A gnawing, nauseous feeling sapped the strength from the notable descendent of John Churchill, the highly decorated victor in the Battle of Blenheim and the 1st Duke of Marlborough. He had prayed that he would not be proven correct in his assessment of five years earlier, but regrettably virtually every element of his dire predictions had come true. The last segment would be war in Europe that appeared to be less than another six months ahead.

They needed to redouble their rearmament efforts, and take every step and precaution toward preparations for war. The protests against the continued inaction of the government mounted. Maybe recognition of Winston's place in history would occur before war started. Maybe war could be averted with a strong, focused military demonstration by France and Britain. An irrevocable line had to be drawn in the sand, or Hitler's hunger for territorial acquisition would remain unsatisfied and undiminished.

Winston leaned toward his friend, Duff. "Why can't they see the obvious?"

"They do not want to see," he whispered back.

"What can we do to help them see?"

Cooper looked into the inquisitive eyes of his friend. "I do not know."

The discussion revolving around the latest transgression of the Nazis in occasional heated language as Members grappled with the enormous weight of events on the Continent. Winston Churchill knew they needed something clear and unmistakable to stop the German expansion in Central Europe. His thoughts could not escape the reality defining their lack of preparedness for what was approaching. The military, except for maybe the Navy, was not ready for general warfare. The Air Defense System of Great Britain was thin, and inadequately trained and equipped. They needed time or at least some edge to mitigate their inferiority to the German armed forces. The nauseous sensations deepened as the debate took on a frenzied, more desperate tone. He asked himself the repeated and inevitable question – what would he do if he were Prime Minister? How would he handle the situation?

Although he maintained a consistent and firm public position, he always questioned whether he might be taking too strong a position. Could his critics be correct? Could his recommendations actually cause the war, rather than prevent it? Only his closest friends heard him ask the question aloud. While few people could say Winston Churchill was a man filled with self-doubt, he never considered himself omniscient despite what some of his detractors thought of him.

Chapter 5

When schemes are laid in advance,
it is surprising how often the circumstances
fit in with them.
-- Sir William Osler

Saturday, 18.March.1939
Wichita, Kansas, USA

The creak of Malcolm's front porch rocking chair working against the boards beneath him set the rhythm for his contemplation. The winter passed quietly and quickly. It was neither bone biting cold, nor pleasantly mild. The winter of 1939 was moderate and about average in the informal words of the weather guessers and farmers. The early rumblings of spring made the flying warmer, and more challenging. The sounds of spring returned to the plains. The birds began to whistle the song of life to all those who would listen. While Malcolm appreciated the season of renewal, his thoughts rested predominately upon one young man.

The time since Brian's plan was set in motion passed through the training of young Brian as effectively as possible given the finite limits. Malcolm knew his generosity and depressed cash flow could not buoy the process much longer. The winter of 1939 had not been kind to Bainbridge Air Service, but he had also been through worse. The motivation came in the form of a brilliant and vibrant reflection of life. He saw so much of what he could have been had he not wasted the years of his youth. Brian had the touch. He had the senses and natural feel for an airplane that should and probably would set him apart from all the others. Brian just needed a little boost to get him on top.

Malcolm made absolutely certain Brian felt the adversity of flight in less than ideal conditions. The cold of altitude was extra frigid during the winter months. The heavy, leather, flying suit with lamb's wool lining barely made the sub-freezing temperatures of winter flight tolerable, and just barely tolerable at that. Malcolm's proverbial neck was going to be stuck out this spring when Brian presented his flying skills to the RAF. There was no question in the old man's mind. Brian's family and friends were going to hold him responsible for Brian running away to join a foreign, armed service. Weathering the recriminations from his parents, Becky and his friends would be tolerable as long as Brian achieved his dream. The element of risk that concerned him most was the federal law establishing neutrality and the punishment for any citizen joining the armed forces of a foreign belligerent power should war breakout. He never faced such a law. Malcolm could not clearly see how Brian would be able to get around that obstacle and there was not much he could do to help the boy. Maybe, even if he made it to Great Britain, the government would extradite him, or revoke his citizenship as the newspapers reported the punishment for violations. Helping Brian would not be easy. Maybe the risks were too great.

In addition to everything thrown up in front of him, Malcolm Bainbridge received numerous indications of the dilemma facing his young protégé. Repeatedly, Brian had asked him not to talk to anyone about their plan and especially Becky. There was no question the lad's girlfriend did not approve of his flying, but Malcolm sensed the pressure was far greater than simple berating by the attractive young woman.

If the expressions and unspoken words in their eyes were even close to accurate, the carnal fires had been lit within both of them. Malcolm had seen the scenario played out so many times, in so many places, in his lifetime. The wanton disregard for the biological realities of their intimacy changed and yet remained the same. The passion of the moment occupied the rational portion of their thoughts. Passion was complemented by Becky's obvious sense of desperation. Pregnancy might be the one bond that would not be broken by Brian's insatiable desire for flight. Although the consideration of the disappointment of her family and the ridicule by the community must have repeatedly passed through her consciousness, the thought of losing Brian in a crash or some other calamity was a more powerful force. Malcolm had to find a way to delicately help the young aviator.

———

On this early Saturday morning as Brian left his parent's house with a good portion of his Mother's pride, a full country breakfast, filling his stomach, the chill of the late winter, or maybe early spring, air made him appreciate the jacket he had hesitantly donned. Brian stopped at the sidewalk standing beside his bike to consider his choices.

Becky was probably doing her house chores with her younger brother and sister. Her parents were already down at their store, General Mercantile, as they were every Saturday for as long as he had known them. The thoughts of her smile, the softness of her voice and the prospect of even a little kiss brought a big smile to his face that no one would see, but he would feel. He also had his own chores. The house chores were mostly complete. The last few items like taking the trash out and cleaning his room could wait until later. Commitment to his agreement with Malcolm also pulled him.

Brian's decision did not take long. This was the third weekend of waiting for some word on the new aircraft he would use for the aerial competition. Mounting his bicycle like a loyal stead, Brian looked over his shoulder one last time as if he considered Becky's companionship. The journey to Malcolm's airfield was uneventful.

Before the young aviation journeyman could jump into his usual Saturday morning task, Malcolm joined him by the storage shed.

"Good news, Brian," was the extent of Malcolm's greeting.

"Oh yea, what's that?"

"Your new airplane is here."

"Really?"

Malcolm did not respond Brian Drummond's rather silly inquisitive remark. Leading the way to the hangar, Malcolm swung open the large doors. As Brian caught up with his mentor, he saw the smooth lines of a bright red monoplane.

"The Mystery S?"

"More or less. Actually, it was a Travel Air Mystery S, but we modified it more than I originally planned. And now, I'm not really sure it has many similarities."

The detailed tour of the aircraft established for Brian all the changes that had been carried out. The biggest change involved replacement of the original Wright Whirlwind 300-horsepower engine with a more advanced and powerful Wright Dynamo 450-horsepower engine. Other changes, the wing reinforcing to eliminate the external support wires; bigger, air-cooled, radial engine with a large, two bladed, wooden propeller; a battery for the electric starter, and significantly improved fairings mainly around the landing gear to improve drag were all described in fine detail. Brian spent considerable time touching, feeling and caressing the aircraft as Malcolm conducted the tour. The cockpit beckoned to the young pilot. The clean, businesslike space enabled good view of the instruments as well was a good field of view except over the nose that was occupied of the radial engine.

"You've obviously flown it. How does it fly?"

"It's a real scooter."

"Fantastic. When do I fly it?"

"Soon. First, we need ta talk a little 'bout the first meet."

"Great," Brian interjected in his excitement and anticipation.

"The first one'll be just 'bout like we practiced. Pylon figures, a circuit race and a few landing precision tasks are 'bout it."

"I can do that."

"You certainly can," Malcolm answered, "but, we ought'a go through these events a few times before Oak City especially with the new bird. Remember, this baby's got nearly three times the power of any aircraft ya've flown.

Ya've got'ta have respect for that."

The hands of an experienced aviator motioned through the descriptive terms associated with higher performance aircraft. Even though heavily modified, the Travel Air Mystery S was a long way from the current breed of high performance aircraft in the world. While it was not the fastest, the modifications hopefully provided the extra edge in maneuverability and precision. More power on an older airframe despite the mods meant more risk.

Malcolm carefully described the techniques for handling the aircraft to avoid mistakes like ground loops, the loss of direction control at low speed caused by the torque of the engine overcoming the force of the rudder. He went through every major problem area with patience, thoroughness and precision. Brian thought he understood.

"Are you ready?" asked Malcolm.

"Sure."

"Then, get in and let's go through a start."

"Isn't this like the other?" Brian asked, remembering he had only flown hand started airplanes that needed someone to pull the propeller through several times.

"Nope. We've got an electric starter in this sweetheart."

"Shouldn't we push the bird out?"

"Nah. It'll be OK. We'll blow some stuff 'round, but no problem," responded Malcolm with an excitement verging on laughter.

Brian had not seen his mentor like this before. Malcolm's almost childlike excitement was puzzling to the young man. He did not quite know why or what had changed Malcolm.

The normal process of training continued as Malcolm Bainbridge stepped through every action required to start the big radial engine. Several new switches had been added to the cockpit to control new equipment like a battery, fuel pump, starter motor and several others. With the absorption of the best sponge, Brian assimilated the procedures quickly and effectively.

Malcolm briefed the specific sequence for Brian's first flight in the new aircraft and demanded strict adherence until he was sure Brian had a good feel for the machine.

Malcolm stepped back off the wing. "All right, give her a go."

Brian looked about to see what was going to be affected by the prop wash. Straw, dirt, some rags, a few tools and various pieces of paper were clearly at risk. This did not look like a good idea to Brian, but it was also not his airplane, nor his barn hangar.

Battery ON. Fuel pump ON. Brian could hear the soft whirr of the motor. Two pushes on the primer button to inject fuel into the intake manifold to assist the start.

"Contact," shouted Brian as he pushed the starter button. He let the propeller turn through three blades, and then moved the magneto switch to the BOTH position. The engine coughed a few times, but did not start. "Again," commanded Malcolm. The sequence was repeated. This time the engine roared to life.

Almost immediately the airplane began to move with a small cloud of whirling debris in the barn pelting him. Once out of the hangar, Brian taxied the airplane, S turning to look around the big nose and keep sight of what was in front of him. At the end of the runway, Brian checked the instruments. Everything looked perfect. He looked down the runway to see Malcolm holding up his right hand with thumb extended high.

"Well, let's go for it," said Brian to himself. He slowly advanced the throttle counteracting the torque of the big engine with right rudder. The airplane began to pick up speed fast. The tail rose off the grass as he moved the throttle to full open. The magnificent machine came off the runway with grace and ease.

"Yahoo," shouted the young pilot as the aircraft began to fly.

The maneuvers prescribed by Malcolm gave him a good opportunity to get the feel of the machine from stall to maximum speed as well as the fundamental characteristics associated with the airmeet events. As Malcolm requested, he also experienced a torque roll, a maneuver resulting from rapid throttle application without the appropriate rudder and aileron inputs to counteract the upsetting force. With all his airwork complete, Brian performed five touch and go landings before concluding the flight. The last maneuver completed just in front of the hangar swung the tail around to point into the converted barn. Brian switched OFF the magnetos killing the engine.

"Great flight, Brian," said Malcolm just after the propeller came to a stop. "Ya're goin'ta do really good."

"Thanks."

"Now, let's go have a Coca-Cola or a lemonade, and talk 'bout what we just did."

Even with the sun higher in the sky, the air was still cool. Malcolm lifted a small chair from the porch of his house moving it into the sun on the leeward side of the house. His words were almost rambling as he covered numerous subjects in essentially random fashion. Brian joined his mentor.

Without the chill of the wind, the heat of the early afternoon sun made the temperature feel warmer than it was. As if on cue, Gertrude Bainbridge appeared with two bottles of Coca-Cola. Brian continued to think it was a bit strange to be drinking a cold soda when the temperature dictated wearing a jacket, but it was like a tradition with Malcolm and just something that was.

"It's after noon, Malcolm. Do you two want a sandwich?"

"Sure, that'd be great, Gerty," he said with a smile looking into his wife's eyes.

"Brian?"

"Yes, ma'am."

Gertrude Bainbridge returned the smile as she retreated to the kitchen. In a surprisingly short time, she carried a tray with a small stack of sandwich halves. All were cold, roast beef on rich brown bread with a slice of cheese. After serving Brian first then Malcolm, Gertrude placed the tray on her husband's lap.

"Don't keep Brian out here too long," requested Missus Bainbridge.

Both the men looked at her as if she were speaking in some foreign language neither of them understood. Malcolm eventually nodded more to placate her than agree. The two aviators still had more to discuss before Brian should leave.

The two men talked for another hour about what was ahead. The practice sessions with the variety of skill maneuvers were required to finish preparing Brian for his trial. Despite his own wealth, Malcolm still had to make a living. Some of the training periods would have to be conducted on working flights. A few of the short flights could be conducted late in the afternoon during the week to allow Brian to join him after school. Most of his training would be performed on the weekends out of necessity.

———

Sunday, 19.March.1939
Chartwell Manor
Westerham, Kent, England

"**A** pleasure to see you again, 'Jumper,'" the short, round-faced man enthusiastically greeted the distinguished, aging, but still fully sharp Director of Naval Intelligence, Vice Admiral Sir Geoffrey 'Jumper' Pike. The venerable and longtime servant of the Crown was often referred to by his nickname, 'Jumper,' given to him affectionately by his shipmates for conspicuous gallantry aboard the destroyer HMS *Spitfire* during the Battle of Jutland – heroism and sacrifice for which he was awarded the Distinguish Service Cross. Pike, and other key intelligence professionals as well as amateurs, were irregular but common visitors to Chartwell, Winston Churchill's family home of nearly twenty years.

"Good to see you again, Winston," Geoff responded.

"The others are here," Winston said.

The others included the pre-eminent, Canadian born industrialist, long-time Churchill friend and Great War fighter ace William Samuel Stephenson, MC, DFC; Colonel Stewart Graham Menzies, DSO, MC, the Deputy Director-General of the Secret Intelligence Service (MI6); Alfred Duff Cooper, friend and now also out of office MP; Professor of Physics Frederick Alexander Lindemann, Winston's scientific confidante; and their focus guest for this special evening, Trevor Andersen, alias Robert Henry Stone Johnson, alias 'Diamond.'

"Good."

With the inconspicuous arrival of Admiral Pike, the Churchill's long-time and faithful butler David Smithfield announced, "Dinner is served, sir."

"Gentlemen," Winston said, looking each man in the eyes, "if you will forgive the impatience of passing on refreshments prior to supper . . ." Most nodded their agreement. "Shall we," the head of the household offered, motioning toward the door through which Mister Smithfield now headed.

The evening meal was cordial, social and unusually quiet. Light words about the autumn colors, the clear, moderate weather of the last few days, and the progress of children and grandchildren. A discernible tension underlay the pleasantries as the seven men waited not so patiently for the evening discussion. The unspoken anxiousness was detectable by Missus Clementine Churchill, Winston's wife and life partner, and the only woman at supper.

Winston Churchill, the 'Lone Lion' as some of his friends referred to him, ended the meal and said, "A most delicious meal. My compliments to Missus Landemare, if you will David." The supper termination words were punctuated by several 'here-here's' and 'Amen's'. "If you will excuse us, Mother," he said nodding to Clementine. "Gentlemen, if you please, shall we retire to the study for a fine Cuban cigar and some delicious French brandy."

Words of gratitude passed quickly to Clementine as the seven men almost ran from the dining room. The trail of notables followed their host up the stairs to Winston's study. The floor to ceiling bookshelves were overflowing with the years of collection and writing that sustained Winston in the valleys of his political career. A small fire added warmth to the cozy room. The formalities of the evening, the passing of the famous cigar humidor as well as the bulbous brandy snifters filled with barely half an inch of the golden liquid, and the ritual lighting and sip concluded the demarcation to the next and more historic segment of the evening.

"Well, gentlemen, I understand the intelligence services have some encouraging news for us."

Sir Geoffrey began, "Winston, if you will permit me, I must say, after this evening, there will only be us who are aware of the subject we are about to discuss. As such, I must enjoin you to the utmost secrecy."

With a slight scowl and a shake of his large, baldhead, the elder statesman answered, "Yes, yes, 'Jumper,' if this lot cannot be trusted, then God help us all."

"Yes, well, this is the closest we've ever gotten to Heydrich's favorite device."

"Then, you have it?" Churchill asked with some pleasure, looking directly at 'Diamond.'

"No," answered Trevor Andersen. "We do not have it, yet, sir."

"Then?"

"We have a lead that a new device will be moved from Berlin to bring the Nazi SS detachment in the Danzig enclave up to standard."

Everyone was silent as Winston lapsed into pensive introspection. Their host considered the meaning and the consequences as he moved slowly about the room with his head lowered. Stopping without raising his head, the old man mumbled softly, almost imperceptibly. "Then, it must mean war will soon be upon us."

The solemnity of the words froze everyone. Trevor Andersen's eyes were locked upon the famous MP who was also a pariah to the Chamberlain government. Admiral Pike stood rigid with his hands clasped behind him and his head raised to the ceiling. Professor Lindemann, the otherwise unflappable intellectual, shivered with the words and felt a mild wave of nausea wash across him.

"We agree," acknowledged Admiral Pike with equal solemnity.

Winston sought a confirmation from his long-time intelligence insider. "Stew?"

"Sir Geoffrey is precisely correct, Winston. Virtually every indicator we have points toward Poland, which means we will probably be at war with Germany before the end of summer."

"How will they move the device?"

"According to our source, by lorry."

"How many troops supporting the movement?" Winston asked with rising animation. His instinctive tactical nature began to take hold.

"The best information we have indicates it will be a single lorry with three SS guards and a driver, all disguised as teamsters to make the movement appear as a routine commercial transit."

The words elicited a deep raucous laugh from Churchill. "Yes, quite right. Leave it to Heydrich to play it cool and cagey."

"If we're lucky," whispered 'Diamond,' but not softly enough to go unnoticed by the others.

Churchill shuffled to stand directly in front of Andersen and looked up into his eyes. "Do you have a plan?"

"Yes, sir," answered Trevor. "We have considered numerous options, but Admiral Pike's quite appropriate constraint that it must not be detected as missing, has narrowed our choices."

"Well?" the old man continued. "I presume the reason you are here other than for my entertainment is, the risk you are going to take." The others stood frozen in time like grand statues of marble. "Then, let's have it."

Trevor continued, "Our best hope appears to be working with a trusted friend of mine in the Polish Secret Police."

"So, you want me to take the onslaught should the plan go awry."

"With your support, sir, we could infer government support."

"Yes, well," Churchill chuckled, "you may not have noticed, I have no seat in His Majesty's Government."

"Quite right, Winston," 'Jumper' Pike interjected, "however, you are the most knowledgeable and influential MP on either side of the aisle."

Duff Cooper, Winston's long-time political ally, added. "He's right, Winston."

Another chuckle. "Yes, well, as our American cousins like to say, that and a dime might get you a cup of coffee."

With the formalities out of the way, the detailed part of the discussion occupied the better portion of the evening. The Prof, as Lindemann was known, offered several technical options, although the original plan stood the test. One critical aspect dealt with the political relationships. The Polish intelligence service had been and continued to be a major contributor to French and English knowledge on German coding hardware and cryptographic techniques. The Poles also recognized the reality of impending doom despite all the efforts to avoid the event. The agreement with the Poles was accepted unanimously.

The device would be held in Poland, first, to determine if the operation was compromised, and second, to allow the Polish cryptanalysts some early exploitation time. Once the device was safely and functionally in Allied hands, control would pass to Stewart Menzies' Secret Intelligence Service and hopefully bountiful exploitation by His Majesty's unique group of cryptographers at the Government Code and Cipher School, GCCS. All aspects were deemed critical to the overall success of the operation. Time would soon tell.

From the humble meeting in the residence of an outcast MP with the

Director of Naval Intelligence, the Deputy Director of the Secret Intelligence Service, one of the most effective espionage agents in His Majesty's Service and three trusted friends, the essence of a small, but dramatic ambush was agreed to and the execution of the plan begun. Everyone knew that should the plan fail and British involvement be established, Churchill would stand before his colleagues in the House of Commons and present himself as the sacrificial lamb for transgressions upon the authority of His Majesty's Government.

As the meeting concluded, Winston quoted Julius Caesar, "*Iacta alea est.*"

"The die is cast," mumbled Lindemann.

Each man paid his respects and bade good night; they knew he would perform the task with distinction, honor and humility. They now needed luck and the grace of God.

———

Tuesday, 21.March.1939
Bank of England
Threadneedle Street
City of London, London, England

The first day of spring in these troubled times proved unusually pleasant. Yet, inside the venerable central bank of Great Britain, it was just another day of business at the focus of the banking industry. For Chief Cashier Kenneth Oswald "KO" Peppiatt, MC, the first portion of the day transpired like all the others until the simple, teletype message, sitting before him on his desk, was delivered by the bank's communication room runner.

```
21 MARCH 1939
TO: BOE LONDON
FROM: BIS BASEL
BREAK
TRANSFER TWO THREE POINT THREE THOUSAND
KILOGRAMS GOLD FROM BIS ACCOUNT TWO TO BIS
ACCOUNT SEVENTEEN STOP CONFIRM EXECUTION STOP
END
```

The request was fairly routine, since the bank provided repository services for numerous national and international banks including the Bank of International Settlements, founded in 1930 to handle the massive reparations transactions dictated by the Treaty of Versailles, ending the Great War.

It was not the request but the timing that bothered K.O. Peppiatt. The news from Czechoslovakia dominated the newspaper and BBC reporting. Bank policy meant he had no reason to know who the owner or operator of BIS Account no.2, or BIS Account no.17, for that matter. However, the events of the last nine years along with various bank transactions suggested the connections. Peppiatt suspected Account no.17 belonged to *Reichsbank* – the central bank of Germany – while Account no.2 likely belonged to the National Bank of Czechoslovakia.

Peppiatt stared at the typed words on the paper in the stone silence of his office, well, except for the faint, rhythmic heartbeat of the pendulum clock on the bookshelf that occupied the entire far wall of his large office. Less than a week prior, German troops marched into Prague in a very public display of domination. This time, there were no excuses about the injustice of the Versailles Treaty, the separation of ethnic German citizens from their Fatherland by the ridiculous retribution of the victors, or *Reichkanzler* Hitler's *Lebensraum* (living space) policy. Peppiatt now felt the pangs of regret for his support of Prime Minister Chamberlain's efforts to preserve the peace in Europe. He shook his head as he lifted the intercom handset.

"Missus Johnson, would you be so kind to see if Governor Norman is available for a matter of some urgency?"

"Yes sir."

He placed the handset back in its cradle and returned to staring at the paper. He wanted to call his friend and counterpart in Basel to eliminate any remaining uncertainty. The buzzer on the desktop intercom ended his supposition.

"Yes."

"Governor Norman can see you now, Mister Peppiatt."

"Thank you, Missus Johnson."

K.O. stood, straightened his necktie, and lifted the message from his desk as if it had some unusual weight. He opened his office door, walked past Missus Johnson's desk and did not make eye contact with anyone. Peppiatt purposely moved up the main staircase to the executive floor, walked down the wide corridor to the anteroom door to the corner office of Governor Montagu Collet Norman, the principal executive of the central bank of Great Britain and indeed the whole of the British Empire. He hesitated to gather his thoughts before he opened the door.

Missus Gathers stood and moved to the adjacent door as she said, "Good morning, Mister Peppiatt."

"Good morning to you, Missus Gathers."

She knocked on the large, stained, oak door, did not wait for a response, and opened the door.

"Mister Peppiatt to see you, sir."

"Yes, yes, please show him in. Thank you, Missus Gathers."

Norman's executive secretary opened the door wider.

"Mister Peppiatt . . . Governor Norman."

"Thank you," Norman said as he motioned to one of four, luxurious, leather chairs.

Gathers closed the door behind Peppiatt. The Chief Cashier sat with his back straight in the right most chair and waited patiently for Montague Norman to complete his reading task. The distinguished face with his well-trimmed, gray, Van Dyke whiskers remained down until he wrote a few notes in the margin of whatever report he was reading. He closed his fountain pen and laid it aside.

"So, Mister Peppiatt, what is on your mind?"

K.O. stood to hand the teletype paper to Norman. He waited and took the paper back when Montague completed his reading.

"What is your concern?"

"Sir, did you note the account numbers?"

With an irritated expression covering his entire face, Norman said, "I have been a banker all my life."

"Excuse me, sir. I meant no offense." Norman nodded his acceptance. "The Germans marched into Prague less than a week ago, and now we have this official BIS request to transfer of £5,600,000 worth of gold from what I believe is the National Bank of Czechoslovakia to the *Reichsbank*."

"And, how do you know all this?" asked Norman, with even more irritation.

"My apologies, sir. Perhaps I have overstepped my place."

Governor Montague Norman stared harshly. "Yes, Peppiatt, perhaps you have."

The Chief Cashier went through the simple message, the process they would execute to fulfill the request, and most importantly, he considered the consequences, the impact, of what they were about to do. He wanted to get up out of the chair, ignore what he believed was behind the routine anonymous request, and just do his normal, boring job. Under "normal" conditions, he would have never made the journey to the Governor's office. These were not normal times. Bank of England Governor Montague Norman did not blink or avert his gaze. Somehow, K.O. did not think this was going to end well.

"If my suspicions are correct, shouldn't we inform or consult Sir John?"

Norman's expression transitioned instantly as he realized the purpose of the conversation with the bank's chief cashier. He stood, turned and looked out the window behind his desk.

K.O. knew they were in a political situation, not a simple financial transaction between international banks. Chancellor of the Exchequer Sir John Allsebrook Simon, GCSI, GCVO, OBE, PC, served His Majesty's Government as the principal minister for economic and financial matters. The message presented a serious political question that deserved the concerted, coordinated, determined response of HMG.

Several minutes passed before Norman returned to the conversation. He turned to face K.O., leaned back against the credenza, and folded his arms across his chest. "I understand and appreciate your concern here. Extraordinary, historic events are transpiring before us on the Continent. We are the repository of choice for numerous foreign banks and nations. We have been the central bank of the United Kingdom since 1694." He paused to let those facts soak in for the bank's chief cashier. "We are not at war . . . yet. The government has not issued any instruction for abnormal operations. We have a proper request for the transfer of funds from a customer bank. The BIS accounts are anonymous for a reason. Unless we question the authenticity of the BIS request for transfer, I suggest we perform our duty without stoking the fire."

Peppiatt nodded his head but he did not move. He recognized that Montagu Norman was also a director of the Bank of International Settlements (BIS), and best mates with Hjalmar Horace Greeley Schacht, former *Reichsminister der Wirtschafte* and recent President of *Reichsbank*, as well as godfather to one of Schacht's grandchildren. Norman's personal and professional life added incredible complication to this particular situation. To go one step farther down this path, he would be questioning the integrity and loyalty of Governor Montague Norman. K.O. wanted this to be done, but he did not want to be crosswise with HMG either. He considered the option of going to Sir John directly. Yet, at the end of the day, Governor Norman had the facts on his side and banking rules were the rules they lived by. He stood. "Yes sir, I will execute the order promptly."

"Thank you, Peppiatt."

K.O. Peppiatt bowed slightly, turned and left Norman's office. The order was fulfilled that afternoon and confirmed by teletype reply.

———

Saturday, 8.April.1939
Tinker Field
Oklahoma City, Oklahoma, USA

Malcolm Bainbridge and Brian Drummond had flown into Tinker Field numerous times during the conduct of the elder's fledgling air courier service. This time was distinctly different. The bright red, highly modified, Mystery S monoplane led the flight of two. Brian had to throttle his airplane back to allow the Stearman C-3R Speedster with Malcolm at the controls to keep up.

As they approached the field, there was a clearly identifiable change. Colors, lots of colors, were arrayed on the north side of the dirt strip. Tents, revival type tents, red ones, blue ones, brown and green tents were lined up behind a string of airplanes. Some of the aircraft were themselves painted bright colors and patterns. Other aircraft like Malcolm's working Stearman had the natural tan color of the varnish that sealed the fabric of the wing and fuselage.

What surprised Brian the most was all the people. Most of them looked like spectators, farmers, families and others, who were out to have a good time and watch the show. Brian had never seen so many people in one place for anything including the traveling circus or carnival.

As they taxied down the line of mostly biplanes with Malcolm's Stearman leading the way, Brian marveled at the variety and beauty of the assembled machines. He could also see heads turn to check out the arriving competitor. Brian could feel his heart beating faster with the thoughts of flying against other pilots. He knew, despite the relatively old age of the Travel Air Mystery S, it still had distinctively smooth lines and the modifications would be a curiosity item for an aviation aficionado who would recognize the basic machine.

The Stearman pulled into the line and turned. Brian moved the rudder to the left deflecting the propeller wash and moving the tail to the right. Brian worked the rudder pedals with skill as he confirmed the clearances for his wing tips and tail to swing around in the limited space.

He remembered to give the airplane a good kick with the prop and then cut the engine as the nose came around. Malcolm taught the flashy technique of parking a tail dragger airplane in a relatively small space to avoid any possibility of damage to the other birds and especially the tents.

As the propeller stopped and Brian made sure all the switches were OFF, he took a moment to gather his feelings before he moved a muscle. Malcolm was out of the cockpit with his sheep skin jacket already unzipped and standing beside the Mystery S cockpit.

A friendly slap to the head broke Brian's trance. "Come on, lad, get out'ta that thing. I'm sure we've got'ta briefin' ta go to," said Malcolm.

Gathering his focus, Brian unstrapped and followed Malcolm off the wing. Another, rather small man with dark, almost black, hair and a matching bushy mustache that nearly covered his lower face approached.

"Malcolm Bainbridge, you old son of a bitch," came the shouted greeting from the little man. "It's about time you showed your ugly face at one of our meets."

"Hi'ya Jimmy," returned Malcolm with a markedly subdued voice.

The two men shook hands before the smaller man looked around Malcolm. "Who's the kid?"

"He's one'a my pilots."

The possessive reference to his avocation did not escape Brian's attention. The young man fought his desire to grin with pride over the recognition, but he knew he had to be cool, reserved and contained. Show no emotion, Malcolm had always told him after earlier expositions of excitement. Never let anyone see what your thinking, he told him many times.

The little man moved around Malcolm. "Jimmy Brown, kid, good ta meet ya," he said extending his hand.

Brian shook his hands with strength. "Nice to meet you, Mister Brown."

Jimmy smiled at Malcolm, then looked back to Brian. "Well, OK, so what's your name, kid?"

Brian saw Malcolm's expression of dissatisfaction with the tone of the question. "My name is, Brian Drummond."

"Well, young Brian Drummond, it's a pleasure." Jimmy Brown turned back to Malcolm. "So, you decided to get back into our little competition, did'ya now?"

Malcolm flashed an unusually communicative smile to Brian, then answered Jimmy. "No. My partner is going to compete."

The laugh surprised Brian letting the air out of his swelling chest from Malcolm's compliment. Brian began not to like the smaller man very much.

"He's just a kid," Jimmy said motioning toward Brian. "How's he gonna compete with real pilots?"

With an even larger grin, now, Malcolm responded, "Well, I guess ya're gonna find out. Aren't ya, Jimmy?"

"Brief time," came the announcement shouted by a man with a large megaphone a few tents down from them.

"Good luck, kid," offered Jimmy as he chuckled and moved off in the direction of the tent.

Neither of the two Wichitans responded. They let the smaller man open some distance between them before Malcolm began to walk toward the tent. Brian followed.

"Don't let weasels like 'im get'ta ya," said Malcolm.

Brian nodded his consent, but knew it was going to be harder to fulfill than a simple acknowledgment. He instinctively also knew Jimmy Brown was not the contact man for the RAF, not just because he acted and sounded like an American, but because he knew Malcolm did not respect the little man. The urge to ask the question of curiosity was too great.

"Is your RAF friend here?"

Malcolm stopped and turned directly to face Brian. "Ya forget that. This day has nothin' ta do with the RAF, yar dream or anythin' else 'cept fl-yin'." There was an irritated quality to his voice almost like he was angry or offended by Brian's question. "Ya've got'ta think 'bout only one thing, flyin'. Ya're gonna have'ta fly the piss out'ta that bird. These guys are good, but ya're better, if ya concentrate."

The strength of his admonition took Brian aback, stunned him for a moment. It also added a seriousness to this endeavor which he had not felt earlier.

"OK," Brian answered.

His mentor felt the need to press the point. "I don't want ya ta know, or even think 'bout, when or where he may be in the audience until after ya've flown. Got it?"

"Yes, sir."

Without another word, Malcolm led the way to the briefing tent. The two men sat at the back of the tent on a couple of rather small, wooden, folding chairs. A rotund man with a bald head and reddish cheeks stood in front of a hand drawn map of the airfield on a 4' by 8' sheet of plywood.

The round man began the briefing with a list of events to be flown. The procedures and scoring took more time to explain so each competitor knew what was expected. All the details were just as Malcolm had told Brian numerous times during his training sessions. They would fly three main events with several variations: landing precision, aerobatics and a pylon race. The landing competition would measure how close the right, main wheel touched down to a spot with both headwind and crosswind, if the wind picked up. Five attempts would be made in two wind directions, the distance off the mark would be measured, and the total accumulated distance would decide the winner. The lowest total being the best. Aerobatics would be judged by five men and would evaluate a long list of characteristics for rolls, loops, Cuban-Eights and Immelmanns. The pylon race involved a triangular circuit, each side a different length, and was run very much like a sailboat race. All the competitors had to cross the start line after a flare was shot into the air. If you crossed earlier, you had to go around and cross the start line again. The race was five times around the course.

A blackboard with chalk marks indicated there were eleven competitors. A warm flush washed over Brian when he saw his name on the board, three from the bottom. There were blocks on the board for the scores of each event along with a final column that was simply marked, rank.

The last element of the briefing acknowledged the prize money: $1,000 for first place, $500 for second place, $200 for third and $100 for fourth. Everyone else would be rewarded with the pleasure of the competition, the round man said as he finished briefing.

"Pilots, man your airplanes," was the final command from the round man.

Except for the race where they would all fly together, the events would be flown in two groups of six and five. Brian was in the latter group.

Preparations took about twenty minutes. The first group took off. The landing spot was a bright red circle about one yard across painted in the dirt at the west end to the runway. When the first group took off, the winds were from the southwest at about ten miles per hour, relatively light winds, but enough to make precision landing a challenge. The landing lines would actually crisscross the runway which was oriented exactly east-west.

Brian and Malcolm walked down near the landing spot to watch the first group perform their landings. Brian was impressed watching the first set of pilots. Occasionally, they would notice a red puff of dirt indicating a bull's eye.

"These guys are good," Brian observed aloud, more to himself than to Malcolm.

"Ya don't worry 'bout 'em, lad. Ya just concentrate on yar flyin'." Brian nodded his consent. "Let's go. We need'ta get ya strapped in." Again, Brian nodded, then began walking toward the airplane.

With the sounds of the first group still performing their precision landings, Brian dropped into the cockpit and began the ritual preparations for flight. Malcolm stood on the left wing beside him just watching his young pupil fasten the harness that made the modified aircraft part of him.

"Concentrate," was all Malcolm could say as he waited with Brian for the other aircraft to land.

The young pilot did as he was instructed. Each step of the process was flown in his head as Malcolm had trained him to do. All the techniques and various cues to assist him with his flying were reviewed to make sure he could seek any last minute advice from Malcolm before takeoff. The faster pace of his heart confirmed the anxiety, but in his gut he knew he was ready. He just wanted to get on with it. His wish was not long in fulfillment.

"Looks like the first group's done," said Malcolm as the string of planes were landing in front of them. "Let's go ahead and get 'er started."

Malcolm jumped down off the wing. Brian placed his goggles over his eyes and rechecked all his switches; fuel cock ON, primer pumped three times and throttle set. A deep breath proclaimed his readiness.

"Clear," shouted Brian as he looked to both sides of the propeller. "Contact," he commanded out of habit as he pushed the starter button, let the three blades of propeller pass the vertical and moved the magneto switch to BOTH.

The engine sputtered a few times, then fired. With the engine running at idle, Malcolm ran to the left wing tip and held up his right thumb. Everything looked good as his hand signal indicated. As the last of the first group taxied to their parking spots, Brian checked his instruments. The engine indications were normal and the sound of the reciprocating engine chugging away was confirmation of the instruments.

Brian found the windsock. The wind was still about the same speed and direction. He would be next to last in line for takeoff. The first three aircraft in his group pulled out of the parking line. Brian added just enough throttle to move the aircraft forward turning the aircraft to the right. The airplanes in front of him were staggered which Brian quickly deduced was to minimize the propwash effects from the aircraft in front of them. The last aircraft was barely moving out of the parking line when the first contestant applied full power and headed down the runway followed shortly thereafter by the aircraft just ahead of Brian.

The young man checked his gages one last time. Everything still looked good. He sucked in a deep breath, blew it out almost in a whistle and said aloud, "Let's go," as he pushed the throttle forward. The sounds of the engine were strong and loud. The swirling torrent of air from the propeller jostled Brian's head slightly as the airplane accelerated down the dirt strip. The wheels responded to the little changes in the ground and the bouncing of the machine became more rapid and pronounced until there was only the smoothness of flight.

The lead aircraft began his crosswind turn when Brian passed over the red dot at the end of the runway. By the rules, they were allowed one practice landing at the dot. Then, they would establish a circuit for the five landings into the wind followed by a 90 degree shift in the circuit for the crosswind landings.

The landing segment of the contest was completed quickly, 'by the numbers', as the old guys would say. Brian actually did better than he thought, but he was not in the top four for this segment, the first portion of the airmeet.

Malcolm was half trotting, half walking as Brian turned the aircraft into the parking line. "Ya did pretty good, Brian," proclaimed Malcolm shouting above the engine.

With only a nod to acknowledge the words of encouragement, Brian proceeded with shutting down the engine. Engine instruments looked good; temperatures and pressures were normal. His left hand reached for the lever that controlled the mixture of fuel and air going to the engine and pulled it to the cutoff position. The engine coughed a couple of times before stopping. Brian completed his task by switching the magneto switch to OFF and the fuel cock to OFF. Only the distant sounds of other engines running remained as Brian unbuckled his harness and used his elbows to raise himself up and out of the cockpit.

"Ya did good, kid."

"I don't know," responded Brian. "I couldn't see the dot."

"By my sight, ya hit the damn thing two or three times, maybe more."

"How about the other guys?"

"A couple of 'em may've done better. It's hard ta say."

A Ford flatbed truck with an elliptical tank laid flat and strapped to the bed with large red letters, FUEL, painted on both sides drove down the line of aircraft stopping in front of the red Mystery S. Brian turned to meet the truck and refuel the airplane. There was not the slightest concern or question. It was a task he had done so many times before.

Malcolm grabbed his arm. "They'll do that," he said motioning with his head toward the fuel truck and referring to the refueling task. "Ya're the pilot."

"Yea?" Brian responded inquisitively. A smile of pride and importance flashed to his face.

The grin and nod from his mentor confirmed the young man's interpretation of the meaning. With nothing to do but wait for the next event, Brian wanted to see the results of the first event. Maybe he had done better than he thought.

"Can we look at the scoreboard?"

Malcolm shook his head in disapproval. "Ya don't check the cake 'til it's done."

A slap on the back knocked Brian forward a step. He turned to see the source. The diminutive form of Jimmy Brown stood behind him. A tinge of blackness tinted his face where his goggles and leather flight cap did not keep the oil mist from the engine away from his skin.

"You didn't do too bad for a kid," said Jimmy Brown.

"Thanks."

Jimmy turned to Malcolm. "You taught the kid well it looks like."

All Malcolm did was nod his acknowledgment.

"Too bad that old Mystery S won't help you in the race," the smaller man said with a devious grin.

Brian had not even considered the issue of speed. Malcolm had never mentioned anything about speed in the practice sessions although a race certainly implied a competition of speed. The emphasis during his training was on technique, skill and tactics. Brian now wondered why the question of speed never entered their earlier discussions of race techniques.

"Why don't ya leave the boy alone, Jimmy?"

"Well, Malcolm, you know this is no different from any aerial fight we've been in."

"Maybe, but why don't ya stop flappin' yar gums and let the flyin' do the talkin'?" Malcolm said with strength and obvious irritation in his voice.

The smaller man stopped, looking deep into Malcolm's eyes as if he was going to find an answer within his older colleague. "How'd we ever get cross-ways?" asked Jimmy.

The response came quickly. "Ya've always done more talkin' than doin', Jimmy."

The words had a definitive effect on Jimmy Brown. He shifted his weight and moved his feet around like he was performing a strange, ritual dance. "I suppose the four Krauts over France was just talkin,' huh Malcolm," he reacted with anger.

"Jimmy, two of those were balloons," Malcolm said almost laughing at the smaller man.

The dance continued and Jimmy Brown almost spit, "You're an asshole," and stomped off in a near rage.

Malcolm turned to Brian who was a silent witness to the verbal confrontation. There was a large smile drawn across Malcolm's face. "He's a little weasel," he said. "Ya just concentrate on what I told ya. Ya'll do OK."

A nod was the only response the words received. Concentrate, concentrate, concentrate -- the instruction began to sound like a broken record on the Victrola, Brian thought. Fortunately for Brian, however, he knew, no matter how tiring the instructions became, Malcolm was correct and wise.

"Was he in Four Three Squadron with you?"

"No. He was in Two Three Squadron for a short time before he was shot down by the bloody Red Baron himself. When he returned to flyin,' he joined the other Americans in the 94th Aero Squadron, the *Lafayette Escadrille*, Eddie Rickenbacker's unit."

"Really?" answered Brian a voice of curiosity.

The discussion was interrupted by the sounds of engines starting signaling the beginning of the second event. The sun was nearly vertical which put the time at about noon. A couple of growls of his stomach confirmed the time of day. A quick, attentive walk around the aircraft established the machine was ready for flight. No damage to the skin or undercarriage, all control surfaces free and smooth, and the tank half full with fuel were the acceptable preflight checks.

Malcolm was nowhere in sight, so Brian climbed into the cockpit lowering his head into his hands with his elbows on his knees. From the contemplative position somewhat hidden from view, Brian began to fly the expected sequence of maneuvers in his head. The entry conditions, the check points and the qualities of each maneuver were mentally rehearsed as Malcolm had taught him. Brian reviewed the specific elements of the scoring system the judges used to establish the points for the aerobatic event.

This time Brian fought the desire to watch the other competitors fly their maneuvers. He wanted to do exactly what Malcolm had told him to do -- concentrate. Each segment of each required maneuver was repeatedly flown in his head.

I wish Becky could see me fly, he thought at one moment. No, no, he struggled within himself, I cannot think of Becky.

A hand touched him on the shoulder startling Brian back to the present. Malcolm was standing on the wing beside him looking down.

"First group's landin'. It's time ta start."

Brian looked around quickly to find half the first group already on the ground taxiing back in with the remainder of the first group lined up on final approach. Brian nodded his acknowledgment.

"Ya got any questions?"

A slight shake of his head and movement of his left hand to set the mixture and throttle for start indicated the negative. Brian completed his prestart checks before Malcolm could walk past the wing.

The engine started promptly. Everything was running correctly. Malcolm offered a thumbs up and a smile which Brian returned. He waited for his turn to taxi out for takeoff. Once again, Brian was number four of the five contestants in the second group.

The circuit pattern was established with all five aircraft spread out around a large racetrack pattern. One pass, straight and level, down the runway signaled the start of the aerobatic maneuvering event.

The first maneuver sequence was a series of four snap rolls alternating to the left and right. Brian began the downwind leg when the leader of the second group began his maneuver. The young man made a conscious effort not to watch the leader as he checked engine instruments. The gages confirmed what the sound and vibration told him. The engine was running normally. Airspeed and altitude were as prescribed by the course rules. The number three aircraft was about a half mile directly in front of him.

The rolls were the easiest of the four required maneuvers, however there was some finesse needed to perform the rolls well. A small pitch up to about ten degrees followed by a slight push forward on the stick to reduce the angle of attack. Then, a full stick deflection to the left or right caused the airplane to roll about the longitudinal axis, the imaginary line down the middle of the fuselage. A little rudder was needed to hold the nose just above the horizon as the aircraft rolled completely over through 360 degrees. A short hesitation was required to mark the end of the first roll, then the sequence of control inputs was repeated to the opposite direction. The roll sequence was repeated three more times.

"Here we go," Brian said aloud to himself as he rolled out of the crosswind turn on the show line, as some of the pilots called the imaginary line along the runway.

The throttle was pushed full forward to gain speed. Brian waited until he had the desired speed and then looked for the appropriate point on the ground before he began the maneuver sequence. The control inputs were smooth and crisp as the airplane responded perfectly to Brian's touch on the stick and rudder.

The successful roll sequence brought a smile of satisfaction to Brian's face as he maneuvered to take up the proper spacing from the airplane ahead of him. The next maneuver was a sequence of two loops.

The basic maneuver was relatively simple, and yet there was a definite subtlety to a loop. The series of two loops required the first loop to be performed well, if not perfectly, to have enough airspeed at the proper altitude to be able to fly through the second loop correctly. Once again, Brian did as he was told and concentrated on the upcoming control inputs, check points and techniques for a good looking loop series.

Brian remembered the advice Malcolm had given him and he had practiced numerous times. He needed to creep up in altitude a little, so he could push the nose over to gain more airspeed prior to starting the first loop.

Everything was going well and just as planned as Brian entered the loop sequence with the right airspeed and altitude. The nose came up with the added apparent weight on his body from the g's, the normal acceleration, of the loop entry. The earth fell away from him.

As the earth began to appear over the upper wing and his head, Brian repeatedly told himself, to keep the nose coming through. As the airspeed began to drop, Brian fed the rudder in to compensate for reduced effectiveness of the tail to counter the engine torque. As he looked over his head to pick up his alignment with the runway below him, Brian instantly noticed he was not perfectly lined up. He had not added the rudder fast enough and the aircraft was now slipping. Brian quickly made the necessary corrections as the nose continued through the inverted position to point toward the ground.

As Brian pulled back on the stick to level the aircraft slightly above the 500 foot desired altitude, he checked the airspeed. 200 miles per hour, perfect, he told himself.

Entering into the second loop, Brian reminded himself to watch the rudder application associated with the airspeed decay. The reminder worked as this segment of the maneuver sequence was virtually perfect.

On the upwind crosswind turn, Brian admonished himself briefly for getting behind the rudder on the first loop, but he knew that was in the past. He had two more maneuver sequences to perform.

The Cuban-eight, when performed properly, looked like a figure eight laying on its side. It was one of Brian's favorite maneuvers to perform since it combined the heavy feeling of the g's required for the loop along with the quick half roll just past the inverted position. Brian completed the maneuver precisely as specified giving him a warm flush of accomplishment and satisfaction.

The last maneuver, a half loop with a half roll on top, was named for *Oberleutnant* Max Immelmann, the German fighter ace who invented the maneuver during aerial combat in the Great War. Brian finished the Immelmann with a slight, but common mistake. The half roll to conclude the maneuver was started with the nose a little too high on the horizon and with a lower than desired airspeed causing the nose to move through a larger arc. The end of the maneuver left the airplane nose low. As Brian tried to pull the nose back up to the horizon, the insufficient airspeed gave a buffet as the airplane shuddered near stall. Brian recognized the situation instantly and carefully lowered the nose to gain flying speed. The mistake would be clearly visible to the judges, but Brian was not thinking of the judges as he coaxed the airplane to fly smoothly again.

The return to landing was quite anti-climactic compared to the invigorating aerobatic maneuvers and the close call at the top of the Immelmann. A stall at full power would have assured a spin that would have been a clear detractor from his demonstration of flying skills.

Malcolm was the first to greet Brian after shutting down the engine. "Good job, Brian," he said and then quickly recognized the disappointment on Brian's face. "Ya handled the stall quite well," Malcolm added with a pat on the shoulder.

All Brian could do was shake his head. There was no doubt about the several errors Brian made during his aerobatic routine.

Several other pilots whom Brian had not met came up to him to shake his hand and offer congratulations. At first, Brian was confused by the apparent contradiction between the compliments and the mistakes he made in flight until he realized the offerings were similar to Malcolm's greeting. In a small way, it was an acknowledgment of common experience. They all had been there before.

"We gotta break before the race," pronounced Malcolm. "Let's go get somethin' ta eat." It was nearly two o'clock and neither of them had eaten since their quick breakfast with Gertrude Bainbridge prior to departure from Wichita.

Walking down the line between the tents, Brian could not resist his curiosity. The young man's head kept moving back and forth looking into each tent. He had never seen so many tents. Some of the tents were plain canvas while most were painted with broad stripes. Reds, greens, blues, and even brown and black were painted on the canvas. Some were faded and others looked brand spanking new. There was activity in almost every tent. The scene reminded young Brian of a traveling carnival. He was too absorbed with his curiosity to notice Malcolm's stoic, almost aloof demeanor. The image was a clear contrast of unimpressed, mature experience against the unabashed, absorbent inquisitiveness of youth.

The aroma of country cooking wafting toward them from a large, double wide tent identified it as the dining area. With the cooking and serving area on one side, the remainder of the tent was filled with slip-together, temporary picnic tables along with portable chairs. Most of the pilots, easily recognizable by the various types of fur-lined, leather jackets and in some cases similar trousers, along with friends and other interested people were in the mess tent.

A variety of foods were available. Fried chicken, smoked barbecue beef and pork along with corn bread, red beans and rice, and several sweets were laid out on large trays upon a long table. It was like a large family picnic gathering on a summer Sunday afternoon.

Malcolm and Brian sat off to the side away from the entrance. The short meal was interspersed with greetings from people, aviators and others, who knew Malcolm Bainbridge. The words were always laden with respect and, in a few instances, with reverence. Brian gained a far greater appreciation for the fame of his mentor through the eyes of others. While the name of Malcolm Bainbridge certainly did not carry the recognition of Eddie Ricken-backer, he was in the same league -- a renowned fighter ace.

Jimmy Brown was not one of the well-wishers.

Some of the recognition bubbled over to young Brian for what he thought was simple association with a good man. Although the words were of his flying, Brian thought they were only being courteous. He had no way to measure the mutual recognition for his own flying skills that was being offered.

One man, obviously one of the pilots based on his attire, larger and about ten years younger than Malcolm, asked him, "Why aren't you flyin' in the meet?"

Without hesitation, Malcolm Bainbridge answered, "It's time ta give the next generation their time in the sun." His firm hand resting on Brian's shoulder and his head motion toward his young pupil were like an announce-ment to the world for Brian.

"Well, you could still beat us all," the man stated.

"That may be, but it's Brian's turn now."

The visitor turned to Brian. "You're lucky to have this man on your side," he said.

"Thanks."

"And, you're doin' really well, I might add."

"Thanks, again," Brian acknowledged.

The round man from the briefing tent stepped into the tent and shout-ed, "Let's get this show going. All pilots, man your airplanes."

A rumble of groans, muffled comments and snorts reminded Brian of the response he heard in school when the teacher announced she was go-ing to give a surprise test. Although there was some degree of sophomoric protestation, the pilots all began to move out of the tent.

The greetings to Malcolm Bainbridge continued until the group of pilots began to disperse. Brian was amazed by all the recognition Malcolm received and quietly he hoped someday people would respect him for his flying accomplishments.

Malcolm must have noticed the expression of adoration on Brian's face. "Let's cut all the bullshit and get back down ta why we're here."

For an instant, Brian was not quite sure what Malcolm was trying to say. Then, the revelation hit him. Brian smiled so big it almost hurt and said, "Right, concentration."

For the race event, they would all be in the air at the same time. As Brian strapped into the cockpit of the modified Mystery S, he remembered the important points he must do to lessen the disadvantage he had in speed. Fly low to take advantage of any ground effect and keep the others in sight. Fly a straight line parallel to and about two wing spans outside an imaginary line drawn between the pylons to account for the turning radius at the pylons. Fly as close to the pylons as possible at the top of the turns. Keep the throttle full open and fly smoothly, don't jerk the airplane, to minimize wasted motion and energy. Above all, keep your eyes in constant scan from wing-tip to wing-tip; keep everyone in sight. It seemed so easy and yet he knew from Malcolm's instruction it was going to be very hard.

Takeoff and marshaling for the start was not too hard although nearly a dozen airplanes in a small area made collision avoidance the number one concern. The start plane, a bright red and white, Stearman, similar to Malcolm's main workhorse aircraft, rose to join them. This particular race, as Brian learned, would be a paced start as opposed to a timed start. The red and white pace plane would fly at 100 feet directly toward the first pylon. The competitors were allowed to be in any position as long as they were not ahead of the starter plane. The start was signaled when the pace plane pulled up abruptly.

Just as Malcolm had told him, Brian took up a position below and slightly behind the Stearman pace plane as the other machines jockeyed for position abeam and above them.

The red and white airplane disappeared from his sight above Brian. The start was clean as indicated by the trail of smoke from the red flair used to signal the spectators.

Most of the other competitors moved out in front of Brian with their faster airplanes. Brian concentrated on what Malcolm had told him. Straight. Smooth. Fly the line.

After the first circuit, Brian was next to last. He kept his hand on the throttle pushing to keep it full open. The other airplanes bobbed and weaved to maintain the course line and avoid hitting one another. From Brian's perspective, the gaggle of multicolored airplanes looked like a disorganized conglomeration of strange birds trying to decide who would lead the flock.

Gradually, Brian's methodical flying began to pay some dividends.

Slowly, ever so slowly, the renovated Mystery S passed one airplane after another as they fought for position above and, for the most part, outside Brian's line. It was almost like they did not know he was there.

The excitement of the race was stimulating and quickly addicting to the novice among the competitors. There was a unique exhilaration associated with flying as fast and as close to the ground and pylons as he could. Feeling the strain of the engine, the rush of the air and ground beneath him were the aviator's narcotic swiftly possessing young Brian Drummond.

By the fourth circuit, Brian was near the middle of the pack. A couple of airplanes fell out rapidly as smoke began to appear from under the engine cowling.

As they began the last circuit of the race, Brian reminded himself again to fly the line, turn smoothly, and keep the throttle full open. Only four aircraft were in front of him as best he could judge. Most of the time he was barely thirty or forty feet above the ground, narrowly missing some of the trees around the course. The last two turns were perfect as he passed two more racers. Brian was in third place as he leveled the wings for the run to the finish line almost passing the second place airplane. Then, the greater speed of the other machines overtook the Mystery S. When they crossed the finish line for the fifth and final time, Brian was in fourth place.

Immediately, Brian backed off the throttle to give the engine some time to cool down before going into land. All the gauges looked OK although the oil temperature was on the high side. Brian was nearly the last to land. Malcolm was waiting for him as he taxied into his parking spot.

The frown on Malcolm's face did not match the excitement Brian felt within. He wondered why Malcolm was not excited as well and physically congratulatory in his manner with Brian's accomplishment. Young Drummond found out soon enough.

"What the hell were ya doin' up there?" Malcolm shouted at Brian obviously angry about something.

Brian was dumbfounded. He had no idea what had upset Mister Bainbridge so much. Brian quickly thought about the race, what he had done and could not think of anything that was contrary to his tutor's explicit instructions. "What do you mean?"

"Ya took too many chances, ya bastard."

Brian was staggered by the vehemence of Malcolm's words. He could not speak.

"Ya flew too low. Yar wing nearly clipped a pylon several times that I could see." Malcolm hesitated to suck in a deep breath and gather strength, and he continued, shouting nearly at the top of his voice, "Ya could'a cartwheeled the damn airplane and spread yar parts all over the place."

Brian still did not know what to say. He did not understand why Malcolm was so angry. He still thought he did exactly what he had been instructed to do, but there was no question Malcolm Bainbridge thought he had gone too far. "I... I..." Brian struggled to speak.

"Do ya know how close ya came ta those pylons?"

"I... I just..." stammered Brian. Malcolm waited. "I was just... I just was trying to do what you told me," Brian finally managed to say.

"Well, God damn'it, ya went too far," he shouted back.

Jimmy Brown was still walking toward them when he spoke rather loudly himself. "Ease up there, Malcolm."

"Ya stay out'ta this, Jimmy. Don't put yar damn snoot where it don't belong."

"Hey, the boy flew a good race."

"He flew too low and too close," Malcolm shouted back at Jimmy Brown with anger still in his voice.

"Isn't that what we're supposed ta do?"

"No," Malcolm spat. "We're not suppose ta do that. We're supposed ta fly safely." His resentment overcame his ability to shout at Brian. He turned and walked off without another word.

Jimmy turned to Brian. "He'll be OK when he cools down." Jimmy smiled to provide some reassurance. "Anyway, you flew a great race, kid. I haven't seen flyin' like that in a long time."

"Thanks," Brian responded to Jimmy's back.

After a quick check of the airplane to make sure there was nothing obviously wrong, Brian walked to the briefing tent. Several of the pilots were sitting and talking about the race and did not acknowledge Brian's presence. The judges appeared to be deeply into the process of adding up the scores. Brian decided to walk around a little before they announced the results.

There was a subdued enthusiasm among the people Brian passed. Everyone seemed to be talking about aviation in one form or another. Men, women and children recounted elements of the competition, or the appearance of an airplane, or the sound of an engine. A few of the spectators talked about a teenager who was flying in the competition. Brian's anonymity among the crowd gave him a warm feeling like a wool blanket on a winter day although some of the people resented the young pilot. Others marveled at the fact that a pilot so young could fly so well.

Aircraft could be seen and heard flying. They were the stunt flyers, the wing walkers and the ribbon catchers. Pilots were willing to try almost any trick or stunt with an airplane to produce a gasp or a sharp pump of adrenaline for those watching the exhibition.

The muffled and intertwined words of the crowd contained speculation about the results of the competition that were about to be announced. With the third indication, Brian looked around him to determine the direction to the briefing tent.

The crowd was drifting off toward the west end of the flight line as he reached the tent. No one was in the briefing tent. Somewhat confused, Brian decided to move toward the assembly of spectators.

The round man stood on a platform with several other people who were probably judges Brian recognized from the morning briefing and subsequent scoring effort. Brian looked around trying to find Malcolm, but the most he could see were hats and the backs of heads. This gathering was obviously the announcement of the airmeet results.

Where was Malcolm, Brian asked himself? Was he still angry? Then, a stirring thought jolted Brian out of the scene as thank you's were being spoken to all the people who helped put on the airmeet. Maybe Malcolm was setting up the meeting with Group Captain Spencer or some other RAF representative. Brian wanted it to be true. Malcolm had said the meeting would not occur until after an airmeet. This was the time, Brian sensed.

Brian's heart rate increased with the excitement of the impending conversation with the harbinger of his dreams – a realization that Malcolm's absence must be a sign of the meeting. He's setting up the meeting or talking to the RAF guy about me, Brian told himself. What am I going to say? What am I going to do, if he tells me, I must leave from here right now?

"Who is this Brian Drummond?" a man standing near Brian asked quite loudly, almost incredulously, snapping the young aviator back to the real world.

For a moment, Brian could only look at the man with an inquisitive expression and thoughts about why the man was asking the question. People in the crowd were looking around as if they were all looking for Brian. The struggle to determine what was going on took longer than Brian felt comfortable with. The moments passed and all he could hear was the rumble and confusion of the crowd.

Then, from the platform the round man shouted, barely above the noise of the crowd, "One last time, is Brian Drummond here?"

Brian still did not know quite what was going on, or why his name was being called out. "I'm here," Brian said not quite loud enough for the meet director to hear. A couple of people in the crowd heard Brian, realized the response did not reach the podium and shouted the location of the competitor.

The sea of the crowd began to part and hands pushed Brian toward the platform. As he moved through the audience, words of congratulations were spoken by anonymous individuals moving Brian forward.

"Are you Brian Drummond?" asked the round man looking down at Brian from the platform.

"Yes."

"Well, get up here, boy."

Brian did as he was told still confused about what was going on. He thought it must be good with the number of congratulations he received as he was ushered to the platform.

"Here you have him, ladies and gentlemen. Brian Drummond, our fourth place finisher, and the youngest pilot in the competition. He's just seventeen. Can you believe it?"

An expression of incredulousness occupied his entire face from his disbelieving eyes to his gaping mouth. For an instant, Brian though there must be some mistake. He had not flown that well, especially in comparison to some of the other pilots.

The round man shook Brian's hand. "Congratulations, Brian Drummond, a great piece of flying." He turned to one of his assistants standing behind the platform to receive an envelope. Handing it to Brian, he said, "And here is the fourth place prize, one hundred dollars." The applause was loud and genuine as Brian accepted the envelope and shook the man's hand, again.

The announcements for the other winners were completed in order, but Brian was not listening. He was looking throughout the crowd trying to find the face of his mentor.

Malcolm's face was not detected by young Brian, but it was there, in the back of the crowd to the right of the platform near the first airplane in the parking line. The smile of his face was a simple expression of pride not meant to be seen by anyone else. His eyes welled up with moisture to complement the emotions of a greater satisfaction.

With the announcements complete, Brian shook hands with several people who complimented him on his flying and wished him luck in the future. The crowd dissipated quickly. Brian still had not found Malcolm. The young aviator began to make his way back to his airplane reasoning properly that Malcolm would eventually show up there since it was the only transportation they had to return to Wichita.

Brian waited at the airplane for what seemed to him to be hours, but in reality, was only thirty minutes. Several people, a couple of pilots and the other spectators, stopped at the airplane to talk about flying. Brian first noticed Malcolm as he walked behind the tail from the other side of the aircraft. The wind was blowing his black and gray hair like a strange hand on his head waving to an applauding crowd. The older man had a stern expression on his face that he had worked hard to achieve. Malcolm did not want Brian to know how proud he felt and the closeness, like a son he never had, that joined the other emotions coursing through his mind and body.

"I was wondering where you were," said Brian as he searched Malcolm's eyes for a clue to his mood. Neutral was the best he could assess. There was no sign of happiness or anger. There was also no response to his words other than Malcolm's continued approach.

The husband and wife who happened to be talking to Brian when Malcolm appeared spoke their adieu and walked away. Even Brian wanted to walk away, but he knew that was not an option.

The old man stopped a little over an arm's length from Brian. The two generations of aviators looked into each other's eyes in search of unspoken answers to a swath of unasked questions. Brian was the first to break the impasse.

"Malcolm, I am sorry," Brian offered with genuine remorse although he was not quite sure why.

As a veteran of the Great War, Malcolm Bainbridge had taken many chances, some necessary, some not. He had also been lucky which was certainly better than good. Many of Malcolm's friends, whom he thought were better than he, were not so lucky. Malcolm knew luck was not something any aviator could count on. Brian's risks during the race were twisted with exceptional skill, clear genius and too much luck.

"I'm sorry," repeated Brian, only this time his apology elicited a hand held up signaling him to stop.

Malcolm waited a few moments continuing to hold his hand up like a traffic cop at a busy intersection in town. "No need ta apologize," he said. Looking down at the ground between them, he continued, "It's hard ta watch when ya're flyin' so close ta the ground, the pylons and the other airplanes."

"I won't do it again."

"No!" exclaimed Malcolm with a sharp voice. "Ya flew a great race against ten other airplanes most of which were faster than the Mystery S." He kicked up a small dust cloud between them. "I've got'ta get used ta watchin' ya fly that close," he said using a hand motion like an airplane flying past a pylon.

"I'm sorry, Malcolm. I just thought I was doing what you asked me to."

"Ya were. Ya did it better than I ever could. In fact, ya did it too well, so forget it."

Several aircraft took off heading home to wherever home was. Both men waited for the engine and propeller sounds to pass.

Brian's mood changed instantly as his thoughts made the jump from apology to pride. "Did you see me? I got fourth place."

"I was wonderin' if ya were ever goin' ta get up on that platform. Yes, I did see ya." Malcolm extended his hand. "Congratulations. Ya flew a hellava meet."

"Thanks."

"Now, what do ya say we get along home?"

Brian nodded and moved toward the cockpit. "You know, I've never held this much money," he said holding up the five $20 bills."

"Put that away before someone decides they need it more than you."

The flight back to Wichita was routine with the winds of the Great Plains giving them just enough turbulence to keep them alert. Both of them separated by several wing lengths shared only thoughts on a common subject considered from entirely different perspectives. Romantic notions about flying the high performance aircraft of the Royal Air Force were balanced by the mixture of dread and resistance of the trauma of combat.

———

Chapter 6

...glory is nothing else but success,
and to achieve it one only has to be cunning.
--Mikhail Lermontov

Sunday, 9.April.1939
The Admiralty
Westminster, London, England

The Director of Naval Intelligence barely touched his first morning cup of tea when the small speaker on his desk conveyed his assistant's voice. "Courier to see you, Sir Geoffrey."

With a frown not observed by anyone, he responded, "Show him in please."

Within seconds and two sharp knocks, the door to his office opened. A smartly dressed Royal Marine entered, stomped to attention before the Admiral's desk and saluted. The older man nodded his recognition of the proper military greeting. The fact that a marine was the courier meant he possessed most probably a signal or dispatch of utmost secrecy from within the Admiralty.

"What have you, young man?"

"An Eyes Only signal, sir."

Sir Geoffrey held his hand out. The marine retrieved the message from his shoulder satchel. The brown envelope with red stripes across it and large lettering, MOST SECRET, over smaller lettering, Director of Naval Intelligence EYES ONLY, passed from hand to hand.

"Thank you, corporal," the admiral said with a tone of dismissal.

"Yes, sir," came crisply with the marine's smart departure.

A quick reading of the short note began the planned and rehearsed set of actions. Sir Geoffrey pressed the lever on his office interphone. "Get Trevor Andersen to my office, immediately."

"Yes, sir," was the only response from his head of operations.

Even at the early morning hour, the summoning of the prized agent took less than an hour. He was standing in Sir Geoffey's office. "We have our sign, apparently," the admiral began.

"Excellent! When does it move?"

"Tonight."

"That is a bit sporty."

"As you well know, you do not always get to choose your time," stating the obvious for both men.

"Right," Trevor paused. "We will need to send out the preplanned signal to 'Blocker'."

"I was simply waiting for you." The admiral pressed another lever on his interphone box. "Lamont," he said to his head of communications, "please send the congratulatory note you have on file for Colonel Pordonski."

"As you wish, sir."

Releasing the lever and looking directly to 'Diamond,' Sir Geoffrey continued. "You will need to get out to Croydon. I shall have the aircraft waiting for you."

"Yes, sir. I guess this is it."

"Yes, it is, my boy. Good luck and good hunting," Sir Geoffrey said, although he wanted to add that the future of the empire was most likely riding on his capable shoulders.

"If I may, Sir Geoffrey," asked Trevor pausing to wait for the admiral approving head nod. "What is the situation in Albania?"

"As you probably know, the Italians invaded Albania Friday morning. They consolidated their position quickly against minimal resistance."

"What are we doing?"

"Nothing, yet, although Winston has been relentless in his pressure upon the government to move several squadrons of the Mediterranean Fleet into the Adriatic in a direct effort to force the Italians out of Albania."

"Any success?"

"None, unfortunately. It appears the extent of action from His Majesty's Government is a Foreign Office letter of protest."

"What about Greece?"

"As I understand the content of the letter, it states we will take direct military action to prevent incursion into Greece. While it falls short of a formal guarantee of Greek integrity, it tries to draw the line."

"Have we detected any connection between the Italian engagement and the timing of Enigma movement?"

"None we call tell."

Trevor Andersen considered the situation, conditions and facts as they knew them. "I suppose that should be sufficient. I should be off, then."

"Good luck," Admiral Sir Geoffrey Pike said to his best agent.

"Thank you, sir. We shall bring this one home for you."

———

Trevor had his travel bag packed for weeks waiting for this moment. The weeks and months of preparation would soon be put to the test. As the admiral's driver worked his way across the River Thames and the streets of South London toward RAF Croydon Aerodrome, Trevor worked his way mentally through each step of the impending operation.

By the time Trevor's airplane took off, Pordonski's men would be moving independently toward Pila. Upon arrival at Warsaw Airport, Stanislaus Pordonski would be waiting to pick him up. The assistant to the Deputy for Cultural Affairs at the British Embassy in Warsaw would be waiting near the British Airways passenger service counter as Trevor and Stanislaus departed. A simple tip of his hat would signal the observed departure of the target truck from Berlin. The earliest the truck could reach the ambush area would be about 20:00, just after sunset. The most probable time was near midnight allowing for moderate speed and formalities at the border. Pordonski had gone to great lengths to make sure several of his men were assigned to the border checkpoint and that one of his men was on duty 24-hours-a-day for the last four weeks. They wanted a normal inspection of the driver's papers and the contents of the truck, so the Germans had no reason to suspect anything unusual. The first man to Pila would be at the police station when the border agent called to pass the crossing time and pin down the trucks expected arrival at the ambush site. In addition, road repairs, detours and delays blocked other possible routes in case the Germans tried to get fancy with their navigation, not likely, but possible given Nazi arrogance.

"We're ready for takeoff," the pilot said upon Trevor's arrival at the flight line.

"Then, let's be off," he said masquerading as a wealthy businessman and the only passenger on this special flight

Enroute, Trevor read through the weather reports for the area from Berlin to Warsaw. It was expected to be clear and unseasonably cold for the next several nights. The moon would be near full and a few days short of its zenith at midnight. Much to Trevor's relief, there was also no recall order. The operation was still on.

———

Sunday, 9 April 1939
Warsaw, Poland

The cold air of the late afternoon bit deep into Trevor's body. The shiver was ignored as his brain continued to race through the upcoming events. The next obstacle was no recall through Pordonski's organization and to pass the passenger service counter with a thumbs up.

"Good afternoon, Mister Johnston," Colonel Pordonski announced in a strong, confident voice. "I have a car waiting to take us into Warsaw," he added for any eavesdropping bystanders.

"A pleasure to see you again, Colonel Pordonski."

The pleasantries of casual conversation occupied their departure from the airport terminal. Trevor discreetly scanned the people moving through the facility. The eyes and face he needed popped out of the crowd at distance of about 15 meters. The man raised his hat which meant the truck had been observed departing from Berlin heading on the expected route.

A sigh of relief softened the tension, well controlled within him. So far, so good. The plan was proceeding as expected. The next gate was the police station at Pila and confirmation the truck passed the border checkpoint into Polish territory.

Pordonski's speed was quite moderate as they headed into Warsaw to check for any followers. In a narrow alleyway, they switched cars allowing the driver to continue with two decoy passengers into Warsaw. With Pordonski driving a Polish Air Force car, they doubled back by a different set of streets toward Pila. After sharing status information, both men rode quietly absorbed in their own thoughts and mental rehearsal. The late afternoon sun shown in their eyes as they moved west. Although the interior of the automobile was warm, the scenery outside was quite cold. The ground was beginning to show through in places, but it was still frozen. Spring was always so much colder in Poland than England, he thought. An icy crust would definitely complicate the task of Pordonski's track covering expert, but Trevor knew he had to trust his friend. He had never been wrong before.

They arrived at Police Headquarters Pila at sunset. Pordonski's lead man opened the door for the two men. Not one word was spoken, or any facial expressions given that might be observed and potentially reported to the wrong people. Even though this was Poland, there were individuals around who were sympathetic to the Nazis. The man led them to the chief's office.

As they entered the office, Pordonski made the introduction. "This is my best man, Carmin Kraczhuk," he said in Polish. "Carmin, this is Mister Johnston."

"Nice to meet you," Trevor said in perfect Polish that surprised Carmin slightly.

"Yes," Carmin answered shaking his hand.

With the door closed, they finally got their next report. "The truck has stopped on the German side of the border," Carmin announced in a low voice.

Both men struggled with their thoughts. What had gone wrong? Had anything gone wrong? Why were they stopped? The questions seemed to be endless and there were no answers.

"Any indications?" Pordonski asked, meaning were there any reasons for the delay.

"None. They simply stopped on their side of the border within sight. Activity appears to be normal."

"Do you think this may be a planned stop to get one last intelligence check before leaving German territory?" asked Pordonski to Trevor.

"I don't know," answered the Englishman again in perfect Polish. "It could be normal. An intelligence check is certainly plausible for a task like this."

"Then, I suppose we should wait to see what they do."

"Our only choice, I do believe."

"We need to leave here. Anymore activity will only draw attention to ourselves. It is bad enough I am in this little town twice in two months' time."

"You have arranged a safe house?"

"Yes, about ten kilometers from here."

Trevor nodded as the three men left the station after thanking the chief for his assistance. They departed the town center toward the South. Out of town, again checking for followers, they wound their way over narrow village lanes toward the safe house. Fortunately, the ground was still frozen. In a few weeks or so, they would surely become mired in the mud of a real spring.

The safe house was nearly a kilometer off the main road, not quite half way from Pila to the forest. The other three men, Lech, Georgi and Milo, arrived a few hours earlier. The three new arrivals caught up with them by eating bread and cheese along with a small amount of wine. Colonel Pordonski used the portable radio to contact his office in Warsaw. They, in turn, contacted the duty agent at the border by telephone to establish the alternative communications link. Within five minutes, a prearranged word code from the border agent confirmed the linkage and the fact that the status was unchanged.

The border agents were briefed to watch the truck continuously for any indications the cargo might be transferred. Use of the code word, FLIGHT, would indicate the contents had been moved. While the Germans still had no reason to suspect any opposition to the movement of their truck, they were a cautious bunch. They were also methodical and in certain ways quite predictable. If there was no reason to alter the plan, they would not. They also wanted to keep the movement as simple and routine as possible so as not to draw attention to the truck. The team had no choice but to assume the Nazis would remain true to form. Each of the agents, in their own private way, prayed for the chance to demonstrate the effectiveness of their planning and preparations.

It was just 21:00 when Stan suggested they all get some sleep. They would rotate watch periods every hour in case the crossing code was given.

It would take the team less than an hour to be in position and have the strike zone prepared while the Nazi truck would need more than three hours to reach the forest of their doom.

—

Sunday, 9.April.1939
Wichita, Kansas, USA

For the first time since they began going steady, Becky seemed to be genuinely impressed with his flying. It was not the money the young woman was astonished by, but the recognition of Brian Drummond's skill. He was fourth among eleven competitors on his first challenge and he was also the youngest of the pilots.

The afternoon bicycle ride out of town provided Brian growing insight into the attitude of his girlfriend. The questions Becky asked, the way she chose her words, conveyed a new and different message. For her, flight was still dangerous, but maybe only for those who were less careful, she admitted for the first time. Rebecca Seward recognized her ignorance and now she wanted to do something about it. The future was too hard to see, however the prize money was real evidence. The news of the Oklahoma City Airmeet spread rapidly among their friends and families with some help from the *Wichita Eagle-Beacon*, the local newspaper. For Miss Rebecca Seward, it was the recognition that changed her mind.

On the other side, Brian felt first hand that for Susan and George Drummond the emotions did not mix well. The newspaper article in the Sunday paper acknowledging the accomplishments of the local, youthful aviator confirmed their suspicions. They were both proud and hurt. Maybe they had not been directly lied to, but they most certainly had been deceived by their only son. Neighbors and friends conveyed their excitement for Brian's effort and achievement. His parents eventually let the disappointment pass and offered their mixture of feelings to their son after Sunday church services. Reluctant acceptance probably best described their view of Brian's activities. They both admitted they hoped their son's obsession with flying would drift into the past like so many other fads.

The difference in Becky's attitude did not escape Brian's awareness or Malcolm's for that matter. For Brian, the change in Becky's attitude was by far the most dramatic. Their intimacy had grown in both frequency and energy. With this change in her attitude, he sensed the coming change in their relationship. The addictive qualities of being wanted and desired nearly overloaded young Brian's sense of purpose. Every time, it was Malcolm who brought him back to reality.

The success of the first competition may have been luck, or it may have been skill. In Brian's case, it was probably a combination of the two with a larger portion of the latter. If he was going to succeed in achieving his closely guarded, declared objective, Brian had to work harder to refine his skills, concentration and competitive technique.

The next meet was just four weeks away at Lambert Field in St. Louis, Missouri. Malcolm knew this meet was going to be different, probably two or three times the size of the Tinker meet. More spectators and more competitors would add to the excitement and the distractions. Brian had to work on his concentration and focus. There was no illusion in Malcolm's mind about the power of young Becky's attentions. At this moment in time, Malcolm saw their young love as the greatest obstacle to Brian's success. The older man had seen all the signs many times before.

Malcolm was also wise enough to know they could not deal with this most personal distraction directly. He chose the path of compromise, a little give and a little take. On this beautiful Sunday afternoon, Brian was taking Miss Rebecca Seward for her first flight in an airplane.

"Are you sure this is safe?" Becky asked with some trepidation.

"Absolutely," responded Brian seeing the complimenting nod from Malcolm Bainbridge.

"OK, then, let's see what all your fascination is about."

A quick thumbs up from Brian followed by a slight bow and sweeping arm motion toward the airplane signaled the final preparation. "You'll be in the front seat, Becky," said Brian.

The faded overalls and bright red plaid shirt made Becky look out of place around the airplane, but her attire made ingress to the cockpit considerably less awkward. Becky thought she was ready for this flight preparing herself for more than a week. Her girlfriends thought she was out of her mind, and yet they also envied her opportunity. After all, Brian was becoming quite the celebrity in Wichita.

Malcolm stood ten feet away letting his young disciple do all the preparatory steps. This flight was against his better judgment and seemed like a waste of time and money, but it was part of the implicit process of give and take. This was the prize for extracting a promise of total commitment for the next four weeks up to the St. Louis airmeet.

With the young couple strapped into the Stearman, Malcolm took up his position at the propeller to assist with the start. After a few last instructions to Becky before the noise of the engine and propeller would make communications more difficult, Brian issued the requisite commands and off they went.

Shouting over the sounds of the engine, Brian said, "Everything looks good back here. Are you ready?"

Becky made no attempt to speak responding only with a simple and singular nod of her head.

"I'll be running the engine up to full power and we'll be off. The noise will decrease a little once we are in the air." He saw no reaction from his girlfriend. "OK, here we go."

The flight lasted nearly an hour including several flirtations with puffy, fair weather, cumulus clouds and a tour of the countryside. Brian flew over their neighborhood pointing out each of their homes. Becky enjoyed herself and Brian detected no signs of her being frozen or scared. He had no way to see or sense the death grip she had on both sides of her seat. Her knuckles were white as if her grip was the only thing holding her in the aircraft. Becky asked numerous questions and pointed to a couple of places on the ground. The buffeting of light turbulence was the worst part of the flight for Becky and she asked twice to be reassured everything was OK. Brian was careful not to do anything fancy with the machine. He knew her acceptance of his avocation depended on this exercise being a pleasant experience for her. His care was rewarded.

Once their feet were firmly planted on the ground, Becky looked at Brian for a few moments, then jumped to him wrapping her arms around his chest. "That was the greatest thing I've ever done," she said.

"I'm glad you liked it," Brian answered as she stretched to reach his lips. Their kiss lasted for quite some time becoming more animated and passionate with each passing moment until interrupted by Malcolm Bainbridge.

"All right, break it up, or I'll hav'ta throw cold water on ya like two dogs in heat."

"Sorry."

Looking directly into Miss Rebecca Seward's eyes, Malcolm asked, "How did ya like the ride?"

"It was really great, Mister Bainbridge. The only scary thing was the bumps."

A hearty laugh brought a lightness to the conversation. "I know whacha mean. I don't like 'em either."

"I really appreciate you letting Brian take me for a ride. I understand now why he likes it so much. There is a kinda peace up there."

"I'd say ya've captured the essence," Malcolm acknowledged.

"Thank you."

Malcolm nodded his head in acceptance of her gratitude. With a simple motion of his arm, the older man directed the young couple toward the house.

The reflection of Rebecca's feelings about her recent experience and the comparisons with Missus Bainbridge's flying experience dominated the discussion over a light lunch. Malcolm recognized the initial signs of a convert. Brian was simply glad his girlfriend was no longer complaining about his flying. With the sensation of her flight still quite fresh in her thoughts, Rebecca was more absorbed in the stories Gertrude Bainbridge recounted about some of her flight experience with her husband. She was amazed at the revelation Missus Bainbridge was herself an accomplished pilot.

The social intercourse eventually transitioned to the approaching air-meet and the need for Brian to continue his practice flights. Gertrude knew why Brian was competing in the airmeets and she wanted to tell Rebecca, but she knew she could not. The betrayal of her husband's trust would be irreparable in light of the relationship Malcolm and Brian had forged over the years. In addition, she had to admit to a reasonable empathy for the desire and ambition of young Brian Drummond. The thought of another generation of America's young men going off to war in Europe was repulsive to the older woman who had sent her husband across the Atlantic twenty years earlier.

"Enough jibber-jabber. Let's go fly," Malcolm pronounced to Brian.

"Sure."

"What do you want me to do, Brian?" asked Rebecca Seward.

A moment's thought provided the answer. "You can stay here and watch, or if you want to go home, I'll see you in about an hour or so."

Rebecca knew it would be more than an hour, plus her parents knew she would be out at Mister Bainbridge's airfield most of the day. "I'll stay and watch."

"OK."

"Then, let's get to it."

———

The two men walked off toward the hangar barns to get ready for another practice flight. Gertrude and Rebecca picked up the lunch plates and glasses returning them to the kitchen. The throbbing harmonic sound of the two different airplane engines was soon heard, followed by the fading sounds of their takeoff. The distinctive tones were a kind of signal for the two women.

"Don't you ever worry about them not coming back?"

Gertrude Bainbridge knew precisely the multiple questions surrounding Rebecca Seward's central worry. "Every time," she responded simply. She wanted the most recent inductee into the aviation-waiting legion to move at her own pace through this process. The intermittent muffled sounds of the airplanes passing by down the grass strip added a sense of connection to the conversation.

A few moments of pensiveness provided the next step. "How do you handle it?"

"You learn to accept what you can't control."

"Can't you just ask them not to fly?"

"To a pilot like Malcolm that would be like asking him not to breath."

"But, still..." she did not finish her thought.

"No buts about it, Becky. We have a choice. We can accept them as they are, or we can leave."

They worked together to finish washing, drying and putting away the midday dishes. There was no doubt Rebecca was seriously considering Gertrude's words. Several thoughts came to the younger woman. Gertrude Bainbridge was certain she saw Rebecca's thoughts...she had the power, the power of her carnal consent. It obviously had a profound effect on Brian. She had discussed the observation several times with Malcolm. He had sensed it as well between the two younger ones. Gertrude could see the gears grinding away...maybe she could convince Brian to stop. Maybe she could convince him, he needed to stop.

"I don't think I can stand the worry," Rebecca said eventually.

"Each of us has to deal with the waiting in our own way. I have just learned to put my faith in God and believe that He will bring Malcolm back to me. When it is time for him to go, the Lord will take him and He will help me accept it."

"But, if he didn't take the risks, the chances would be reduced."

"No, honey. It doesn't work that way."

"Why?"

Gertrude knew this was the time when she should paint a graphic picture to help Rebecca deal with the risks, and even more importantly, the trauma she was about to face when Brian left for England. "Because things happen, Becky. Things we can't control. The world could be at war next month for all we know."

"What does that have to do with keeping Brian from taking chances?"

"If you try to change Brian into something he is not, he won't be happy and I guarantee you won't be happy, either. About the only thing you can do is tell him what you feel when he is flying, but if you ask him to stop, you probably won't like the result."

"What do you mean?"

"You can ask him and he will probably quit, only for a short time. He would most likely leave you before he would give up flying all together."

"No."

"Yes, Becky. I've seen it before. It almost happened to me."

"Noooo."

"It may hurt to think that it might happen and you may think you can hold him tight with your body, but it won't work."

Rebecca flushed with embarrassment that another person would even think such a thought about her. "I don't do that," she stated with considerable emphasis on the indirect reference. A soft laugh from Gertrude Bainbridge was not the response Rebecca Seward was looking for.

"I see the way you look at each other and I have seen the changes in Brian. I have also been there before, Becky. It is nothing to be embarrassed about although I think you are too young, but it is part of life."

"Oh, my gosh."

"It's OK," Gertrude said putting her arm around Rebecca's shoulders. "We've all done the same thing."

"Oh, my gosh. I am so embarrassed."

"Don't be. It is good to be close to the man you love, but don't use it against him, or you will lose."

Rebecca Seward's face was still red at the thought someone knew she and Brian had been intimate. She struggled with her emotions. There was no way she was going to be able to look Missus Bainbridge in the eye again. Rebecca threw the dishtowel on the counter and started to run out of the room.

"Wait. Don't leave like this."

Rebecca did not hesitate or stop.

"Rebecca, please," shouted Gertrude Bainbridge.

This time the young woman stopped in her tracks, two paces from the kitchen door as if she had been frozen by some supernatural force. A torrent of questions and thoughts were flashing through Rebecca's mind. None of them provided her guidance on what to do. She was still torn by the predominant questions whether she should continue to run, what would she say or what could she say to Missus Bainbridge? Then, she heard a voice.

"It's OK."

The process of recognition took several seconds since Rebecca was so fully absorbed in her own self-deprecation. Slowly, she began to return.

"It's OK," Gertrude repeated as if she was soothing a puppy scared by a clap of thunder.

With the realization the voice was still Gertrude Bainbridge and she was coming closer, Rebecca Seward found that she could not move and the now searing heat of embarrassment was returning. Rebecca collapsed to her knees dropping her head into her hands and began to cry, almost wail, uncontrollably. She felt a pair of hands touch her and begin to stroke her soft brown hair, her shoulders and her back. Gertrude patiently let the sobbing subside before she gripped her shoulders and pulled her up.

"Come over here, dear. Let's sit at the table."

Rebecca slowly did as she was told.

"It's OK. We've all been through it, in one form or another."

"Oh, right," cried Rebecca.

"Now, don't misunderstand me. I don't condone pre-marital relations although I did it as well. I believe, now, you should wait until the marriage bed. But, what's done is done."

"Please don't tell my parents," she howled.

"I'm not going to tell anyone."

"Please."

"You'll have to trust me. I have no reason to tell anyone. I just want to help you."

Ever so slowly, Rebecca began to swim her way out of the whirlpool of self-pity she was in. The words Gertrude Bainbridge offered were knowledgeable, caring and comforting. Once Rebecca regained control of her emotions and her breathing was nearly back to normal, the two women, separated by a generation, began to talk. The tone of their conversation was more like friend to friend, or sister to sister, rather than mother to daughter, but the content was essentially what a mother-daughter talk about the facts of life should be. Their talk was interrupted only once.

Malcolm and Brian came in through the kitchen door laughing and joking about something.

"No," snapped Gertrude. "Get out. You guys go fly another flight."

"We just got finished," responded Malcolm.

"I don't care. Just go fly another flight."

Recognizing the significance of the moment, Malcolm wisely chose not to argue. "OK. We'll be back in an hour."

The flick of her hand like she was shooing a fly was the only response they got. They turned and left. Brian looked over his shoulder as Malcolm grabbed his elbow and pulled him out the door. Brian wondered if Becky had done something wrong or was in trouble. He had not been able to see her face. Missus Bainbridge did not look like she was angry or upset. Gertrude, and certainly Becky, could hear Brian ask several questions himself as they walked to the airplane and prepared for another flight. All Malcolm said in response was not to worry and concentrate on the flight. Soon, the two men were back into the world of the eagles.

The talk between the two women concluded before the men returned, again. They had discussed everything from the emotions of intimate relations to pregnancy and contraception. Gertrude kept her knowledge of Brian's goal as well as her feelings about abstinence from pre-marital sexual relations out of the conversation. Rebecca felt more at peace with herself now than she had for many months. She felt like she finally had an enormous burden lifted from her shoulders.

Gertrude Bainbridge served cold bottles of Coca-Cola to Malcolm and Brian after their hesitant return. The words were sparse despite several attempts by Gertrude Bainbridge to stimulate some conversation in a neutral direction.

"Thank you, Missus Bainbridge," Rebecca offered as the younger couple began to leave.

Both men noted the extra meaning behind her words. Both of them knew something important had happened in the Bainbridge kitchen and neither was certain he would find out.

"You are most welcome, Becky. We look forward to seeing you both real soon."

"Thanks," was all Brian said as he raised his hand to wave good-bye.

In characteristic fashion, Malcolm provided only a nod of his head for acknowledgment. He waited for Brian and Rebecca to disappear down the road back into town before he turned to his wife. "What's all that 'bout?"

"We had a sister to sister chat, Malcolm. It is just as we suspected. They have been intimate and she wanted him to stop flying. I think she understands much better now. I don't know what she'll do, but if you're going to help Brian, you'd better watch closely. They playing with some powerful tools."

"Thanks, Gertie. At least, it's somewhat in the open, so we can deal with it. I'll watch for the signs."

———

Monday, 10.April.1939
Pila, Poland

The night passed uneventfully for the team of five Polish and one British agents. One sunrise communications check confirmed the situation was just as they left it last night. The waiting game continued.

The fact that the truck was still at the border was considered a good sign by both Trevor and Stanislaus. If the Germans were suspicious, they would have moved the truck back to Berlin immediately. The delay enroute looked more and more like a planned breather to make sure all arrangements and safeguards were in place for the journey to Danzig. The journey from the Polish border to Danzig through Pila, the shortest route, normally took about eight hours by truck. The Germans would either do it all by day, or all by night judging from past performances. The two senior agents compared thoughts in private. Both of them were suspicious about the German motives for the delay and wondered if they had managed to somehow switch the contents.

By mid-morning, instincts told them it would probably be by night since the truck was still at the crossing with no signs of activity. Plus, movement by night provided less traffic, fewer obstacles to be negotiated and some degree of anonymity with the cover of darkness.

To pass the waiting time, all six members of the team rehearsed their individual roles, alternative actions, and immediate actions should conditions change. This was the first time all six men had rehearsed together. The acquired and practiced skills of the Polish agents with the blowgun were impressive. Jokes about the usefulness of the skill lightened the waiting. The preparations were flawless. Trevor and Stanislaus both recognized their readiness. Their only prayer, now, was for the Germans not to wait too long. A long wait would dull the edge the six men had finely honed.

Their prayers were answered just after sunset, at 19:52. The phrase, THE HOUSE BURNED DOWN, received from the border via Warsaw established that the truck crossed the border. Smiles and an OK hand-sign from Colonel Pordonski set the gears in motion for the next phase of the operation.

Each man checked and rechecked his equipment. Each of the strike team carried two blow tubes, ten Curare tipped darts, any one of which was instantly lethal to a human, as well as a Curare tipped dagger and a British Sten submachine gun with three clips of ammunition. Trevor Andersen carried the Enigma copy in a special backpack. Stan carried another backpack with the radio and several grenades. They would listen to the radio until one hour prior to the expected time of arrival for any special messages. The radio would be switched off to avoid any crackling even by a handset receiver that might alert someone, or startle any wildlife that could raise suspicions in the plain clothes, *SchutzStaffeln* guards in the transport truck.

The team used two automobiles to move to the strike area. The cars were parked off the road about 500 meters east. A small pine tree was easily pulled down so that its bows lay across half the roadway. The truck could easily pass, but would have to slow down to avoid the tree and the possibility of slipping over the edge into the stream. Small clumps of snow were carefully arranged on the 'fallen' tree to make it appear to have come down prior to the last snowfall. All their tracks were expertly removed.

The foliage of the 'fallen' tree was not sufficient for a man to hide behind which hopefully would make the Germans feel a little easier as they approached the obstacle. Lech would have to wait behind a small boulder and dash the two meters to the truck. Carmin had the streamside front position while Georgi had the rear position. Milo took the hillside rear position across the road from Georgi. Each man checked their footing. The small spikes in their boots gave them the traction they needed. The team had one last meeting to confirm the signals and the strike commitment. No messages meant the plan would be executed.

A thumbs up followed by a pump of his right fist by Pordonski signaled the team to take their positions. Without words, the four members of the strike team moved carefully to their positions covering their tracks as they went. The process took 30 minutes.

The next hour, plus or minus 30 minutes or so, would be spent in motionless waiting ready to spring into action. The warmth of the white and dark gray winter camouflage suits would soon disappear without movement, but it was a risk they had to take.

Pordonski moved to the high ground behind them where he could see the better part of two kilometers to the West. He expected to see the headlights of the truck moving like any other commercial transport.

Trevor waited behind a large pine tree about twenty meters back from the road. The cold was already stabbing at his feet and working its way up his legs. He kept telling himself the pain would be worth it if they captured an Enigma machine to go with the operating manual they already had. Access to the Nazi encrypted military communications would probably prove to be of incalculable value when war came. With the signs of war so close, they may never get a chance like this again. He could only hope the dedication of Pordonski's men would be sufficient to sustain them through the pain of the cold. The moment of destiny inched ever closer. They absolutely must be successful. Even the enormous size of *le Armée de Terre* did not make the French feel less nervous although they still possessed a unique arrogance regarding their invincibility and impenetrable strength of the Maginot Line. Since September 1938 and the Four Powers Munich Accord, Churchill and several others inside and outside of the government had been convinced war with Nazi Germany was now inevitable. It was simply a matter of time. Not one of them could see peace lasting through the summer.

They needed Heydrich's Enigma machine. This operation had to bear fruit.

The pain migrated up both legs and arms. His joints began to ache. In a strange way, it was a good sign. The worst sign was the lack of pain in his feet. The numb sensation was the first indication of frostbite setting in. Trevor knew the other men had to be in the same condition. The question of whether they would be able to run and jump with the agility they needed began to occupy his consciousness.

The stone cold silence of winter in the forest brought additional concerns about whether his hearing had been affected. If it were not for the moonlight and starlight, the dark might have left him questioning his eye sight. All his senses seemed dull. Even the pain in his extremities was diminishing which was by far the greatest concern, now.

The soft, slow crunch of a single man moving through the forest behind him brought the first sign of relief. Hopefully, this was Pordonski returning to the ambush site with news of the truck entering the forest. Trevor's supposition proved correct. The quick thumbs up hand signal contrasted with the death in Stan's eyes. The moment of vengeance was near.

The sound of the laboring, Mercedes-Benz, diesel engine provided the first clear sign of their target. A few minutes later the truck's headlights began to filter through the trees. The truck was moving at a moderate speed for the road conditions. Even if they did not slow up at the tree and as long as they did not speed up, the strikers would be able to do their job.

Adrenaline began to fill their veins. Any remaining pain disappeared in the rush of impending combat. Muscles began to tighten in anticipation of the instant they had waited and trained for.

Among the trees to his left, Trevor could see the silhouette of the medium size, dark colored, canvas covered bed, Mercedes-Benz truck. The tone of the engine remained the same as the tree had to be visible to the driver, a very good sign. To his amazement, the sounds of the engine slowed as the truck approached the tree. The preparations of the area to make it look like a natural tree fall were about to pay off.

Like a bolt of lightning without the light, Trevor heard the doors of the truck open and almost instantly the engine went to idle as the driver's leg on the accelerator went limp with death. A short moment later, a German voice shouting a question from the back was greeted by the sound of canvas being pulled back. Then, silence. The four men moved quickly to secure the truck and confirm the deaths of the four Germans.

"All clear," Carmin said in a normal tone.

Colonel Pordonski and Agent 'Diamond' moved quickly toward the truck. The ambush took four seconds, surprisingly faster than the expected and rehearsed seven seconds. The four darts had already been removed from the bodies that were purposefully left where they died.

The next phase demanded speed as well. They needed to find the Enigma machine among the other cargo, replace it with the copy, stage the driving accident, and initiate the fire that would incinerate the combustible contents before rigor mortise set into the bodies. The SS troopers needed to burn in a position commensurate with an unfortunate road accident.

Milo and Georgi held the flashlights on the interior while Pordonski and Andersen deftly searched the contents of the cargo. Most of the supplies were administrative, like common office typewriters, letterhead paper, a mimeograph machine, pencils, ink pens and erasers. None of the boxes were locked, sealed or even remotely secured. The first search yielded nothing. A thought flashed to Trevor although he could not speak it. They might have risked starting another world war over office supplies. Intelligence was rarely perfect and he prayed this was not one of its failures.

The second search produced the same results. Ten minutes elapsed since the ambush. Only enough time for one more search remained. Whether they found Enigma or not, they had to complete the plan, or this incident would surely be the excuse Hitler was looking for.

Trevor looked into Stan's eyes for the first time. "I'm sure you're thinking the same thing I am. Any ideas?" he asked in perfect Polish.

"This looks like routine office material."

Both men ground away at possibilities. Pordonski was the first to speak. "What about false floors?"

"You're right."

"Carmin, you and Lech search the bottom of the truck, and the cab and engine compartment for any hidden compartments."

They moved swiftly without speaking. Pordonski and Andersen went back through the interior boxes one last time. Each of them tapped listening for the hollow sound. Nothing.

A sense of desperation filled his entire being. Trevor wanted to keep looking until they found the device somehow he knew was there.

Pordonski was the first to state the obvious. "It's not here. We must stage the accident. We've used too much time."

"I know. I know. Have we covered every inch of the vehicle and its contents?"

"Yes."

The other answers came in the form of reluctant nods. Each of the six men took a few moments to scan the truck one last time.

"Wait. Did you tap the truck wall between the bed and the cab?"

"No."

Trevor jumped up to the bed moving over the cargo as carefully as possible. He pushed the boxes back away. Tapping carefully, he neither heard nor saw anything unusual. As he reached the bottom of the wall behind the driver, the sound changed. He tapped the area several more times. There was something behind that spot.

"I think I've got something. Check behind the driver's seat. Let me have that torch." Before either of the men could reach the cab, Trevor found the opening crease. The compartment opened exposing a wooden box. Pushing the cargo further back, Trevor extracted the simple wooden box. Several over-center, loop latches secured the lid.

There were no signs of any locking or sealing measures. Damn if these Nazis aren't arrogant, Trevor thought to himself. A device so important and yet they thought it was invulnerable to compromise. It needed no special protection. Thank God all mighty for German arrogance, Trevor shouted to himself.

Agent 'Diamond' cautiously raised the lid. It was not beyond reason for the Nazis to booby trap a box of this importance. He found no evidence of explosive devices.

With the lid fully open and the light brightly illuminating the contents, the excitement was nearly impossible to contain. The red and black switch plugs below the typewriter keyboard with the lighted letter code lights and, under a wooden panel, the infamous seven code wheels betrayed the box as their target. This was Enigma. The little known, but highly regarded coding device invented, developed and produced by *SS-Obergruppenführer* Heydrich and his small team of respected cryptographers. Trevor knew exactly what he was looking for, thanks to the operating manual provided by Agent 'Ash,' the French run, German espionage agent.

"Excellent! This is it!" exclaimed Trevor. "Let's clean this up."

The men moved about their chores while Trevor placed the Enigma copy in the compartment, closed the door and very carefully returned each cargo box to the condition and position they found them.

"The truck is ready," Trevor said continuing to use perfect Polish.

Carmin continued to work on the tracks around the area. Milo re-started the engine, carefully checked the intended point for leaving the road, and sat in the dead German's lap. Backing the truck up, he moved forward at a normal speed, turned the wheel toward the stream, and leapt from the cab slamming the door behind him as the truck crashed violently into the stream bed. The men waited for a fire to start naturally. When none did, Milo jumped into the frozen water, searched for and found the fuel line from the tank and pulled it away.

When Milo was safely back on the roadway, Colonel Stanislaus Pordonski lit a special, large wooden match and tossed it into the stream igniting the fuel. The remains of the match would float down stream and dissolve by morning as it was designed to do. It served its purpose, although at first, only the fuel in the stream burned.

"Let's move quickly," Colonel Stanislaus Pordonski commanded. "Carmin, make sure you cover our tracks. This thing should blow soon."

The men moved with the precision of an agile mountain cat. Carmin followed the team down the road covering the last of their tracks. Several times, Trevor stopped to inspect Carmin's work. There was no question as to the expertise of Carmin Kraczhuk. The only tracks discernible anywhere were the wheel marks of the truck leaving the road into the stream.

They were only a hundred meters or so from the truck when the fuel tank finally exploded. The fireball rose quickly into the air temporarily blinding the men. All six stopped to evaluate the extent of the conflagration. The entire truck was burning nicely. The German inspectors would find only the melted wires of the Enigma copy. The Polish constabulary would unconsciously obliterate any remnants, if they existed, of the team's presence.

While the light from the fire would be seen for several kilometers and would ultimately attract the attention of the police, one final evaluation of the fire marked the movement of the team around an obscuring bend in the road. The fire had fully engulfed the truck and all its contents. The success of the mission now rested with the effectiveness of the covering task and the thoroughness of the Nazi investigators. By prior agreement, Colonel Pordonski and his men would remain well clear of this place and this event. Every normal and usual effort would be made by the police as well as Pordonski's Secret Police to treat the incident in the forest west of Pila as an unfortunate and regrettable road accident.

The egress portion of the mission continued according to plan. Each of the men would shed their camouflage attire while in the automobile. Carmin Kraczhuk, Stanislaus Pordonski and Trevor Andersen split from the others prior to reaching Pila. Georgi would drop Milo and Lech at two different rail stations to the South. Carmin would be dropped off outside Warsaw. Until then, the extra firepower was considered wise for the protection of the small box inside the backpack held firmly on Trevor's lap in the front passenger seat. Carmin sat in the middle of the rear seat with his Sten gun resting comfortably on his lap. The Polish agents would meet back in Warsaw within three days.

Not one word was spoken during the journey to Warsaw. Carmin was dropped off at the last rail station before entering the outskirts of the Polish capital city.

———

Tuesday, 11 April 1939
British Embassy
Warsaw, Poland

The first pinkish, orange smears of dawn greeted the leaders of the Enigma strike team as they made their way through the city streets to the gates of the British Embassy. The Polish guards snapped to attention with some surprise upon recognition of the famous Colonel Pordonski, Polish Secret Police, at such an early hour of the morning. The guards instinctively wondered what they had done wrong to warrant such a visit.

Both men walked into the embassy reception room. As the door closed behind them, they turned to each other. Smiles finally adorned the fatigue drawn faces.

"Protect my country with this prize," Colonel Stanislaus Pordonski said reverting to English for the first time in three days.

"We will. It will be time soon for the geniuses to go to work. I'll trust you will notify your experts as agreed. We'll try to make the most of this gift."

"Then, the risks shall have been worth it."

"History will probably never recognize the enormous contribution you and your men made tonight toward defeating Hitler and his dogs, but rest assured it will last until my last breath."

The refreshment of the light chuckle brought the first humor in several days. "Then, I pray you shall breath for many years."

The two men embraced holding each other as brothers and parted.

"Good bye, Stan."

"Until the next time," he answered waving his hand and looking over his shoulder as the door was opened for him.

The senior orderly in the reception area waited patiently watching the curious exchange. As Trevor turned toward him, he said with a heavy Scottish accent, "Mister Johnston, I presume?"

"Yes."

"Mister Carlyle has been waiting for you." The words were spoken in a distinctly condescending manner as if to say, why are you so late arriving. "Follow me, please."

The path took them down a long, segmented flight of stairs into the basement to a heavy metal door otherwise unmarked, although the two, large, heavily armed, Royal Marine guards conveyed the importance. The orderly pressed the buzzer beside the door. A small slot opened in the door and a pair of eyes peered out.

"Mister Johnston to see Mister Carlyle."

The slot closed and the unbolting process could be clearly heard. As the door opened, the man motioned for Trevor to enter alone although he really needed no prompting. The precious burden was now inside the safest, most secure area of the British Embassy, the communications center. The teletypes were busy clattering away. The radio room occupied a closed, glass room with banks of electronic dials, switches and displays. Three men tended the communications equipment.

"Mister Carlyle is in his office," the man said over his shoulder as he led Trevor to another door. He knocked twice.

"Enter," came the response.

"Mister Johnston to see you, sir."

Carlyle leapt to his feet. "Thank you, Rearson." He closed the door behind him. "Good to see you again, Trevor. We were beginning to worry about you. 'Jumper' Pike has queried us twice. I trust your business was successful."

"Yes, indeed, Ian."

"My God, what this will mean."

"Quite," he paused for a short smile. "I need you to send an Eyes Only immediately to Admiral Pike simply stated, MAGIC SHOW CONCLUDED."

"Right away." Carlyle moved quickly to fill out the proper form.

"I'd like you to code it yourself using the SIS grade one cypher."

"Yes, right, no problem." Ian Carlyle left Trevor alone in his office while he proceeded to the code room, encrypted the message and sent it himself. "It's away."

"Very good. Thank you, Ian."

"I know you will tell me if I am out of line, but do you think I might be able to have a peek at the device?" Ian asked as a connoisseur might ask a famous gourmet chef to sample a unique creation.

"Admiral Pike has classified anything and everything associated with this mission, this device and any product from it as, MOST SECRET - ULTRA. You have been cleared for ULTRA since you have helped me and will continue to help me until the device is safe in England. One last personal note,"

Trevor said pausing for emphasis, "this may be the single most valuable secret in the entire British Empire, if not the world." Trevor knew he did not need to insult the communication officer and faithful servant of British Intelligence with the consequences.

"As you say."

Trevor opened the backpack for the first time since the ambush. With the box resting on Carlyle's desk, Trevor let his fingers caress the stained oak wood like it was the finest silk, or most luxurious velvet. Ian Carlyle watched the accomplished agent with a mixture of annoyance, curiosity, impatience and respect. In time, Trevor slowly opened the lid for only the second time, this time with less caution.

Both men stood staring at the orderly array of keys, lights and switch plugs. Trevor chose not to expose everything. The code wheels remained covered. There was no reason to go too far with the revelation.

"My God, man. Is this truly the real thing?"

"Yes."

"My God."

"I know the feeling. It's quite like seeing the Holy Grail."

"Yes, it is," Ian Carlyle said extending a finger to touch it as if it might be burning hot. "Oh my God. How on earth did you obtain this?" he asked more out of reflex than conscious thought.

Before the career diplomatic communications expert could catch himself, Trevor Andersen responded with cold, surgical precious. "You know better than to ask that question."

"Terribly sorry, old boy. A slip of the tongue."

Without further discussion, the lid was closed and latched. "Your sealing materials, if you please."

Ian Carlyle did as he was requested.

"Two on each side," Trevor instructed referring to dripping two globs of sealing wax over the crease between the lid and body.

From his pocket, he produced his own imprint block. Each imprinted one of the wax globs. Carlyle blew on them to solidify the wax more quickly. The corners were supported by two pencils to avoid breaking the seal while they did the other sides. With all four sides now sealed, Trevor again lay the box flat.

"How many people have access to your security safe, or the code safe?"

"Seven have access to the code safe, three to the security safe."

"Then, the box will be stored in the security safe and I'll need to brief all three access individuals immediately."

"Certainly, however the other two are off duty. We may not be able to locate one of them on short notice."

"Give it a go, if you will."

"Yes, sir."

Carlyle made several telephone calls to issue immediate recall commands to the correct people to execute the process. As Carlyle continued his efforts, Trevor's thoughts returned to the Enigma device sitting on the desk before them. The temptation to leave Poland immediately with the machine was overwhelming. Leaving the box behind just did not seem appropriate. However, the plan was well thought out. If the Nazis were even the slightest bit suspicious, they would have every exit point from Poland covered with SS undercover agents. The safest place for the machine was in Warsaw, secure in the safety of the communications center. The only critical element remaining entailed getting the Enigma device out of Poland before the war started. The prayer for now would be for the Nazis to wait at least until summer to invade Poland. At least a month was needed to evaluate the Nazi response to the accident and measure the possibility they might be suspicious. Beginning in a few weeks, assuming no drastic action by the Nazis like invading Poland, several dummy runs would be made by various agents with marked and controlled luggage. Any violation enroute would measure the suspicion without exposing the agent to arrest, or worse, assassination. When several unmolested runs were completed hopefully prior to significant darkening of the already present clouds of war, Agent 'Diamond' would return to Warsaw to move the box to England.

Trevor knew quite well the struggle with impatience and anxiety that lay ahead. The geniuses at the Government Code and Cypher School would soon be pushing to move the box as quickly as possible. Their reasoning would undoubtedly be to minimize the risk of losing the device and give them the maximum time to work with Enigma. They did need the time to figure out the code wheel sequence, the change interval and any other variations to the wheels themselves. The wiring plugs added another although less complex element to the assessment task. But, he was still the expert until the Enigma was safely in their hands. Until then, they would have to be patient.

The only concession to the impatience of the cryptanalysts in both Poland and England allowed a short exploitation by a small team of two specialists each. The Poles possessed more detailed knowledge of German coding practices than any nation. They were the well-source for Agent 'Ash' and provided key bits of information regarding technique that enabled the Allies to progress as far as they had. They deserved the privilege.

Ian Carlyle returned. "You are lucky. The other two will be here shortly."

"What is shortly?"

With some poorly disguised irritation, Ian answered, "About one to two hours."

"That's the soonest?" Trevor asked.

"Look, Mister Andersen. These blokes are off duty. Both were asleep. It is rather early in the morning, you know."

With his own irritation beginning to bubble to the surface, Trevor responded, a bit harshly. "We have the greatest single key to our ability to defeat the Nazis and you, or anyone else, have the audacity to talk to me about sleep. What's more, I've only had a few fitful hours of rest in more than twenty-four hours. So, don't talk to me about sleep. I want those men here as soon as possible."

Ian Carlyle knew he had overstepped his position and did feel some remorse for barking at Trevor Andersen, despite the rebuke from the accomplished agent. He also felt somewhat intimidated by the man. Ian wanted to avoid any further confrontation.

"I'll go work on it."

"You do that."

The drop after the massive adrenaline rush of the capture along with the fatigue of inadequate sleep provided a fertile environment. Losing one's temper usually accomplished nothing other than alienation of the person or group that was the focus of the anger. Trevor felt his own remorse over his loss of control, but the importance of protecting their recent acquisition helped him rationalize his sharpness with Ian Carlyle.

Without knowing how long the communications officer would be away, Trevor placed his right hand on the box and allowed himself to doze off, to find whatever recuperation he could. There was no way to tell how long it might be before he got a decent night's sleep.

To Trevor, Carlyle's return seemed like a mere few minutes. Actually, his absence was not quite an hour. The latch of the door opening was enough to bring him out of his cat nap.

Behind Ian were two other men, presumably the other communications officers. Trevor stood extending his right hand as the introductions were made.

"Well, here we are."

"Yes, right. My apologies for disturbing your off duty hours, but this is of vital interest to His Majesty's Government and potentially to the free world."

"We can dispense with the melodrama."

"This box has been sealed by Mister Carlyle and myself. It will be stored in the security safe and will not be disturbed until I come to retrieve it."

"What is in the box?"

"That is not relevant to these instructions."

The two newcomers appeared to be a bit offended by their exclusion. While Trevor noted their discomfort, the only one of the three selected for access was Carlyle as the principal intelligence operative within the group.

"What happens if you die?"

"Then, you shall receive accreditation for my replacement via cable and a properly authenticated letter from the Director of Naval Intelligence." Trevor paused. "Any other questions?" None of the three provided any indication. "Right, then, Mister Carlyle would you be so kind to open the security safe?"

Ian Carlyle complied with the request. Trevor lifted the box and placed it in the space cleared by Ian. With a last soft pat, he stood. "Close the safe, please." After the door was shut, latched and the dial spun, Trevor added, "Thank you."

"When do you expect to return for the item?" asked Ian Carlyle.

"I suspect it shall be about a month, maybe more, maybe less."

"What do you want us to do if any of the seals are broken?"

"You will notify the Director of Naval Intelligence by encrypted message, classified MOST SECRET, and at that point this safe will not be opened for any reason until either myself or a properly authorized individual arrives to reseal the box."

"Wait a moment. This is a working communications security safe. You cannot take it out of operations just because a bloody wax seal on a little wooden box has been broken."

Trevor could feel the rage within him, but this time he fought to control it. "I not only can, I have given you a proper command to perform. If you have even the slightest question, you are quite welcome to ask the ambassador to query the Foreign Minister regarding the validity and authenticity of this command."

"I just may bloody well do that."

"Be my guest. Now, if there are no other questions, you are welcome to leave and return to your off duty pursuits."

"I'll be damned," was the last exclamation Trevor heard as he departed the communications center. He returned to the reception area to ask the duty security officer for transportation to the airport. It was still rather early in the morning although the embassy was coming to life. The prompt response was indicative of the authority the security officer knew Trevor to hold.

The journey to the airport was direct and uneventful. He wanted to ask about any reports from the border or any other location. Had the Nazis reacted with any suspicion? Trevor knew he could not ask despite the temptation to avoid bring any attention to any association between himself and the Germans. He would have to wait until he was safely back in London. Trevor Andersen breathed a deep sigh of relaxation as the aircraft lifted into the air.

Chapter 7

The secret of success is constancy of purpose.

-- Benjamin Disraeli

Friday, 5.May.1939
Saint Louis, Missouri, USA

The great city at the confluence of the Missouri and Mississippi Rivers being further from Wichita than Oklahoma City dictated a Friday afternoon, after school, departure. Susan and George Drummond reluctantly acquiesced in their son's drive in the hope the foolishness with aviation would pass like a childhood fad or crush. Rebecca Seward could not be so circumspect. She worried about the only boy she truly loved. Brian Drummond accepted the status quo at home with his eyes, mind and spirit clearly focused on the event just ahead.

The flight to Lambert Field took even longer than planned as a result of several deviations to avoid thunderstorms. They arrived after sunset, but before the end of evening twilight. The large concrete runway loomed out of the humidity haze of early evening. A long row of smudge pot flames illuminated the edges of the long runway to assist the pilots landing at night.

Brian had landed at Lambert Field once before with Malcolm on a working flight to deliver a box of unknown contents for a customer and pick up several special parts for Beech Aircraft Company. The size of the airfield was still impressive to Brian. It was the largest field and one of the few paved runways he had flown into.

Brian could not see all the other aircraft that were already there for the airmeet. What he could see was at least three or four times the number of airplanes as there were in Oklahoma City. Some of the aircraft were probably not competitors, but it was still an impressive number of flying machines.

Some of the tents typical at Oklahoma City were replaced by more permanent buildings made of wood and corrugated tin. Brian tended to securing the aircraft for the night while Malcolm checked in with the airmeet control officials in one of the larger wooded buildings.

After the airplanes were tied down to ground anchors and the appropriate entry procedures completed, Malcolm took young Brian Drummond into town. They registered and settled into a nice room at the prestigious Gateway Hotel before they went out to see the sights of the city. The lights and motions of the city fascinated Brian. The more he saw, the more he wanted to see, but Malcolm knew the limits.

On the banks of the greatest American river, Brian marveled at the experience. "I can barely see the other side. My golly, the Mississippi is a whole lot bigger than I expected."

"Yep."

"Seeing it from the air, it didn't seem so big, but standing next to it makes you very small. I imagine in the daytime it is even bigger."

"Ya're right."

"Even at night you can see the currents. Wow, this is big."

They walked along the bank talking about the river, but mostly about flying. Brian's natural curiosity kept interjecting questions about London and Paris, exotic places for his fertile imagination. The widening world the young man had experienced since he began flying had enormous seductive power drawing him further and further from the environs of one of the Midwest's historic cow towns and now budding aviation centers.

The two aviators returned to the hotel before midnight.

———

Saturday, 6.May.1939
British Embassy
Warsaw, Poland

Less than a month passed since the capture of the Enigma device. Key intelligence operatives listened and watched the Nazi apparatus for any sign the capture operation and the device had been compromised.

The Nazi SD investigative team completed their examination of the accident site. Colonel Pordonski's shadow agents reported nothing unusual. The accumulating indicators provided the confirmation of the success of the capture operation.

Although the expected delay time had not entirely expired, the threat of war and all the misery it brought along with no detectable compromise convinced Vice Admiral Sir Geoffrey Pike and Colonel Stewart Menzies along with their direct advisors that it was time for the next phase. Possessing the coding device along with the operating manual acquired earlier, served no purpose without exploitation. The small team of cryptanalysis experts needed time to scrutinize the machine and determine how it worked in every respect. While the operating manual told them physically how the machine worked, it did not tell them how often nor in what sequence the code wheels were changed, nor how the plugs were altered. The wheel sequence, change interval as well as the relationship between each subsystem like an elaborate combination to a bank safe was critical to the operation of the device. Any one item out of proper alignment would yield only gibberish. For the box to be of any use to the Allies, they needed to use it like the Nazis. They needed to think like Heydrich and his code specialists, a bit demented and ruthlessly devious. After all, they did not call the damn thing, Enigma, for nothing.

Trevor Andersen returned to Warsaw for the first time since the April capture operation. Agent 'Diamond' would soon set the exploitation phase in motion.

Through the security checks into the bowels of the embassy, Trevor reached his objective. "Good afternoon, Mister Carlyle."

"Good afternoon, Mister Johnston," Ian Carlyle answered, using Trevor's public alias. "I presume you have some good news for us?"

"I certainly do." The experienced agent motioned toward the communications center supervisor's enclosed office. With the door closed behind them, Trevor continued. "All indicators are positive."

"Very good."

"We've decided to start the exploitation early."

"Who's the team?"

"Five experts, two Poles, one Frenchman and two Brits. The team will be led by Roger Baldwin from the Golf, Cheese and Chess Society," Trevor said, using the quasi-public reference to His Majesty's Government Code and Cypher School.

The GCCS was His Majesty's most secret and protected cryptanalysis agency. The men and women of the GCCS hoped to give key leaders direct insight into Nazi plans and orders. Enigma was the primary coding device for the SD, the SS, and significantly, the *Oberkommando der Wehrmacht*. Cracking the encrypted messages of the German High Command had such tantalizing possibilities. The anxiety and impatience were almost too much for some to bear.

"That is quite a mixed kit, isn't it?"

"Yes, it certainly is. I suppose the composition of the team is recognition of the contributions of each government."

"Isn't that more risk?"

"According to 'Jumper,' each member of the team has been involved with this problem for quite some time. None of us can predict what is going to happen in the next few months, so I imagine this team is also a hedge against several potential actions. The boys at GCCS as well as 'C' know each member of the team personally and professionally."

"When do they begin?"

"Monday, day after tomorrow."

"The room is ready. Do you want to see it?"

"Yes, if you please."

Ian Carlyle led the seasoned field agent out of the communications center and down the basement hall. A room that a few weeks ago functioned as a disused storage room with a mixture of mops, old files and various diplomatic artifacts was now a secured, closed, sealed facility. Monday morning after the exploitation team was all present and inside the new room, the Enigma machine would be brought in by Trevor.

"This is it."

The exploitation room was well lit and freshly painted with several workbenches, typewriters, mechanical calculators, chairs, blackboards and other tools of the cryptanalysis profession. The brief discussions regarding the readiness of the facility established the status as well as the extraordinary efforts of the embassy staff. The two men also discussed the administrative security procedures. Every piece of material generated directly or indirectly from the exploitation of the Enigma machine must be classified, MOST SECRET -- ULTRA, an appropriate moniker for intelligence material of such importance. Access to any of the material associated with or derived from the ULTRA Program would be strictly controlled by 'C' – Director-General, Secret Intelligence Service. In actuality, even the use of or reference to the ULTRA Program would be classified SECRET. Everything about the program had to be strictly, religiously, jealously protected if the value was to be preserved.

"We will need an around-the-clock guard of Royal Marines on the door until the device is moved. There is no point to installing a proper security door system."

"Already arranged."

"Excellent. Now, I would like to inspect the seals on the box."

"As you wish."

———

Saturday, 6.May.1939
Saint Louis, Missouri, USA

A small bus picked up some of the pilots at the hotel for the nearly one hour drive out to the airfield through the city and rolling hills of the Missouri countryside. Brian was still amazed by the size of everything around him and the numbers of people involved with this airmeet.

This time the pilot's areas were separated from the remainder of public displays and facilities. Only entrant pilot's were allowed past the cordons which meant Brian would be on his own.

"Remember what I told you," said Malcolm. "This is no different from the Tinker meet. Ya're equal ta any a these guys and don't let 'em get ta ya."

Brian nodded his head in acknowledgment.

"Ya just make sure ya note what yar position and flight numbers are and the sequence of events. They'll brief all the procedures, so just pay attention."

Brian nodded again.

"One last thing," Malcolm paused to make sure he had Brian's eyes and attention, "all ya hav'ta do is fly. Ya've gotta concentrate and forget all the bullshit goin' on 'round ya."

"Thanks."

"Good luck, Brian. Enjoy yarself."

A nod was all Malcolm received from Brian as the young man passed through the gate into the briefing building. While the pilots were going over the rules, procedures and requirements for the meet, Malcolm used the free time to walk the line of aircraft. There was a wide variety of aircraft. Contrary to Oklahoma, most of the contestant airplanes were new monoplanes with smooth, polished surfaces. One bright red monoplane had a transparent canopy completely covering the single cockpit. The quality of aircraft on display and about to compete was exceptional and a marvel to behold independent of any actions their pilots were about to make them perform.

Malcolm checked the angle of the sun. The time was near mid-morning and the pilots were still briefing for the competition. It was near the appointed time for Malcolm to meet his old friend and squadron mate.

The rendezvous took about twenty minutes to achieve. In their last letter a little over a month ago, they agreed to meet at the center of the flight line. Royal Air Force Group Captain John Henry Spencer, DFC, was at the designated location. As soon as Malcolm spotted his friend, a broad smile washed across his face. Their eyes met in recognition across a distance filled with numerous spectators. He had gained noticeably more weight and lost most of his hair except for a well-trimmed, laurel of dark brown hair around his shiny skull.

"My God, John, it's great ta see ya," Malcolm shouted over the rumble of the crowd around them.

"Good to see you, Malcolm."

"Did ya have a pleasant journey?"

"Quite nice, actually."

"Good," Malcolm said. "I hope the effort will be worth it."

"Let's walk, shall we?" Spencer said with some anxiety. "I get nervous standing in one place these days."

Malcolm nodded and the two men began to slowly meander through the crowd. The caution, or paranoia some would say, of his friend was an ominous sign.

"I would not have come if I did not trust your judgment, dear fellow. I look forward to watching your protégé."

"They're in briefin' as we speak. They're supposed ta start the meet in 'bout an hour or so."

"Malcolm, I must ask you again before we go too much further down this path, is this really what the lad wants to do – the American Neutrality Act and all?"

A passenger carrying, Ford, Tri-motor transport airplane with the markings of American Air Lines took off for some major destination, like Chicago or Columbus.

"I believe he's convinced and committed."

"You know quite well what he is getting himself into."

"How bad is it?"

"Well, if you listen to the government and the majority of politicians and press, it is much ado about nothing. According to my Uncle Winston, and a few others, war with Germany is as inevitable as the rising of the sun, and modern fighters are nasty business."

"From my distant perspective and with what we're told, I suspect Winston is correct."

John thought for a moment. "Quite so. A few of us believe this is going to be a particularly bloody sodding row."

"John, come on. How could it possibly get any worse than it was in France?"

A short, cynical laugh was about the only reaction Malcolm's question produced. "From the information we have received, the German Army and Air Force are superior to the French, and our own services for that matter. We have been and are struggling to develop adequate armaments fast enough. My boss, Dowding, privately thanked the PM for Munich, for God's sake, because it gave us a little more time to prepare. However morbid it may seem, I think he is correct."

Malcolm listened with interest, but wanted to hear about more exciting topics. "I've heard rumors 'bout yar new monoplane fighters."

"I am not sure what you have heard, but the new fighters may be the only tools we will have."

It was Malcolm's turn to laugh. "What about the Royal Navy?"

"Oh, the Navy will play an important role, but modern aviation will take the dominant position over land and sea."

"That's a pretty big statement."

"Yes, it is. Your air force general, Billy Mitchell, was spot on, regarding the importance of air power. Just imagine aircraft like that antiquated Tri-motor that took off a few moments ago, carrying several 2,000 pound, high explosive, or incendiary bombs, and fighters with heavy guns flying in excess of 400 miles per hour."

"Ya're kiddin'?"

"No, I am afraid not. Those aircraft are flying today."

"My God."

"And, there is so much more to look forward to." The sarcasm thickened with each word.

"I've tried ta talk Brian outta doin' this, John. But, he's this romantic notion."

"This will not be a pleasant war," John repeated. The RAF officer looked off across the airfield to some distant place. He wanted to tell his friend to keep the young pilot safe, but reality would not allow it. "He should stay here and be safe, but I am not certain there will be any safe place in this war. Dear God in heaven, the government initiated conscription a month ago for the first time in several centuries. So, unfortunately I must say, we need young pilots who can deal with the speeds and quickness of modern aerial combat."

"In that sense, ya'll like what ya see."

"If he's as good as you say, we will accept him with open arms."

"Good."

"Malcolm, we think things are so grave we are taking almost anyone who indicates an interest," he said with a grave tone to his voice. "We have some pilots who will never survive a single air engagement, but we need to get the airplanes into the air."

"That bad?" Malcolm repeated like a broken record.

"Yes."

Malcolm thought about the consequences of the words from his comrade from the Great War. There was an air of desperation to the picture John Spencer painted. Thoughts of resisting Brian to keep him out of the mess in Europe and the conflagration that seemed so imminent passed through his mind. Malcolm wanted to think of something else besides the tragedy of the coming war.

"Tell me a little 'bout yar new fighters."

"They are not what we must have just yet, but they are capable machines with beautiful lines. Two types. We call them, Hurricane and Spitfire. Both monoplanes with a thousand horsepower, supercharged, ethylene glycol cooled, petrol engines, retractable undercarriage, closed cockpits and can do 400 miles per hour or better as I said earlier."

"So I've heard."

"Eight Browning, thirty-thirty, machine guns in the wings."

"Jesus."

"What's worse, Gerry's got a high speed fighter, similar to ours, that is currently faster and carries a 20 millimeter cannon. Willie Messerschmitt, you may have heard of him, calls it the model 109. The actual designation is Bf109 for *Bayerische Flugzeugwerke*," he said in perfect High German, "but, most of us cannot seem to pronounce it correctly, so we just call the beast, Me109, in Willie's honor."

"Didn't I hear, they used that fighter in Spain?"

"Yes, they did with devastating results. The damn thing is maybe slightly faster, harder hitting and possibly less maneuverable than our best fighter, the Spitfire."

"My God."

John stopped to face his friend and look him directly in the eye. "Do you see why we are saying this is going to be a nasty war?"

Both men knew the implications of the speed and firepower. Malcolm also knew without asking why they were looking for young men to fly these new airplanes. The RAF needed pilots with instant reflexes, no fear and cold, calm, purposeful thought under the worse conditions. Thoughts of keeping Brian out of such a grim situation returned to Malcolm.

John Spencer clasped his hands behind his back and turned to walk back to the center of the line without saying another word. Malcolm caught up to his friend in a few steps.

John spoke with his head held high and his eyes focused into space. "It looks like they are getting ready to start."

"Ya're right. I'd better get over ta the plane and help Brian get started. He's flyin' a red, modified old Travel Air Mystery S monoplane."

John stopped again. "We will split then, I should think."

"Yes." Malcolm looked around and then pointed to the tallest building with a small room surrounded by glass on the top. "Let's meet at the base of the control tower after the meet's over."

"Very well, Malcolm. I look forward to meeting your young pilot."

Malcolm nodded his head in response. John walked away into the crowd that was getting bigger by the moment. For Malcolm, John's words brought to his mind's eye, the image of a calf being led to slaughter. It was not a pretty or pleasant image, and it made his stomach turn with revulsion. Maybe this was not such a good idea, he told himself, with slightly more question than statement to his thoughts.

The thickening crowd made progress toward the aircraft more difficult than just less than an hour earlier. Brian stood dutifully by the airplane waiting for his mentor's return. The Mystery S had looked so capable in Oklahoma City. Now, it looked like an old, tired veteran trying one last time for glory.

"I was beginning to wonder where you were," said his young pilot.

Malcolm waved his hand as if to say, you worry too much.

"Where were you?"

The question struck Malcolm like something his wife might ask. "I was just walkin' 'round," he answered not wanting to give Brian the slightest clue the young man's inquisitor was in the crowd.

"I'm in the second flight. The first is getting ready to go shortly."

"How many flights?"

"Four."

"Good. Then, we should be finished later this afternoon, so we can get back home."

The thought was attractive to Brian although there was a touch of resistance. He wanted to get the pressure of the impending meeting with Malcolm's British air force friend over with. Brian wanted to know whether his dream of recent months would be fulfilled.

The events for this meet were identical to the airmeet in Oklahoma City except there was three times the number of competitors. Progress through the events and flights was quick. Several of the pilots he recognized from Oklahoma City. Most were new to him. The caliber of pilots in general was considerably better. The quality of aircraft was also well above the previous meet. The Mystery S was underpowered and less maneuverable than most of the other aircraft. The lack of a more capable aircraft frustrated, but did not deter young Brian from doing the best he had ever done in the precision landing, aerobatic and pylon race events. Out of 32 pilots in the competition, Brian placed 3rd in the landing event, 7th in aerobatics and could only manage 22nd in the race. Overall, his final standing was 9th place with only the top five receiving monetary awards.

The good part about the day's events was Brian's feeling of accomplishment. He had competed against exceptional pilots with a relatively old airplane and he felt good. He had done the best he could.

As Brian taxied the bright red, Mystery S to his parking spot after the final race, Malcolm waited for him with a great smile and pride in his eyes. The young man had improved so much in such a short time. He had truly become an accomplished aviator.

"Ya did real good, Brian," said Malcolm. "Ya made that ol' bird sing.

I'm prouda ya."

"Thanks."

"Any problems with 'er?" Malcolm asked motioning with his head toward the Mystery S.

"No."

"Good." Malcolm put his arm around Brian's shoulder pulling him away from the airplane. "Let's go for a walk."

"Where are we going?"

"I want ta show ya somethin'."

"What is it?"

"Ya'll see."

———

Although John Spencer had never seen a Travel Air Mystery S, he recognized it was not a new airplane. Without asking Malcolm, he suspected his former squadron mate acquired the machine, probably just for Brian Drummond, and modified it as best he could to give the young man a fighting chance in competition with newer, faster, more maneuverable aircraft.

Watching Brian fly, told him just about everything he needed to know. First, the recommendation and endorsement were from one of the best pilots he had ever known and one of the few pilots in the world he would trust without question, reservation or second thought. Second, the broad smile on his face reflected the demonstrated skills of Malcolm's protégé. Brian's impressive combination of precision, grace, aggressiveness and determination worked like a Lord Tennyson poem in the air. Although Brian did not win the competition, he appeared to be the most skilled pilot in the air. Third, desire, simply desire. Attitude, commitment and enthusiasm could overcome just about any obstacle. When mixed with skill and instinct, the boundaries were limitless. The only element he had yet to judge was instinct. According to Malcolm, the boy was a natural hunter. If Malcolm was correct, Brian Drummond could be the 'Bloody Red Baron' of his generation...the best, most successful fighter pilot...and... "He would be on our side," John said aloud to no one in particular as he saw Malcolm, tall by RAF standards, walking with a taller by nearly half a foot, trim, strikingly handsome young man with light brown, wavy hair and magnetic, blue-gray eyes. "This kid is going to be a killer of more than just Germans," he said aloud again to only himself.

"Brian," he said, "I'd like ya ta meet a very dear friend, Group Captain John Spencer of the Royal Air Force."

John Spencer could see the excitement in the young man's eyes along with a slightly startled expression. Malcolm undoubtedly had not told him about the meeting that obviously had come unexpectedly.

"John, this is Brian Drummond."

"A pleasure to meet you, my boy."

The young man still did not know what to say. His hesitation was even more embarrassing when he realized the elder gentleman had his hand extended. Taking his hand, he shook it firmly.

"You are an impressive pilot."

"Thank you...sir."

John decided to get right to the point. "Malcolm tells me you want to join the Royal Air Force to help us fight the Germans."

There were too many thoughts packed into the simple sentence. Mister Spencer was obviously convinced war was inevitable unless it had already broken out and the word had simply not reached America.

"Yes."

"Do you know what you are getting into?"

"Yes. Malcolm told me what is going on and what is probably going to happen. I think what that man, Hitler, is doing is wrong."

Brian appeared to be surprised by the strange laugh his words caused. "Yes, I should say so. *Herr* Hitler is gobbling up territory like a hungry wolf and all Chamberlain and Daladier can seem to do is feed him more."

"Where d'ya think it'll stop?" asked Malcolm.

"It won't stop until we stop him. Uncle Winston believes, and I agree with him, Hitler will take us into another bloody world war in twenty years, and blindly, the appeasers are helping him along the way."

"How soon?"

"Within the year, I should think," responded Group Captain Spencer not wanting to acknowledge the latest intelligence estimates that put the time at this summer, certainly within a few months.

"Not good."

"Quite so."

"John, tell Brian what he's askin' ta get into."

"My boy, you are asking to join a weak, but growing Fighter Command that will probably be the only bulwark between Hitler and his conquest of all Europe and maybe the world. This is going to be a bloody row to a far more heinous standard than the world has ever known. And . . . we need all the young pilots we can find." John wanted to ask Brian to join them, but knew he could not. Brian had to volunteer, had to want to be in the fight, for his conscience to be clear.

Without any familiarity with the Englishman's phrase, Brian knew what he meant.

"Can I join?"

"We will take you with open arms, my boy. But, in deference to my honored friend, I want to talk you out of this notion."

The expression of elation quickly changed to anxiety. "Why?" protested Brian.

"Many of these young men will be killed or seriously injured. Modern fighters do not leave much to the imagination. This will be, kill or be killed, and in very fast order. Do you want to kill your fellow man?" he asked bluntly to test the young man's resolve.

The slap of his question stung Brian. This short man who spoke with a melodious accent was very graphic. There was a morbid quality to the raw words.

"If I have to."

"Oh, I'm afraid you will have to, my boy. There will be no choices." Spencer paused to find the right words for both Malcolm and Brian. "This new German fighter aeroplane with their young, aggressive pilots, tested in Spain, will make the 'Bloody Red Baron' shrink further into history."

The words hurt. They enveloped Brian like a steaming, wet blanket sucking all the air out of his lungs. He was not talking about pheasants, squirrels or ducks. He was talking about human beings who spoke a different language and were themselves only following the orders of their leaders, however misguided that leadership might be. Brian instantly had an image of a young German man, just like him, flying one of their fighters in combat over France like the previous generation had done twenty years earlier.

"Can you do it?" John Spencer persisted.

Brian swallowed hard. "Yes, I think I can."

"I'm afraid that won't do," said Spencer quite strongly. "You cannot think. You will either kill or be killed," repeated the Englishman.

"Yes, I will do what has to be done."

"Oh really."

"Yes. I think what the Germans are doing is wrong and if I can help stop them, I will."

"Good," John said with a dramatically different voice. "We need you, young Brian Drummond, and if you are as good as your flying, you will do well."

Brian could only manage a nod as he tried to choke back the adrenaline pumping through his veins. The contrast in moods was almost more than the young man could handle.

"With your permission, Malcolm, I should like to go fly with young Brian, here. I have made arrangements through an acquaintance, for us to fly a couple of two-seaters in mock combat."

"Whatever you like," Malcolm responded. "We do have the Stearman, which I flew over on Brian's wing."

"It would probably be better to use an unfamiliar airplane for my purpose."

"Sure."

The challenge of a new airplane would give Group Captain Spencer a true view of young Brian's adaptability as well as his airmanship and instincts since he would not be able to rely on known or rehearsed actions.

With that consent, the three men returned to the flight line. A man introduced to them as Bobby Joe Sales would be their adversary in the mock aerial fight. Sales owned two surplus, Navy/Grumman FF-1, carrier, biplane fighters. Although only six-years-old, the retired two-seat fighters provided a new challenge, which was part of the evaluation, and an equal couple of pretend combatants.

The rules were simple. Several starting points were picked. Head-to-head, on top, underneath, behind and in front of the adversary aircraft, flown by Sales, with the object being to achieve an imaginary firing position about 100-200 feet behind his opponent. Brian had flown these maneuvers so many times. He did not expect the engagements to be easy, but he was confident he would do well.

"Brian, I shall ride in the rear cockpit." Everyone knew the forward cockpit was more difficult because of the obstruction to the up and forward field of view by the proximity of the upper wing. "Please pretend I am not there except for my instructions on the starting position. It is solely you against your opponent." Spencer paused to receive an acknowledgment from Brian. "Mister Sales, if you have no objections, we should offer Malcolm the open seat in your aircraft."

"No problem," responded Bobby Joe Sales.

Group Captain Spencer turned to Brian Drummond. "Are you ready?"

"Yes, sir."

"Oh Brian, also please remember, this is not a test. There is no pass/fail criteria. I simply want to see how you fly in an adverse situation. We will build the rest."

"Yes, sir."

John Spencer gave a thumbs-up to Bobby Joe Sales and all four men slipped into their respective seats. With little delay, the airplanes were off the ground, heading to the farm fields across the Missouri River.

"Hold your heading until I say, go," shouted Group Captain Spencer over the drone of the engine and the rush of the air passed their heads.

Brian nodded his acknowledgment without looking back at his companion.

The first setup placed Bobby Joe Sales about a quarter of a mile directly behind Brian. Repeated looks over his shoulder kept the other aircraft in sight until he heard the signal to commence the engagement.

The twisting, turning gyrations of the mock aerial fight between the two airplanes more closely resembled an intricate ballet in the sky than what would be a deadly serious confrontation safe only from the lack of guns and bullets. Brian worked hard with precision movements and carefully timed actions to negate the superior position of his opponent.

Fifteen different segments were flown by the two pilots. The flight occupied 95 minutes from takeoff to landing.

With his aircraft firmly on the ground, Brian became aware for the first time the sweat soaking his clothes and the fatigue in all his muscles. It was not the longest flight he had ever flown, but it was certainly the most demanding and tiring.

The crowd had not thinned very much during their absence, but several of the competing aircraft were missing from the flight line.

Bobby Joe Sales stopped to talk to a friend while the other two, older aviators gathered around Brian and waited for the dominate sound of the aircraft engines to die away before speaking.

Malcolm was the first to ask, "How d'it go?"

All Brian could do was shrug his shoulders with indifference since he lacked the experience to know how his evaluator viewed his performance. He felt good. He certainly had worked hard during the flight.

Without providing his own answer to Malcolm's question, John Spencer turned to Brian looking directly into his eyes. "You have a lot to learn, young man," he said pausing to see what response he would receive. There was none. "However, you have had an exceptional tutor." A smile, ever so slightly, came to Brian's face. "As Malcolm knows," nodding toward his friend, "it is rare for any of us to find a natural, instinctive pilot. You are one of those rare gems."

"Thank you."

"No . . . thank you."

The confused expression on Brian's face was an obvious clue he did not know why this senior officer in the Royal Air Force was indicating his gratitude. After all, Brian was the one asking for something, not John Spencer.

Taking the sign, John added, "His Majesty's Government shall be immensely grateful for the services of your skills in the defense of Great Britain."

Brian could not quite comprehend the Englishman's words. "Does that mean I am in the air force?"

A short chuckle made Brian feel a bit foolish. John answered, "No. We cannot recruit you directly. Agreements between our governments, you understand. But, if you take certain actions, in essence making your way to the Commonwealth country of Canada and volunteer, we shall take care of the rest."

A broad smile came and went just as quickly. "Are you pulling my leg?" asked Brian in a very serious tone as if he was passing judgment upon a cruel prank.

"Let me assure you, Mister Drummond, I am not pulling your leg, as you Yanks say."

"Does this mean I've done it?" Brian asked Malcolm.

"Not quite, but close."

The conversation was interrupted as Bobby Joe Sales returned to the small group. John Spencer shook his hand and thanked him for his effort.

Sales faced Brian. "Great flyin', kid."

"Thanks."

"I hope you got your money's worth, Mister Spencer."

"Indeed. I am quite satisfied. We appreciate your services."

"Good luck, kid," said Sales recognizing the reservation in his employer. Bobby Joe put his right hand to his forehead in a quasi-salute and disappeared into the crowd.

Brian wanted to return to the singular topic on his mind. "How do I get to Canada? Where do I go in Canada? When do you want me?"

"Well, now, let's take your questions one piece at a time." John paused for a moment to consider his response. "I'm afraid you must make your own way to Canada. American law is quite clear on this point, and we certainly do not want to upset our American cousins. I might suggest a train to Chicago, and then on to Detroit." Malcolm nodded his agreement. "You will cross the border at Detroit. There is a small office in Windsor, Ontario on the northwest corner of Maple and Lewis Streets with a sign outside the two-story building called, the Commonwealth Exchange Office. The office you need is on the second floor. The door is lettered with the same name. Our agent's name is, Mister Reginald Blackwell. His secretary is, Miss Helen Riser. When you arrive, simply tell him your name, from that point on, we will take care of everything else. Do you understand?"

"Yes."

"Do you need to write any of this down?"

After considering the question for an instant, Brian answered, "Maybe I should write down the names."

John Spencer took a card from his shirt pocket and the fountain pen from a pocket inside his suit coat. He wrote the two names along with the city and office names on the card and handed it to Brian.

"Do I leave now?"

"Well, Brian, that is up to you. His Majesty's Government needs you as soon as possible. However, we fully recognize your need to set your affairs straight."

Brian nodded with some relief.

"When can you get to Windsor?"

"I don't know," Brian responded looking to Malcolm for some help. A flood of thoughts about his family, Becky, his schooling, filled his head.

"We kin probably get 'im there in a coupla weeks. He graduates from high school the middle a this month and he's already of legal age."

"That is quite acceptable."

"Thank you, sir," responded Brian.

"You are certainly welcome," said Group Captain Spencer. The RAF officer looked intently into Brian's eyes trying to find some answers, or at least an indication of intentions. "Brian, you must ask yourself if you genuinely want to do this, and if you are willing to take the risk and make the commitment required. You will not be happy nor will we, if you are not committed to this endeavor."

"I am."

"Excellent. However, if you should change your mind, we will most certainly understand and appreciate your interest."

"I won't."

"If you should, a short letter would be appreciated."

"I won't change my mind. This is too important."

"Then, we shall see you in England soon. I shall meet you upon your arrival."

Brian's smile was so broad it looked as if his cheeks would tear. He could not stand still as he danced around like a small child trying to find a place to urinate. The young Kansan pilot was decidedly a happy fellow.

———

As Brian Drummond reveled in the prospects for the future, Malcolm Bainbridge and John Spencer moved down the flight line with a slow, effortless walk. The words touched on news of their comrades-in-arms who flew with the Royal Flying Corps in France, the boiling clouds of war in Europe, again, and as all good pilots eventually do, the wonders of the newest generation of flying machines. Brian walked behind listening intently, but not participating in what was quickly and clearly becoming the subtle and personal good-bye between two close friends. By the time the three men worked their way back to the Mystery S and Stearman, the crowd strangely seemed to disappear. The bodies were still walking around, but their existence seemed to evaporate. The two older men stood face-to-face. Brian felt like he needed to fade away as well.

Malcolm and John embraced and held each other for the longest time. Brian had never seen two men embrace like that before, but he also knew they were on a higher plain of friendship. What he did not fully appreciate was the feelings each veteran had for the other man, men who had saved each other's life more than once. The dependence of each on the skills of the other was a reality difficult, if not impossible, to communicate to those who had never been there. The bond was just as strong, maybe even stronger, than it was in the skies over Eastern France.

Holding each other's shoulders, John Spencer was the first to conclude. "Take care, my friend."

"Ah, we're both goin' ta live forever."

"Maybe so."

"Ya headin' back ta England?"

"Yes, tomorrow morning. I'll leave out of New York."

"I'll miss you, John."

"I as well." A brief smile flashed across John Spencer's face. "Now, get in your aeroplanes and get on home."

"Sure."

"Malcolm, thank you for helping us," John Spencer said with a nod to Brian. "I shall take good care of him as best I am able."

"Ya do that for me, John."

"Thank you, Brian. I'll see you again soon, I hope."

"You will, sir. Thank you, sir."

Spencer faded into the mass of remaining spectators.

"Let's get on home ta those who love us," Malcolm said to Brian.

The start up was normal. Brian taxied his aircraft away from the line to takeoff followed shortly by Malcolm in the Stearman. They waited patiently for their turn to takeoff and were eventually given a green light from the control tower.

The journey that would change Brian Drummond's life forever was about to begin. The imaginings of what was ahead filled Brian's head on the flight back to Wichita. The weather was clear. The flight was effortless. The welcome upon their return was provided by Gertrude Bainbridge. Brian would have to wait to see Rebecca. He wanted to tell her of his excitement, his honor and his future. The urge was almost impossible to overcome, but the feeling would pass.

"Before we call it a day, Brian," Malcolm said as Brian was about to pedal his bicycle back into town, "I want ta remind ya, current U.S. law forbids any citizen from joinin' the armed forces of a belligerent nation. I don't know what kinda enforcement there may be, but ya're goin'ta hav'ta be careful. Newspapers say they could revoke yar passport or somethin' like that. This isn't goin' ta be easy no matter how ya cut it."

"I understand, Malcolm, but that doesn't change my mind."

"I didn't think it would, but I needed ta say it, nonetheless."

"Thanks."

"Ya won't be thankin' me when yar in the middle a this thing, but I'll do my best ta help ya, and I know John Spencer is a man a his word. He'll do his best ta help ya, as well."

"I couldn't ask for more."

"Then, so be it. Off with ya, now. Ya've got a coupla weeks ta enjoy yar family and Becky, then ya'll be on yar way."

"Thank you, Malcolm," Brian said, and gave his mentor a strong hug.

"Ah, what now. Yar turnin' European on me already. Get outta here before either of us gets a tear."

The ride back to town in the late afternoon was jammed with so many thoughts as it had been virtually every time recently. Things seemed to be happening much faster now. The question of wisdom did come to Brian several times. Was he doing the right thing? Was his dream so selfish? What would his parents and Becky do when they found out what he had done? Would they try to stop him by calling the police, or FBI, or something? The experience with Group Captain Spencer made his decision, his dream, all the more real, and made it feel exactly correct. This was what he was meant to do.

———

Wednesday, 17.May.1939
Wichita, Kansas, USA

"**T**his is a great day for you and a great day for the family," Missus Susan Drummond told her only son, her only child. "You've completed more school than anyone else in the family. We're real proud of you, Brian."

"You can say that again," added George Drummond.

"Oh, it's not that bigga deal," announced their only son.

"It most certainly is," objected Susan. "You've worked hard despite the distractions, Brian. You deserve the credit."

"OK." Brian knew he had to go through the motions of high school graduation, but his thoughts were on the big day now just over two weeks away. He was eager to start the journey to his future. The discussions with Malcolm about the speed and capability of the Spitfire brought an irresistible temptation. Malcolm made sure Brian did not forget the deadly seriousness of what lay ahead. He was not afraid. He was more curious about what to expect in real aerial combat. Leaving Becky, his mother and father, and the rest of his family and friends always brought a solemnity to what he was about to do.

"You seem to be very distracted. Are you all right?"

"Sure, Mom."

"As soon as Becky gets here, we'll go down to the school."

"Sure, Mom."

Brian's thoughts returned to the future while his parents rambled on about the importance of school and the anticipated next stage of Brian's education. Rebecca Seward had already announced her acceptance to the University of Kansas in Lawrence. His parents continued to press him for a commitment to go to KU, as well. He made the motions without conviction. The most pressure came from Becky. She wanted their relationship to continue and she knew their best chance was probably at the same university.

The knock at the door returned Brian to the present.

"Here's Becky," announced Susan Drummond.

Rebecca Seward's new spring dress illuminated the figure of the young woman and increased her attractiveness. Brian was impressed.

"That's an incredible dress, Becky. You look gorgeous."

"Thanks."

"Congratulations, by the way."

"Thank you, Missus Drummond."

"Shall we go?" asked George Drummond.

Without answering, all four people rose to leave. Rebecca decided to go to graduation with Brian and his parents disappointing her own parents who resigned themselves to attending their daughter's high school graduation without her.

The ceremony for Brian and the Drummond's presumed future daughter-in-law provided great pride for the Drummond family. Recognition for their son's scholastic and athletic accomplishments made the years of attention and extra care worth every sacrifice. Brian's achievements added to his parents' sense of fulfillment. Although he was not the highest standing student, Brian's top quarter ranking gave them plenty to be thankful for. They shared their pride with the Sewards.

The two families had been neighbors of a sort for nearly twenty years. They had been friends for more than a third of a century. The friendship seemed only natural to offer the basis for Rebecca and Brian to grow from. The pride in their children was truly and mutually shared.

Rebecca Seward stood number three in the class of 23 graduating seniors. Both sets of parents had plenty of reason to boast, to smile, to talk, to enjoy. The future looked so very bright for both families through the potential of the next generation.

While the parents and most of the other attendees at the ceremony derived their own enjoyment, Brian agonized over the decision he had made. He loved Becky. He wanted to be with Becky, he thought, for the rest of his life. She was, without a doubt, everything he had ever dreamed of. He also wanted to be around his parents and family. He wanted to continue flying with and for Malcolm Bainbridge. The young man could not reconcile the contrast, the conflict, of his familiar environment with the aviator's opiate of the ultimate challenge looming in the not too distant future. The stories and evolving mythology growing around R.J. Mitchell's pride and joy, the Supermarine Spitfire, some said the best fighter airplane in the entire world, were almost more than Brian Drummond could bear. He knew he had to go to England, but part of him did not want to leave home, family and Becky.

The cheers of his classmates brought Brian back to the event and signaled the conclusion of the ceremony. The processional retreat ended with a hug and a kiss on the cheek from his mother. Handshakes from the men and hugs from the women mixed with the words of congratulations. Gertrude and Malcolm Bainbridge also attended the graduation and added their own praise for both Brian and Becky.

The two families left the school auditorium for the best steak house in Wichita. The excellent meal complemented the expressions of praise, hopes, dreams and expectations. The words did not make Brian feel good. They added to the conflict he held within him and could not share with anyone. Only Malcolm had a clue. Every word seemed to be calculated to add to the pressure within the young aviator. Even the clandestine touches under the table from Becky did not make him feel better. Brian was eager to finish the evening meal and get on to the graduation party. Becky must have sensed the distraction in her boyfriend. When the touches did not have the desired effect, she resigned herself to wait for their privacy later in the night.

The two families split returning to their respective homes for the two graduates to change clothes for the traditional party to close out the right of passage. The preparations did not take long. This was also the first night neither graduate would have a curfew to meet. Both were eighteen and of legal age. The parents offered the appropriate words of caution about responsibility, moderation and respect.

"Since we probably won't see you until breakfast, there is just one more thing I'd like to say on this day," Susan Drummond announced. "We're depending on you, Brian. Please don't do anything foolish."

"Mom," her son protested. "I'm just going to the grad party with Becky. I'm not running away with her."

"I wasn't thinking of that. I was thinking of your flying."

The topic surprised Brian especially since the whole issue of his avocation had not come up all day. He hesitated struggling with the thoughts occupying more of his consciousness as the day of his departure approached.

"We've accepted your flying despite our better judgment, but we are both concerned about your interest in the events in Europe. Please don't do something foolish now that you are able."

Brian wanted to change the subject, but could not. "Like what?"

"Like joining the Army, or something."

"I'm not going to join the Army," he responded technically telling the truth, but not admitting to or accepting the intent of his mother's admonition.

"Just remember that, Brian. Now, go on, get on to your party. Have a good time, son. Enjoy yourself and take care of Becky."

"Be good," George Drummond added.

"Goodnight. I'll see you later."

Once out of the house, Brian felt some relief. The audible exhale as he walked down the street toward the Seward house eased the strain like the weighted valve on a pressure cooker. The feeling was good. With each step, his thoughts returned to more pleasant topics like the party and Becky.

"You ready?" Brian asked as Becky answered the doorbell.

The answer came with a kiss and a pair of arms around his neck. Becky practically pushed Brian off the porch. The mood was clearly light, positive and happy which also helped Brian forget the impending events.

The two graduates, friends and lovers celebrated with their classmates the accomplishment as well as the future. Most of their friends planned to work with their families either on farms or in stores. Only a small number were going to college. Only one was planning to volunteer to fly fighters for the Royal Air Force. Only one of the graduates considered the probability of war in Europe.

Congratulations, bravado and dreams filled the conversations. Dancing, touching and kisses occupied the moments of silence. The gathering storm in Europe could not cast a shadow upon the Great Plains of Kansas. As the evening approached midnight, established as well as newly formed couples disappeared into the darkness.

The quiet of the solitary night up to the first streams of dawn provided the backdrop to the repeated, prolonged and protracted intimacy between the young lovers, Rebecca Seward and Brian Drummond. Sensations, feelings and pleasures they had only shortly begun to experience grew into full bloom before the sun rose above the horizon. They needed each other for different and yet similar reasons. Their needs could not be denied.

—

About the Author

Cap Parlier

———

Cap and his wife, Jeanne, live on the Great Plains of Kansas, along with three dogs and a cat. Their four children have begun their families. He is a graduate of the U.S. Naval Academy, a retired Marine aviator, Vietnam veteran and experimental test pilot, and currently serves as a senior principal project engineer for an aerospace company. Cap has numerous other projects completed and in the works including screenplays, historical novels and a couple of history books.

———

Interested readers interested in Cap's essays and other projects may wish to visit Cap's website at:

http://www.Parlier.com

Or you may wish to subscribe to Cap's weekly Blog: *"Update from the Heartland"* at:

http://heartlandupdate.blogspot.com

Cap can be reached at: Cap@Parlier.com.

Books by Cap Parlier

___

Anod series
The Phoenix Seduction (1995)
Anod's Seduction (2004) [reprint of The Phoenix Seduction]
Anod's Redemption (2004)

___

Sacrifice (2000)
The Clarity of Hindsight (2016)

___

To So Few series
To So Few – In the Beginning (2013)
To So Few – The Prelude (2014)
To So Few – Explosion (2015)
To So Few – The Trial (2016)

___

and with **Kevin E. Ready:**
TWA 800 - Accident or Incident? (1998)

___

Coming soon from Cap Parlier, **To So Few – The Verdict**, the fifth book of the series novel of flight and a warrior's life.

Web address: http://www.SaintGaudensPress.com

Visit Cap Parlier's Web Site at: http://www.Parlier.com

SAINT
GAUDENS